RAINTREE: ORACLE

LINDA WINSTEAD JONES

Published in Great Britain 2015
by Mills & Boon, an imprint of Harlequin (UK) Limited,
Eton House, 18-24 Paradise Road, Richmond, Surrey, TW9 1SR

© 2015 Linda Winstead Jones

ISBN: 978-0-263-25405-1

89-0315

Harlequin (UK) Limited's policy is to use papers that are natural, renewable and recyclable products and made from wood grown in sustainable forests. The logging and manufacturing processes conform to the legal environmental regulations of the country of origin.

Printed and bound in Spain
by CPI, Barcelona

Linda Winstead Jones is a bestselling author of more than fifty romance books in several subgenres—historical, fairy tale, paranormal, contemporary and romantic suspense. She is also a six-time RITA® Award winner and (writing as Linda Fallon) winner of the 2004 RITA® Award for paranormal romance. Linda lives in north Alabama with her husband of fifty-two years. She can be reached via lindawinsteadjones.com.

For Linda Howard, fabulous writer, partner in crime,
travel buddy, and most of all, good friend.

Prologue

Autumn in the North Carolina mountains was always special. Even after serving six years as keeper of the Raintree Sanctuary, the beauty of the place and the season was not lost on Echo. The days were cooler now, and she liked that. The leaves on the trees had turned enticing shades of gold, orange and red. These early-morning walks along a wooded trail were for her and her alone. The rest of the day might be spent handling Sanctuary business, but each day began just this way, with a long walk and blessed solitude.

Suddenly her vision dimmed, and an instant later a burst of bright light blinded her. Echo dropped to her knees, hard, then fell forward, grasping at the dirt and small stones on the trail with her fingertips, trying to hold on so the world wouldn't spin out from under her. For a split second she was able to think, and what initially came to her was *I'm too young to have a stroke!* But then thought was gone, the images bombarded her and she realized this was no stroke.

There was water, lots of it. Icy-cold salt water filled her nose and her mouth; she choked on it. It burned. She could not breathe. The two worlds—hers and theirs—merged. She was prone on a dirt trail on Sanctuary land, holding on for dear life, but she was also *there*. And she was drowning.

The boat was sinking, going down fast. Water rushed in, sweeping people off their feet and away, pushing them under the cold water. The forceful and icy water swirled around her legs, pushing and pulling until she, too, fell and was washed deep into the sea. She screamed, and water filled her lungs.

There were one hundred and three souls on board; she knew that in a way she could not explain. Though she was underwater and for all intents and purposes drowning as so many already were, she heard the panicked cries of those who had not yet been swept under the dark waters. They were all screaming for help, and they were all going to die…

And then it was over.

Echo felt as if she'd been kicked by a mule, but she blinked twice, three times. She caught her breath and rolled onto her back. Her entire body trembled; her knees were weak, and she remained cold. So cold. She wasn't sure how long the vision had lasted. Even though it had seemed like seconds while she'd been caught up in it, she noticed that the sun had moved a bit higher in the sky. The morning was growing warmer.

She didn't sob, but silent tears streamed down her

face. Her lower lip bled; she'd either cut it when she fell or had bitten it during the vision.

All her life she'd dreamed of disasters as they were happening. Sometimes she'd go a few days without a nightmare, but she'd never gone more than a week, maybe eight days, without one. Now and then she might see a disaster before it took place, but not often. Not nearly often enough.

This was new. For the third time in a little over a month, a vision had come to her while she was awake. Each one had stopped her dead in her tracks, had thrown her to the ground—or the floor—and had twisted her body and mind as she suffered along with the victims. She'd always hated the nightmares; she'd dreaded them. But this…this was so much harder. This particular vision had been far more vivid than any of the others, much too real. What if they were getting worse?

If she had not been pulled out of the vision in time, would she have drowned with the others? Would she have died on the trail that had, until a short time ago, been such a place of peace?

As with the other instances she would go back to the house, sit at her computer and try to piece together when and where the disaster was happening. Or had already happened. In her heart she knew that once again she would be too late. Her true curse was that she was *always* too late.

Being keeper of the Raintree Sanctuary—this blessed land that was so special and necessary to her family, her clan—had not been her idea, but she'd done her best to embrace the assignment. She'd left the band she'd loved and quit her waitress job. She didn't miss the job, but she did miss the band and the girls she'd played with. Most of all she missed Sherry, her friend and roommate, a pretty good drummer who'd died in her place. Sherry had been murdered by a psycho Ansara soldier who'd thought she was killing Echo Raintree. A lot had happened six years ago, when the Ansara had attempted to take on the Raintree clan. Changes, upheaval, the beginning of a new era. The end of the evil leadership of the Ansara clan, the beginning of a new Rainsara clan with Mercy, Echo's cousin, the previous keeper of this Sanctuary, at the helm with her husband.

At the time, getting away from it all had seemed like a good enough idea. Some days she could almost forget that the idea hadn't been hers.

Even though she had initially argued a bit—she'd never been a fan of being told what to do—she'd thought being here, living in this safe place, would help her learn to control her ability. Being honest with herself, she admitted that her "control" wasn't just poor, it was nonexistent. Instead of learning, she was getting worse.

The Raintree clan was by far the most successful—and powerful—in the magical world most people had no idea existed. There were other clans, other groups held together by blood and by bond, but none were as old or as organized as the Raintree. Echo's cousin Dante was Dranir, leader of the Raintree clan. With her husband, Judah, cousin Mercy led the closely affiliated Rainsara clan. Gideon was always there to help his siblings, if help was needed. That branch of the family was all amazingly powerful. Why couldn't she control fire, or lightning, or heal the sick and wounded? Why was *this* her so-called gift?

Echo jogged back to the house, breathless and hurting, her knees knocking. It was always possible that this time was different. Maybe she wasn't too late.

By the time she pieced together the clues, the story was on the newsfeed. *Russian Ship Sinks, Search for Survivors Under Way.* Echo's heart dropped. Tears filled her eyes, blurring the words on the computer screen. "There are no survivors," she whispered to the screen, and then, without a second thought, she wiped away her tears, snagged her cell phone off the desk and thumbed her way to the contacts list.

Her cousin picked up on the second ring. "Hi, Echo. What's up?"

Gideon sounded cheerful. He was so happy with his life! Too bad she was about to ruin his day.

"Are you busy?" she asked, as if this were an ordinary call. Her heart pounded; her breath caught in her throat as she suffered second thoughts. This was her family, after all. She loved them; they loved her. She would do anything not to hurt them or cause them distress. *Almost* anything.

"I have a few minutes," Gideon said. "Everything okay there?"

She probably should have called Dante directly, since this was about to be his problem, but she was closer to Gideon. They lived in close proximity and had for years. He was the one she always turned to in times of trouble. Gideon was only a dozen years older than she was, but he was more of a father to her than her real father had ever been. Half the time she never knew where her parents were, and she had learned long ago not to bother them with her troubles. They didn't like it. Her troubles put a damper on their fun.

Besides, cousin or not, Dante scared her a little when he was mad. And this was definitely going to make him mad.

She started with a casual, "How are Hope and the kids?"

"Everybody's fine," Gideon said. "Emma is playing softball this year. Fall ball, they call it. Tournament this weekend. She'd love if it you came to a game." He laughed. "I promise you, softball at this age is absolutely hilarious. It'll be worth the trip."

Unfortunately, hilarity was not in her immediate future. Echo hesitated. She ran a lone, dirty fingernail across the top of her desk. She'd always been a little bit of a rebel, but this...this was going to take real courage. "Any chance Emma is ready to take on her role as caretaker of the Sanctuary?" she asked. After all, Emma was destined to one day take on this job. It was what she'd been born to do.

Gideon's tone changed; she could hear the seriousness over the phone lines, could *feel* it even before he spoke. "She's five years old, so no. Not yet." His voice lowered, making her wonder if there was anyone else around. "Dammit, Echo, she deserves as normal a childhood as we can give her."

Echo paused. She took a deep breath and let it out slowly. No one was going to be happy about this, but what choice did she have?

She'd never had control over her powers of prophesy, and she'd actively fought the empathic powers her cousins insisted she possessed. Powers they said would grow in time. She didn't want to be an empath, didn't want to suffer the feelings of others. She didn't want to be a prophet, either, suffering their disasters, as well, but there wasn't much to be done for that. Was it too much to want control over her *life*? No, it was not. For all she knew the same magic that made this land a safe haven for others in her clan was causing the distressing shift in her abilities.

She had to start somewhere and this was it.

"Call Dante and tell him there's a position to fill," she said, calling on every ounce of bravery she possessed. She took another deep breath. "I quit."

Chapter 1

One year later

Ireland. Echo had always wanted to visit, it was on her short bucket list, and now here she was. This trip was hardly a vacation, though. She was on a mission. She needed help, the kind of help her cousins had tried—and failed—to give her.

The village of Cloughban was well off the beaten path. She'd gotten turned around three times trying to find her way here. The GPS on her phone seemed to think the place didn't exist, but she had a map. An actual paper map that was so old she handled it carefully so as not to tear it along the folds. Still, she'd taken more wrong turns than she cared to admit to. She'd almost given up once, but at this point she couldn't afford surrender.

Echo parked her rental car in a small space beside the village pub—the Drunken Stone, a name which made no sense at all—exited the vehicle with purpose and walked toward the center of town. It felt good to stretch her legs, as she tried to decide how to proceed from here.

In spite of her troubles, she was instantly charmed. She'd left behind the stifling humidity of a North Carolina autumn heat wave for a cool breeze and...this.

The village might've come right off a postcard. The road was narrow, barely wide enough for two small cars. There wasn't a single building in town taller than two stories high. They were all very old, that was evident in the weathered stone-and-brick walls. The buildings were dull grays and browns, but the doors had been painted bright colors—red, purple, blue and green—and there were flowers everywhere. In window boxes and large tubs along the sidewalk. Hanging near shop entrances, stems loaded with blooms flowing from earthenware pots to the ground. She slowed her step, momentarily caught up in the simple beauty of the place.

The windows of the shops along the main road were all enticing, their offerings tempting. Candy, colorful scarves, hats and jackets, cheeses and wines. Ice cream and coffee. If she stayed here for a while, if she found what she was looking for, that might become her favorite establishment.

The sun was shining, but thanks to an increasingly stiff breeze it was cooler than Echo had expected. She hugged her arms to herself, wishing she'd grabbed her lightweight jacket out of her duffel bag. She didn't want to go back to the car to get it. The walk back would hardly be a long one, but if all went well she might be here for a while, and she needed to be properly equipped for the weather. This trip was not much more than a whim, and in a fit of frustration she'd just thrown a few clothes into her red duffel without giving much thought to the weather. She stopped in front of a boutique with her eye on a dark blue sweater in the window.

How did a store like this survive in a town so small? She supposed the locals had to have a place to shop other than the next town over, but still, through the window the boutique looked to be stuffed to the gills with really nice, upscale merchandise.

Echo stepped into the shop, which was smaller than she'd thought it would be as she'd peeked through the window. Small, but crammed with shelves and racks of colorful clothing. And hats! There was a very interesting collection of hats on a rack at the back of the store. The clerk behind the counter, a middle-aged woman with reddish-blond hair and an easy, wide smile, said, "Hello. Can I help you?" Her accent was lovely, lilting and almost musical. Echo realized *she* was the one with the accent here.

"I saw a beautiful blue sweater in the window."

The woman waved her hand dismissively as she stepped around the counter. "Ah, you don't want that sweater. It's far too expensive and the color is all wrong for you. It's too dark. You'll look best in pastels or jewel tones. Definitely jewel tones." She crossed the small space between the counter and the rack near where Echo stood and grabbed a green sweater. "This one will suit you much better." She lifted the price tag. "And it's on sale. What luck."

The green was a better color for her, she supposed,

and who could pass up a sale? Half price. It was meant to be. Echo bought the sweater, which was folded neatly and with great care before being placed in a brown paper bag. Already she was eyeing a raincoat and a matching hat, but she supposed she should wait and see how long she'd be here before she made any more investment.

The cashier cleared her throat and asked, her tone a bit too carefree, "I don't believe we've met. Are you new to Cloughban? Are you visiting a relative or a friend?"

"Just visiting," Echo said simply as she counted out the euros.

"My name is Brigid," the saleslady said. "I hope you'll come back while you're here and look around some more. Do you expect to be here for a while or will yours be a short visit?"

"I don't know yet," Echo said honestly.

"Well, do come again."

"Thank you, Brigid. I'm Echo Raintree, by the way. It's very nice to you." She didn't have any idea how long she'd be here, or if she'd need more clothes, but it was a good sign that she'd made a friend right off the bat. She offered her hand for a handshake. Was that the protocol here? It seemed like the right thing to do, and since Brigid took the offered hand for a shake, she figured she wasn't too out of line.

The handshake didn't last long. It was, in fact, oddly brief. Brigid's smile faded.

Echo left the pleasantries behind and got down to business. "Maybe you can help me. I'm looking for a man named Ryder Duncan. Do you by any chance know where I might find him?" Cloughban was a small enough town. Maybe it was one of those places where everyone knew everyone else.

The once-friendly woman's smile faded; the change in her mood was instantaneous and complete. "No, sorry. I can't help you." Brigid's speech was clipped, the crisp words passing through pursed lips. Gone was the wide smile. Her eyes narrowed. "You'd best be on your way. I'm about to close for lunch."

Echo was ushered from the store, all but thrown out as if she were a bum and Brigid a brawny bouncer. In seconds she found herself on the sidewalk, shopping bag in hand and her head spinning from the rejection. All she'd done was mention Ryder Duncan's name!

Duncan was, if her research was correct, a powerful and rare teacher. A professor of magic. A wizard, a sorcerer, a shaman. He was a stray, unaffiliated with the Raintree or the Rainsara or the now-defunct Ansara clan. It wasn't as if you could use Google to search his name and come up with "wizard" but if you knew where to look, and she did, a small amount of information did exist. Not enough to paint an accurate picture, but enough for her to know that she had to at least try to find him. His last known place of residence was here in Cloughban. *White Stone.*

Being keeper of the Sanctuary had put her in control of a vast number of proprietary computer records. After she'd announced her resignation, she'd started her research.

In the past year, her cousins had tried to help her control her abilities so she could live a somewhat normal life. With books, charmed amulets and a number of meditation techniques, they *had* tried. A couple of times she'd actually thought it was working, but the results eventually faded away. Maybe they were too close to her. Maybe she needed to work with someone who was not family.

She hoped.

Echo stopped on the sidewalk and pulled her new sweater from the brown bag. Brigid had been nice enough to cut off all the tags, so all she had to do was pull it on and toss the bag in a nearby trash bin. That done, she glanced around again. Either everyone in this village took lunch at the same time, or there was an impressively fast phone tree and she was being shunned. Closed for Lunch signs were posted on doors and windows. As she walked around the small town square she heard locks being thrown, one after another. Why would an ice cream shop close for lunch? She couldn't be the only person who occasionally opted for an ice cream sundae.

Just as alarming, where were the pedestrians who'd been on the square when she'd walked into the clothing shop? They were all gone. *All.*

Frustrated, she turned about, around and around, looking for a sign of life. Any sign. She saw no one. She could almost swear a gray pall had fallen over the entire town in a matter of seconds. Even the once-bright colors seemed dimmer, though she knew that was impossible. The square no longer resembled the picture on an inviting postcard. Instead, it looked like a place wide-eyed pale children with axes and an appetite for brains might live. Great, just what she needed. She turned toward the rental car, trying to decide what to do. If the very mention of Duncan's name caused this kind of reaction…

No. It was coincidence. Nothing more. With the

sale done there was no more reason for the clerk to be
friendly. It was lunchtime. Maybe Brigid was hungry.
Maybe everyone was hungry! The weather had simply
taken a turn. Everything that had happened in the past
few minutes was explainable. She'd just have to wait
out lunchtime and ask again. Someone else, this time.
Someone not so sharp.

She'd almost reached the car when the first drop fell.

If you could call it a drop. Soft Irish rain, more mist
than true rain, was cool on her face. It felt good, she
had to admit, though she had no desire to be soaked to
the skin. Not in this cool weather. She should've bought
the raincoat instead of the sweater.

Echo's stomach growled. With the time difference
she didn't know what meal her body was asking for, but
it was definitely time to eat. Given the way the town
square had suddenly become deserted, it would be a
waste of time to head back that way. Instead of getting
behind the wheel of the rental car she turned left and
ducked into the pub with the weird name. The stone
building, which didn't have a single first-story window,
wasn't exactly what she'd call inviting, but surely the
pub served food of some kind. At this point anything
would do. Maybe her head would clear once she'd had
something to eat.

The Drunken Stone was dimly lit, all dark wood
and dark leather and beer advertisements. One table
in the far corner was occupied by three older, gray-
haired men. Was Ryder Duncan sitting there? Not that
any one of them looked like a powerful wizard. She
didn't look much like a prophet, so what did appear-
ances mean? Nothing, really.

While she had found mention of Duncan in the Raintree records, there weren't many details. There definitely hadn't been a photo. All she really knew was that he was a teacher, and he lived in—or at least had once lived in—Cloughban.

One of the men actually looked like a garden gnome come to life, with a squished face and a tremendous nose, but he was a bit taller than any gnome she'd ever seen—just a bit—and he didn't wear a pointed hat. The other two were thinnish and looked enough alike to be brothers, or maybe cousins. The similarity was in the nose and the slant of the eyes.

The man behind the bar was not older, gray-haired or gnomelike. He was good-looking, tall and lean with wide shoulders in a snug gray Henley. She'd guess he was in his mid-thirties, just a few years older than she. He had a nice head of thick, dark hair that hung just a little too long. There was a bit of wave in that hair that looked as if it was begging for a woman's fingers to straighten a few misbehaving strands. Adding to the mystery was a leather cord just barely peeking out from the collar of his shirt, and a leather cuff on his right wrist.

He was, in fact, quite nice to look at. Just what she needed.

No, just what she *didn't* need! She had the worst tastes in men. Her romantic history was more tragedy than comedy, and in the past year she had not even dared to get involved with a man. After a lifetime of dealing with her own so-called gift, when it came to men she much preferred those who were unencumbered by magic. She didn't even want them to believe that true magic existed. It would be easier that way. But what if she allowed herself to hook up with a serious boyfriend and had an episode in front of him? How would she explain it away?

"Can I help you?" the too-good-looking barkeep asked.

Considering the reception she'd gotten when she'd initially asked about Duncan, she decided not to go there just yet. She'd passed a lot of nothing on her way to Cloughban. If the bartender was no friendlier than Brigid, it would take her at least an hour to find her way to the next small town. And that was if she didn't get turned around again.

"I'm starving. What do you recommend?"

"I recommend a very nice café in Killarney," he said, his Irish accent not as pronounced as Brigid's had been. And then he continued. "Are you lost, then?"

"No, why do you ask?"

"You're American, and we are far off the beaten path. You won't see a tour bus on the streets of Cloughban."

No tour bus would be able to make it down the narrow, winding road she'd taken to get here, but that was beside the point.

She stepped to the bar and took a stool. No matter what, she was not going all the way to Killarney for lunch! This was a public place—a *pub*—and she was hungry. If the bartender tried to send her away, she'd plant her feet and insist on being served.

Well, it was never a good idea to piss off the people who were going to handle your food, but still…

"I'm looking for someone, but first I really want something to eat. A sandwich should be safe enough. Please," she added as sweetly as she could manage.

He smiled at her, but the smile did not touch his dark

eyes. Not Irish eyes, she knew in an instant. Not entirely. There was a bit of Romany in those eyes. Tinker, to those less kind. She shook off the empathic abilities that had been trying to come to the surface in the past several years. Dammit, she didn't want them.

"Safe enough, I suppose," the hunk and a half said in a voice of surrender. He didn't try again to send her to Killarney. "Beer?"

"Tea," she said. "Sugar, no milk." She needed to be completely clearheaded for what was coming, judging by what she'd encountered so far.

Rye hadn't known who the woman was, not when she'd first walked through the door, but it hadn't taken long for his instincts to kick in and alert him to the trouble she was bringing his way. His instinctive reaction had been to suggest that she lunch far from his humble establishment. For all the good that was going to do. She was a stubborn one; he saw that right off.

She'd been well into the room before he'd realized more precisely who she was. *What* she was. Up close the eyes gave her away. Her brilliant green eyes and the voice that whispered in his head. *Raintree princess*.

Too bad. She was a pretty girl, petite and fair, with soft, pale blond hair cut to hang to her jawline. He didn't normally care for short hair on a woman, but he had to admit, the neck revealed was nicely tempting. Long and pale and flawless. She had amazing eyes, a very nice ass and breasts high and firm and just the right size for his hand.

He'd feed her, but then she had to go. Killarney was likely not far enough away.

Doyle Mullen was working in the kitchen today, as

he did six days a week. He cooked, swept and manned the bar when Rye had to step away for a few minutes. His was not a particularly demanding job, but it was one that had to be done. The pub menu was limited. The single laminated page offered ham and cheese sandwiches, chips, vegetable soup and brown bread. There was also fish and chips, but he could not in good conscience recommend them to anyone. Not even her.

After delivering the order to Doyle, Rye returned to the bar and made the tea himself. It gave him the opportunity to turn his back on the Raintree woman for a few minutes. Dammit, he could still feel her eyes on him.

She hadn't said so, not yet, but she was here for him. He felt it as surely as he would feel rain on his face if he were to step outside. The question was, why? What did she want?

Even without the talismans he wore, Rye was not the most powerful psychic in the world, not by a long shot. He had learned as much or more as he'd been born with, learned at the knee of his Romany mother. Sometimes knowledge slammed into him and he knew it was truth. Other truths were muddy, or hidden from him entirely. He'd often thought it would be better to see nothing at all than to be given only the occasional glimpse. It would ease his frustration considerably.

He had other gifts, gifts he kept dampened, but his psychic ability had never been his strength. If he were honest, he'd admit it was often more annoying than helpful.

He delivered the Raintree woman's tea, then went into the kitchen to check on her meal. It was not quite ready, so he waited there until it was. Doyle tried to make conversation but Rye was in no mood to participate. Eventually the cook went silent. No one else came into the pub; he knew without watching the door. No magic was involved in that knowledge. A bell sounded when the front door opened. Usually a shopkeeper or two stopped in for a bowl of stew or a sandwich about this time of day, but so far all was quiet. Because *she* was here.

They knew. Someone among them had realized who she was and the word had spread like wildfire. He wondered if the pretty girl realized that her family name had the power to strike fear into the hearts of others. They would hide from her if they could. If she wasn't careful, someone might do more than hide.

His life here in Cloughban was orderly. Predictable. He liked it that way. More than that, it was necessary. Thanks to an ancient protection spell, stray tourists didn't find their way here. Only those who possessed magic could make their way to this special village. If anyone—tourist or wandering Irishman—was going to get lost, they got lost on another road in another county. But then, the Raintree woman wasn't exactly lost, was she?

When the sandwich was done Rye delivered it as he had the tea, but again, he did not linger. While the Raintree woman ate he left his station at the bar to check on the regulars in the corner. Three grumpy old men who had been a part of this community for as long as anyone could remember. In a town population that was ever changing, these three were constant.

He stood close to the table and crossed his arms across his chest. "Are you fellas ever going to buy anything? Do I have to depend on strangers to wander into the place in order to make a living?" Tully, Nevan and

McManus had been fixtures in this pub since long before Rye had taken it over. They'd probably be here long after he was gone.

Nevan, who was short and squat and looked as if his face had been scrunched together by two overly large hands, grinned. Not a pretty sight, considering that the old man was ugly as sin. "There'll be a good enough crowd here tonight, and you know it. You don't need our business in the middle of the day."

His friends agreed with him.

"Maybe I shouldn't open until four, then. I could sleep late if it suited me."

Tully nodded. "That would be fine. I still have a key to the back door. You haven't changed the locks, have you, son?"

Rye scowled and took a bar towel to empty tables, just so he wouldn't have to face the Raintree woman. If he were lucky, she would eat, pay and leave.

He didn't feel at all lucky today. She was trouble, and in his experience when trouble came for him it never walked away. It usually planted its feet and stayed awhile. He hadn't experienced trouble of her sort for a long time. A very long time.

Her stool scraped across the floor as she pushed it back so she could stand. Coins were carefully counted out and placed on the counter.

And then she walked to the corner. All three old goats smiled at her; he saw that out of the corner of his eye.

"Perhaps you gentlemen can help me," she said.

Rye stifled a snort. They would be instantly charmed. They would tell her whatever she wanted to know. To a point.

"I'm looking for a man," she said.

McManus cackled. "Lucky lass, you've found three."

She smiled. Good Lord. Dimples. "I'm actually looking for a particular man. Ryder Duncan. Do you know him?"

"I do," Tully said in a booming voice. "And so do you, pet."

Rye turned, ready to face the inevitable. Nevan pointed a crooked finger in his direction. The Raintree woman turned around slowly. Maybe she paled a little.

There was no running from it, he supposed.

"I'm Duncan. What the hell do you want?" he asked sharply.

Yes, she definitely paled. She took a deep breath and closed her eyes.

If someone was going to come for him—for the child more likely—why her? She was alone, she was not particularly powerful in that special Raintree way, nor was she physically strong. But she was a woman, and a pretty one at that. Did the Raintree think he was that weak?

More importantly, *did they know*?

Chapter 2

Oh, no. Not him! Echo was no fool. Well, she was occasionally a fool, especially where men were concerned. She already knew it would not be a good idea for her to spend too much time with this one. There had been an instant attraction. Nothing she couldn't handle, of course. He was kind of a jerk but he was a pretty, sexy jerk.

He was also her last chance. She hadn't come all this way to flake out because Ryder Duncan was not at all what she'd expected him to be.

"Maybe we can have a word in private?"

"No need," he said sharply. "You can say whatever you need to say here and now, before you're on your way."

Yes, definitely a jerk. "I'm looking for a…a…" How much could she say in front of the three older men?

Duncan wouldn't expect her to know who and what he was, so he wouldn't be worried about what she might say. "A teacher," she finally said. "A trainer."

"For you?" He all but scoffed. His lip curled a little.

She wanted to call him a very bad name and walk out with her head held high. But then what? Where would she go from here? Maybe he wasn't her absolute last chance, but she didn't have a plan B at this moment. She took a deep breath, swallowed her pride and said, "Yes, for me." More swallowing. "I need your help."

He turned and walked toward the bar, calling out as he went, "I don't do that anymore."

The three old men listened closely. They no longer bothered to even pretend to engage in their own conversation. The one on the far end must be hard of hearing, because he leaned over as far as he could, tipping in her direction.

Echo didn't want to say anything that might give her true intent away. It was best to keep magical abilities hidden from those who did not have them. That was a bridge difficult to cross, and anyone who found themselves human in a supernatural world almost always became resentful, in time. In the end, they wanted what they could not have. No ordinary human could ever understand her desire, her *need*, to be rid of all magic.

Gideon's wife, Hope, was the exception to that rule. Ungifted to the bone, with a husband and two little girls who were anything but, she was fine with who she was. More than that, she didn't want magical abilities. She said she had her hands full enough as it was. And she wasn't wrong.

Echo followed Duncan to the bar. Slinking away after one or two rebukes was not her style. "You're too

young to be retired. I'll pay you." This was one pur-
chase she would gladly dip into Raintree family money
for. "I'll pay you well."

He didn't even bother to turn to look at her, which
offered an interesting view. Echo tried not to notice
the nicely shaped butt, the way his gray shirt stretched
across broad shoulders, the thick, wavy hair.

"I don't need your money, and I certainly don't need
the hassle," he said as he rounded the bar.

"But I need…"

From behind long expanse of scarred wood that
stretched between them, he turned to look her in the
eye. Big hands on the bar, he leaned forward in a way
that was unmistakably threatening. His expression
alone stopped her words, made them freeze in her
throat. "You *need*. You *want*. You have my answer,
love, now be on your way."

She lowered her voice, edging toward desperation.
She had no idea what might come next if he continued to refuse her. "You don't even know why I'm here,
what I need."

He was unmoved. "I don't care."

Echo turned, mustering what little pride she had left
to walk out the door before the tears came. She could
not speak another word without losing what little control she had left. Dammit, she would not cry in front of
that jerk! He wasn't her last chance, couldn't be. There
had to be another way.

She just didn't have any idea where to look for it.

Once she was outside, the heavy wooden door closed
solidly behind her, the rain began to fall harder. It was
still what they'd call a soft rain, but she'd get soaked
in the short walk to her car. Just as well that she wait a

few minutes. She needed to calm down before she got behind the wheel. And went…and went *where*?

Echo backed against the rock wall of the pub, protected by a small but sufficient overhang above. She leaned there, boneless and shaking with a mixture of anger and frustration. She looked to the right. The square was still deserted, but given the rain that was not unusual. In her mind she continued to ask, *Now what?* No answer came to her. None.

She was lost. Far from home, alone, desperate for help—and lost. Worse than simply turned around, she didn't know where to turn next, didn't know which direction to take. She'd come to Cloughban so sure Ryder Duncan would help her. She hadn't realized how deeply she'd believed him to be her last and only hope. Now what?

"Hello." The small voice from Echo's left-hand side startled her so much she twitched as she turned to glance down. The voice belonged to a child, maybe ten years old, with an impressive head of curly red hair, a smile that would surely light up any room and deep chocolate-brown eyes. As ordinary as she appeared to be, it was definitely odd that in spite of the steady rain, the little girl was not wet.

"Hello," Echo responded. "Who are you?"

The question went unanswered. "You're American," the girl responded. "I can tell by your accent. Sometimes I watch American television."

Yes, she was the one with the accent here. "You're right, I am American." The fact that the girl had come out of nowhere and was oddly dry was the least of her worries. The kid was, at the moment, a welcome distraction. "My name is Echo."

"I *love* that name," the child said with enthusiasm. "My name is Cassidy, but most of my friends at school just call me Cass. I like Cassidy better, but I don't want to tell them. It might hurt their feelings. There's no way to shorten Echo! You're so lucky. No one will ever call you Ech."

In spite of herself, Echo found herself smiling. "While I'm here I'll call you Cassidy, since that's the name you prefer." Again, there was that uncomfortable sensation of being lost and not knowing what came next. Her voice was lower, less steady, as she said, "Though I'm afraid I won't be here much longer." The rain was letting up a bit. It would end soon, and she'd have no reason to stand here and wait. No, not wait, *procrastinate*.

"Yes, you will," Cassidy said. "You're going to be here for a very long time." She seemed sure of herself, but then she was a child, a child who knew nothing about what had brought Echo to this place. Or what—who—was sending her away.

Cassidy leaned toward Echo a little and lowered her voice. "You need to go back inside. He will help you, he's just scared. Only a little scared, but still scared."

For a long moment Echo couldn't speak. How did the kid know about Duncan and his refusal to help? Duh, the child had been listening in somehow. That's why she wasn't wet. Cassidy hadn't appeared out of nowhere; she'd been inside, hiding in a dark corner or behind a booth, and had slipped out of the pub quietly either right before or right after Echo.

"No, I can't stay here."

Cassidy was not at all put off by that statement. "Yes,

you can. You will! Besides, you really shouldn't drive in your condition."

"My…"

Echo stopped speaking because Cassidy disappeared. The kid didn't run away; she literally vanished into thin air. Here one second, then poof, gone the next.

Was Cassidy a vision of what would be, like those Gideon had once had of his eldest daughter? A delusion, brought on by her own frustration? An incredibly gifted child? She'd never known anyone to be able to disappear that way.

It was possible the child had not been there in body at all, but had somehow manifested from a distance. Or didn't exist at all. Yes, she was right back to delusions. Great.

You shouldn't drive in your condition.

If she had an episode while she was on the road…

It began with a sensation of intense heat. She felt that heat on her face and in her blood. Instinctively she raised her hands up to protect her face. Her vision dimmed, her knees went weak. Echo turned clumsily. It took all her strength to throw open the pub door. It didn't matter that Ryder Duncan had sent her away; she would *not* fall to the wet sidewalk. She would not expose herself that way.

She lurched into the pub and took four steps before she fell to her knees. Her last clear look at the here and now was of Duncan's unhappy face.

Rye was about to ask the Raintree woman what the hell she was doing back in his pub when she dropped to her knees. Hard.

"Not now," she whispered.

"Not now what?" he snapped. "If this is some kind of a trick to get me to change my mind, forget it."

She fell forward, drew in her knees and covered her head with her hands, drawing herself into a ball. She shook violently. What the hell?

McManus lifted up slightly and peered over the top of the table to get a better view. "I think she's having a fit."

"Sure looks it," Nevan said.

"Looks like a seizure to me," Tully said.

Nevan chimed in again. "What's the difference between a seizure and a fit?"

"What difference does it make?" Rye dropped beside the Raintree woman, placing a hand on her shoulder. She felt hot, as if she had a fever, and she continued to shake. Hard. Dammit, she'd been fine when she'd left a few minutes ago.

Whatever was going on, she was not faking.

He let loose a stream of foul language that had Tully laughing and Nevan crossing himself. She was light enough, easy to pick off the floor and carry to the back of the public room.

"One of you fetch Doyle from the kitchen and tell him to watch the place for a bit," he said. All three men agreed, without question. Not that he expected any actual customers this afternoon. They knew to steer clear; they would know Raintree was here.

That was why no one but her had come in for lunch. Did Echo know her family name sometimes elicited fear in others of their kind? In the past, Raintree royalty had sometimes been imperious and even dangerous. Not in the past couple hundred years, maybe, but independents remembered their history, they had heard the stories. They came here, more often than not, to be left alone.

Rye dipped down just enough to open the unmarked door at the back of the room. Steep, narrow stairs loomed ahead. He carried the Raintree woman up, into the room where he slept some nights, and lowered her to the unmade bed. Dull afternoon light streamed through the windows.

Already she was cooler, and the trembling was lessening. He backed away from the bed to stand by the door, arms crossed and scowl in place. It had been a long time since he'd had a woman in this bed. Just his luck, she was not there for a pleasant reason.

What the hell did she really want with him? Why was she here? No Raintree, especially not one of the royals, would need his help. None of them would leave the clan looking for a teacher when they were surrounded by some of the most gifted individuals in the world. No, she wanted something else.

Rye hadn't been lying when he'd told her he didn't teach anymore. He no longer had the patience for it, and besides, his attention had to be focused elsewhere. He was also no longer wild about bringing strangers into his circle, even for a few days. The last time, a good four years earlier, things had not ended well. He had to be so careful.

It wasn't long at all before the woman on his bed opened her eyes and looked at him with tear-filled, hope-filled, impossible eyes. Those eyes had a way of cutting through him, of touching him deep down in a way he did not wish to be touched. He knew he was screwed even before she whispered, "Please, make it stop."

Chapter 3

Fire. She hated the visions of fire more than anything else. This one—a true inferno—had taken place in a warehouse of some kind. China, Echo thought. Not that it mattered. The disaster was over. The fire had been waning as she'd fallen to the floor.

She looked at Ryder Duncan as she pulled herself back to the present. Straightening her sweater was as much a nervous gesture as anything else. It was a way to remind herself that this place and time were real. *She* was real, and safe. Unburned, no smoke in her lungs…

As was usual, she felt as if she were caught between a dream and reality, as if she were dreaming that she was awake but wasn't quite there yet. The feeling would pass, she knew, but it usually took several minutes. She clutched the sheet beneath her hands, holding on to this world for dear life.

Her greatest fear was that one day she'd leave this world behind for much more than a few minutes. What if she stayed within a vision of disaster? Drowning or on fire, caught up in a violent earthquake or a trapped in a war zone. Would she die with those around her? It was that fear that had driven her here, away from her family, away from home and her responsibilities. The only way to handle that fear was to gain enough control so that she knew she'd always come back to herself.

Duncan had been her last sight before the vision, and now he was her first sight after. Even in her distressed state, she could appreciate that annoying as he was, he was a fine sight. Focusing on him allowed her to leave her fears behind. For now.

Normally she was alone when she came out of a vision. She'd always thought that was best. Her dreams of disasters, her visions of pain and suffering, they weren't meant to be shared. Who would want to share them? Still, she had to admit, it was nice to see Duncan's face waiting. Even if he did look pissed.

He was not at all what she'd expected when she'd flown to Ireland. It had been silly of her to expect anything at all! She hadn't been able to find much in the way of detail about him. A mention in a story from ten years before, a second- or thirdhand account. In the real world, the world she lived in, "wizard" didn't necessarily mean an old man with a long gray robe and long white hair and a magical staff. Though that was not impossible...

She sat up, uncomfortable to be on what was obviously his bed but too weak to stand just yet.

He continued their conversation as if there had been no break, no pause for her vision.

"Make what stop?" he asked, his voice cold.

She was probably wasting her time, explaining why she'd come to him for help. He'd already turned her down flat! But he had asked the question—*make what stop?*—and she knew better than to lie to him. She didn't know exactly what powers he had, what gifts he possessed. He might realize she was lying; he might already know why she had come.

The truth. What else did she have to offer?

"My name is Echo Raintree. I'm called the Raintree prophet, but everyone knows I'm a poor excuse for a prophet." That was her curse, as much as the visions. Always a disappointment, always less than she should be. "My visions come too late. There's never anything I can do to help the people I see and hear... and feel. There was a time when I only saw these horrible things in my dreams, but as you just witnessed that is no longer true." She shivered, then pulled the front of her sweater closed as if that might warm her. "They come all the time now, day and night, without warning, just..." She shuddered. "I don't know what to do."

He did not move closer or drop his arms. Jaw tight, dark eyes cold, he responded. Somehow, his Irish accent was more pronounced than it had been before as he asked, "You want me to train you to be a better prophet?"

Her heart leaped. In the beginning, even just a few moments ago, that had been her plan. But as she lay on his bed, shaking, feeling as if she'd blink and be back in the burning building, she realized she wanted more than control. Much more.

"No. I want the visions gone. I want them wiped

away, erased. I want…help. The kind of help only you can offer."

There was an uncomfortably long pause before he responded. "You want a lot," he said without emotion.

"Yes, I do."

Anger flashed in his dark eyes. "Are you telling me there are no Raintrees who can help you?"

Again, she had to stick with the truth. If she lied to him and he found out, there would be hell to pay. One did not try to pull the wool over the eyes of a wizard. "They've tried, but…no luck." Not knowing how much he knew, how much he saw, she had to tell all. "My cousins have attempted to teach me to control the visions. When I asked they said it was impossible to get rid of them entirely." Gideon had refused to even discuss that possibility. "Maybe I'm too close to them, too connected. A st—" She caught herself. "Someone outside the clans seems like a better option, at this point."

He didn't respond for a few drawn-out seconds, and then he said in a lowered voice, "Poor Raintree princess can't get her way at home so she flies across the pond to ask a *stray* for help."

Her chin came up a bit. "I didn't call you a stray." Though she almost had. *Caught.* Echo swung her legs over the edge of the mattress, taking a deep breath in an attempt to regain her strength. If only her knees would stop knocking. It was impossible to be strong when her entire body was weak, shaking, drained. She didn't want Duncan to see her as weak. Not that she should care what he thought of her. She'd never see him again, once she drove away from Cloughban.

Which would probably be very soon. It was looking as if her trip had been a complete waste of time, as if Ryder Duncan was not all he'd been rumored to be. Any decent teacher would see that she needed help and offer it!

"No, not out loud," he said. "But isn't that what you call those with magic who are unaffiliated with your clans?"

She stood. Anger helped her find her legs. "Okay, fine. I almost called you a stray. Sorry if that offends you. What would you prefer?"

"Independent."

He remained angry; he'd called her a princess with disdain…yes, this trip had been a waste of time. She wanted to run, she wanted to hide from those dark, condemning eyes. "Stray seems more appropriate to me." She walked toward the door he blocked, trying not to let him see how devastating his refusal was. She would not beg!

"Sorry to have bothered you." She thought about the little girl—real or imagined—she'd been talking to before the vision began. Beneath her breath she mumbled, "I guess Cassidy was wrong."

Duncan didn't move away from the door. Echo had to stop a couple of feet short. It was that or physically move him, and given his size and very nice solidness, *that* wasn't going to happen. After a few seconds, she waved her hand in a dismissive gesture. He still did not move. Dammit, did he want her to go or not?

"Cassidy?" he said in a lowered voice.

Echo sighed. "A little girl that was probably all in my head. I saw her, or imagined her, outside the pub right before this latest vision. She said I'd be here for a long time." Wishful thinking, a real child with magic, a new precursor to the visions? She didn't know. Cassidy had obviously been wrong when she'd said that Duncan would help her.

"What did she look like?" he asked.

She wanted out of here before she started to cry. She wanted to walk out with her head high and a smidgen of her dignity intact. A smidgen was all she could hope for at this point. If she stood here too long, neither would happen. "What difference does it make?"

"Indulge me."

Echo backed away a little. Duncan could get under her skin much too easily. Just standing close to him made her shiver. Then again, maybe that was no more than lingering physical weakness thanks to her latest episode. Might as well give him what he wanted so she could boogie on out of here and have her nervous breakdown in private.

"Curly red hair, dark eyes, a few freckles. Maybe ten years old. She was on the sidewalk and then...she wasn't." She didn't feel the need to explain anything more to him.

Instead of ushering her out of the room and down the stairs, Duncan stayed in place. He seemed to be contemplating her. Why? He'd already turned her down. Not once but two or three or four times.

"You give up far too easily, princess. Don't you want to hear my answer?" he asked, and for the first time there was some humor in his voice. Dark humor, but at least a bit of his anger was gone.

"Fine." She crossed her arms, much as he had. "Give me your answer." Maybe it would make him feel better to tell her off before he let her go. Jerk.

"I will not strip away your gifts."

"You wouldn't call this a gift if you had it," she snapped.

He held up a stilling hand. "It's possible—I won't tell you it's not—but it isn't an easy process. There would be a high price to pay. Your cousins were right to dismiss that option if they care for you at all."

Well, *that* was interesting. Apparently what she wanted most of all was possible. She hadn't been entirely sure. "What kind of price?" No price was too high; she'd do *anything.*

He ignored her. "I can teach you to control your abilities."

Echo sighed. "I've tried, I really have. That's not…"

"Of course it's not what you want," he interrupted. "You're spoiled and undisciplined, and I suspect you have been all your life, *princess.* The gift of prophesy is rare and difficult and precious, and you have squandered it. I will not strip your abilities away, but if you do precisely as I say I will help you learn to master them."

That was what she'd planned to ask for when she'd walked into the pub, but now she realized it was not enough. Duncan would do no more than her cousins had done for her, and that wouldn't do. She'd tried talismans, meditations, exercises. In this case she'd have to face *him* each and every day, and she didn't think she could take it. Besides, she did take a perverse pleasure in being the one to walk away. She'd bet no woman had ever told Duncan no.

"Thanks, but no thanks." This time when she shooed him aside, he moved. She opened the door, started down the long, narrow stairway. Her knees were still shaky, and she had no idea where she'd go from here. Ryder Duncan was not who she'd thought him to be, and she could not, would not, put herself in his hands. One good thing had come out of the encounter. He wouldn't do it, her cousins wouldn't do it, but someone could remove her abilities entirely.

She had almost reached the bottom of the stairs when his soft voice stopped her. "It will only get worse."

She didn't turn to face him, but she listened.

"The pain, the frequency and intensity of the events. Because you fight it, because you are spoiled and untrained, because you fear your gift rather than embracing it, what's happening will eventually kill you."

After a moment of complete silence, Echo turned and looked up. She didn't know Duncan at all, she didn't even like him much, but she didn't doubt the truth of his words. "You can take it away. You said..."

"I said there was a price you and those who care for you would not wish to pay for such a miracle."

It wasn't what she wanted, but what choice did she have? She had nowhere else to turn. Besides, when he discovered that she could not master this curse no matter how hard she tried, maybe he'd agree to strip it away. No price would be too high.

"When do we start?"

Rye sat at a table with the woman on the other side. The old men had left, and so had Doyle. They were alone, though that would not last. In an hour or so the late-afternoon crowd would start to arrive.

He should've sent Echo Raintree on her way, should've let her go to another part of the world searching for another stray who might be willing to do as she asked. He could've and should've sat back and allowed her to implode. It wasn't as if he had any love for the Raintree clan.

But apparently Cassidy had said Echo would be here for a while. Cassidy was never wrong.

Echo rambled. About her problems, about her struggles with her abilities. There was something about a band, and parents who liked to gad about more than care for their only child. She was tired of seeing horrible things and never being able to do anything to stop them or influence them. He listened, but he was also distracted. Beautiful face, feminine figure, bright eyes. Any man might be understandably distracted.

He knew a bit about control, more than he was willing to share with her or anyone else. It was the reason he clung to routine, one of the reasons he remained in this quiet, enchanted village. The question was, could he *teach* control again? It had been more than four years since he'd taken on a student, and the last time hadn't ended so well. There had been successes in the past, but were even a hundred successes worth the risk of a catastrophic failure?

Finally he interrupted her. "You're stalling."

She looked guilty. Rye had spent so much of his life hiding who and what he was, her easy-to-read expressions were a puzzle to him. The Raintree woman was an open book. How had she survived to this point? He knew she was twenty-nine years old. At one point in her rambling she'd said something about starting a new life at the age of thirty. A life without visions, a life without nightmares.

She was a mere six years younger than he was, but listening to her...it was as if they were not even of the same generation. Their lives to this point had been so very different.

He would help her if he could, but he couldn't promise her a life without nightmares.

"Sorry," she said in a lowered voice. "I didn't mean to go on and on. We need to focus on the future, not the past. How do we begin?" She looked more than a little apprehensive.

"We don't, not yet."

"But you said…"

"I don't know you and you don't know me. Our first step is to get acquainted."

Now the open book was suspicious.

"That doesn't mean I want to get you into bed," he clarified. "Though I imagine nearly every man you've ever met has tried."

"I didn't say I thought…"

"You didn't have to."

She pursed her lips. "I didn't know mind reading was one of your abilities."

He started to say, *It's not*, but kept that piece of knowledge to himself. True, some thoughts jumped out at him on occasion, but it was damned hard work to go around reading the minds of others. It was also potentially dangerous.

But perhaps it would be a good idea to let her believe he could peek into her head at will. Did she not know she was an open book? Did she not realize that everything she thought was written on her pretty face for the world to see?

"So, there's not a file on me back at Raintree headquarters?"

He expected her to laugh at the idea of Raintree

headquarters and files on independents, but she didn't. "Not much of one," she admitted. "I didn't have an easy time finding any detailed information on you."

"Good." Before she left he'd find out what—where and how—she had discovered about him, and make sure no one else could follow in her footsteps. He couldn't make it impossible for someone gifted to find him—those with special abilities found their way to Cloughban all the time—but if there was any kind of a paper or electronic trail it would have to be eliminated.

She straightened her spine. "So, how do we get to know each other?"

"Among the many jobs you've had, have you ever waited tables?"

"Many times. When my band was playing in Wilmington…"

Not that again. "I don't need to know the details," he snapped. "You start tonight, princess." With that, he slid from his seat and stood. He'd spent too much time looking at her. She was starting to get under his skin, and that was the last thing he needed.

She stood, too, more than a little angry. "I've had about enough of that. You can call me Echo or Raintree or pain in the ass, but do *not* call me princess."

"Why not? Isn't that what you are, a Raintree princess?"

Echo lifted her chin in obvious defiance. She'd probably deck him if he told her she was cute when she was mad.

"Some might say so, but that's not who I want to be. I just want… I just want…"

A normal life. A life without pain. Ordinary worries,

ordinary dreams. He knew very well what she wanted. "It doesn't matter what you want, love."

"Besides, you make *princess* sound like an insult."

"Maybe it is," he admitted.

She took a step closer, angrier, tense. "And another thing—you can stop interrupting me."

"If you would get to the point in a timely manner, love, I wouldn't need to."

She punched him in the chest. "And *love* is no better than princess. I am not your love. I am not your princess. If you can't call me Echo or Raintree, don't call me anything at all. I'll be happy to answer to *hey, you*."

"As you wish. Be back here ready to work in two hours. You'll need a place to stay. Maeve Quinlan rents out rooms by the week. She should have a vacancy." He gave her directions, which were quick and easy. The Quinlan house was within walking distance, as was everything in Cloughban.

"How long will I need that room?" Echo asked. "One week? Two?"

One week or even two might be manageable, but he was not optimistic about that timeline. What had Cassidy meant by a long time? To an eleven-year-old, a month might be a very long time.

"I haven't any idea." He still wanted to send Echo Raintree on her way, but why fight it?

Like it or not, his daughter was never wrong.

Chapter 4

The rain stopped as suddenly as it had started, leaving Cloughban looking freshly washed, sparkling and clean. Echo drove the short distance to the bed-and-breakfast. It would be an easy enough walk—she could see the two-story house from the pub—but she needed to park her rental car. Duncan had told her there was parking available behind the boardinghouse.

It would cost her a small fortune to keep the rental car indefinitely, but what choice did she have? It would be a day's trip to return the car to the Dublin airport and then get back to town. She didn't know anyone in Cloughban well enough to ask for that kind of favor.

She would've been better off to fly into the Shannon airport, but it wasn't as if she'd taken her time and planned this trip well. The flight to Dublin had been the next with an available seat, and she'd taken it.

Besides, she didn't want to be stuck without an easy and immediate mode of transport. If things didn't go well she could leave at any time.

Always have an escape route...

Echo carried her bag up the narrow stairway, half listening to her new landlady, who led the way with a sway of her hips and a bright smile she occasionally cast over her shoulder. Maeve Quinlan was fiftyish, tall and pleasant looking with salt-and-pepper hair and a sturdy build. She wore a calf-length skirt in a girlish pink print, a matching blouse and a white cardigan. She could easily pass for a 1950s housewife.

"Breakfast is at seven." Mrs. Quinlan's voice was as bright as her smile. As soon as she'd confirmed Duncan had sent Echo, she'd been much more welcoming. "If you're not an early riser there are always pastries in the kitchen, and you're welcome to help yourself. I make a fabulous lemon blueberry scone." The word *fabulous* was accompanied by an expressive wave of her hand. "Lunch is on your own, but you're welcome to join us for dinner if you'd like. Just be sure to let me know if you'll be here so I can set a place at the table for you. There's nothing sadder than an empty place at the table, is there?" She walked briskly down the second-floor hallway to open the second door on the right. "Here you are, love. I hope the room suits you."

The easy way *love* rolled off the lady's tongue made Echo cringe. Duncan's *love* had probably been meant in much the same way. These people used *love* the way her Southern aunts used *honey*. Anyone and everyone was called *honey*. Great. She'd made a fool out of herself insisting that he not call her *love*.

Well, it wasn't the first time she'd been a fool. Wouldn't be the last.

"It's lovely, Mrs. Quinlan."

Again, that expressive wave of a hand. "Call me Maeve, pet." Before Echo could respond she continued with, "The bath is at the end of the hall. You'll be sharing with Maisy Payne, who's staying in the room next door. She's our new librarian. Not that the Cloughban library is much to brag about, but we do have one. Maisy is a lovely girl. I'm sure the two of you will be the best of friends."

Echo refrained from telling her new landlady that she didn't need or want any new friends. She needed to get what she'd come here for and then get the hell out of town.

Maeve left her new tenant on her own, in her rented room. A small but nicely furnished room that, with any luck, would be home for a short while. Echo stared longingly at the narrow bed that was pushed up against one wall. She dropped her duffel on the floor and plopped down on the bed. Not too hard, not too soft. Just right.

Echo sat there for a moment, bouncing gently. It had been a long day. The longest. She'd slept on the plane, but that had been hours ago! With that in mind she laid back, stretching out. She might as well rest while she could. The time difference was going to be a bear, and the vision of the fire had drained her.

She was here and she'd found Duncan. It was too early to know if she'd get what she needed from him or not, but there was at least a chance. That was more than she'd had yesterday.

The bed was narrow and short, but it was also really

comfortable. She'd just close her eyes for a few minutes…she'd take a moment and unwind a bit…

A banging on the door woke her. Disoriented, she noted a couple of things at once. She'd been sleeping hard. It was dark outside and it was completely dark in her new room, until the door flew open and someone switched on the overhead light. Echo's instinct was not to be afraid. Instead, she was annoyed. Who would do such a terrible thing? The light was far too bright. She pulled the pillow over her face to block it.

Someone snatched that pillow away.

"If you're going to work for me, it's best not to be two hours late for your first shift."

Duncan. Of course.

"I fell asleep."

"Thank you for informing me," he said dryly. "I never would've figured that out for myself."

"There's no need to be sarcastic." She opened one eye. Too bad he was such a jerk. He was more than a little cute. No, not cute. Handsome. Sexy. Brooding, like her own Rochester.

Yeah, because every modern woman needed a boyfriend who kept a crazy wife in the attic…

"Can't I start tomorrow?" She yawned and began to stretch again. Then she squealed as Duncan picked her up and slung her over his shoulder. The world spun. How dare he!

"No, you may not," he said as he carried her from the room, slamming the door shut with one foot. "This is exactly what I was talking about when I said you were spoiled and undisciplined. You will be on time. You will do as you are told. You will not be late again!"

"Great. You're one of *those* bosses."

"One who expects his employees to actually do their jobs? Yes!"

She bounced hard as he started down the stairs. Hanging on to the back of his shirt for support was necessary.

"Wait. Wait!" she called as she tightened her grip.

He stopped in the middle of the staircase, and Echo took a deep breath. "Let me wash my face and brush my teeth, maybe throw on a clean shirt." And pee. Not that she would share that detail with *him*.

Duncan turned and carried her up the stairs. He moved more slowly this time, giving her a moment to appreciate the solidity of the body against hers and the tempting wave of his hair. He had a nice neck, she admitted to herself, a strong jaw and broad shoulders. He carried her as if she weighed nothing. It would be beyond foolish to get involved with him, and since he obviously didn't like her much that wasn't a concern. That didn't mean she couldn't appreciate his finer attributes. Not that she would ever admit aloud that he had any.

He placed her on her feet near the door to her room. "You have five minutes."

"Five?" The expression on his face stopped her from saying more. "Fine, five minutes."

And then he tossed a black shirt that had been slung over his shoulder—much as she had been—in her direction. "Wear this."

If she had any objections to wearing the tight black T-shirt with the pub logo on it, she hadn't said a word. He'd realized it was a bit too small when he'd chosen it from the stack of shirts in the storeroom, but it did show off Echo Raintree's fine figure to its best advantage.

The customers didn't complain, either. Every eye of every male in the place, young and old, married and not, followed her as she served drinks and food and brilliant smiles. Complete with dimples.

Yes, she'd done this before. He might think her a fine employee if she hadn't slept through the first two hours of her first shift.

He could've cut her some slack, he supposed. She'd had a long day. He'd been to the States a time or two himself and he knew very well that the trip was a challenging one. He could empathize. To a point.

If he cut her some slack, they'd never be finished. And he wanted to be finished. He wanted to get this done and send her on her way. If she got too curious, as his last student had, she'd have to go. Finished or not, on the verge of an ugly death for a pretty young woman or not, it was a risk he could not, would not, take.

The crowd began to clear out half an hour before closing time. It was a weeknight, after all. Echo cleaned tables without being told. She handled a bar towel like someone who'd done it before. The way she moved was oddly tempting. Graceful but strong. She flowed from one table to another, easy and, at least for now, unworried. Yes, tempting.

He could not afford to be tempted, not by her. If he was ever stupid enough to get involved with a woman again, if he allowed his body's demands to override his brain, it would not be someone with the last name Raintree.

One thing he could say for her. Princess or not, she did not shy away from work.

As the last customer left, Echo walked to the counter and took a stool there, directly across from Rye.

"If I was wearing a shirt this tight at home I'd get a ton of tips. Here? Nada."

"We don't tip."

She pursed her lips in what he assumed was mock displeasure before saying, "So I noticed. I think tipping is a practice that should be instituted ASAP. Barmaids across Ireland would be ecstatic."

In spite of himself, he smiled. Her complaint was lighthearted, and had been delivered with her own smile.

He didn't allow his smile to last. She was not his friend; she was not going to stay in Cloughban.

"Be here tomorrow at eleven."

"I'll be working a split shift?"

He nodded.

"It's not like you do any business at lunchtime," she argued. "You don't need me."

He glared at her, just a little.

"Fine, fine, I'll be here by eleven."

If tonight's reception to her was any indication, his noontime business was about to pick up. Not that he would tell her that. She might take it as a compliment. As they got to know her, his customers seemed to forget that her last name was Raintree. Most of them, anyway.

"Don't be late."

She headed to the back of the room to grab her sweater. "Never again, boss, I swear. I'll be here early. I'll stay all day. Whatever it takes to convince you that I am not spoiled and undisciplined, I'll do it."

"I'll believe that when I see it. Good night, Raintree."

"Night, boss." She exited by the front door, and when she was gone the pub felt suddenly and completely empty.

Even satellite phones were not entirely secure, but all things considered…there was no other choice.

"There's a Raintree in Cloughban."

After a short pause, the man on the other end of the line asked, "Which one?"

"Echo, the prophet."

The sigh of relief on the other end of the line could be heard from miles away. Hundreds or thousands of miles? That was a mystery. "She's no threat. They worried about her during the conflict with the Ansara, but she was not a factor."

The Raintree clan was always a factor! "I can kill her if you'd like." It was a thrill to watch someone die, and a Raintree! Not just any Raintree, either, but their prophet. The keeper of their Sanctuary. At least, she used to be keeper. What was she now? Why was she here?

"No!" The sharp command left no room for argument. "A suspicious death would only bring in more of them. Just watch, for now. Alert me to any unusual activity."

Too bad.

There was a short pause, then, "Does she know?"

"I don't believe so."

A pause, a gentle hum. "Perhaps she's there to recruit Duncan."

That was a startling thought. Ryder Duncan, part of the Raintree clan? That would be a disaster for all who opposed them. "If you let me kill her…"

Again, "No."

In the past, hundreds of strays had been called to Cloughban. No, not hundreds. Thousands. This place, the stones that fed the energy that surrounded and flooded it, had been here for thousands of years. Maybe longer than anyone knew. Was it possible that Echo had been called here by the power of the stones, as others had? If she knew everything, if she suspected, she would not have come here on her own.

Echo Raintree walked toward the house where she was renting a room. Her stride was slow and easy. Was her presence here really a coincidence? She didn't seem to be on alert, and she *was* here alone. If she knew what was coming, if any of them knew, others would be with her. An army of Raintree would be swarming the countryside.

"Keep an eye on her for now."

"Of course."

The call ended abruptly. It was just business, after all.

Echo walked into the house. A few moments later, the light in a second-floor window came on. She was there. Right there. On her own and unprepared. It would be so easy...

Maybe killing the Raintree woman wasn't approved just yet, but a good scare to make her leave town would probably be seen as clever initiative.

The whisper was caught on the wind that picked up. "I'll be watching."

Chapter 5

Echo walked through the front door of the pub, ready to get to work. Already the place felt a little like home to her. The warm atmosphere, the smell of ale and wood polish, gave a kind of comfortable aura. Ryder Duncan stood behind the bar in his usual place, and he did not look happy. He glanced up, shot some seriously dark eye daggers her way, then shook his head.

The Drunken Stone was a lot busier than it had been yesterday. The same three old men were in what was probably their usual spot, but today four other tables were occupied. At this time of day there was more food and tea being served than cider and beer. It truly was a village gathering place. Every town needed a place like this one.

She dropped her sweater and purse in the back room, then headed toward a grumpy Duncan. "What's up?"

"You're twenty-three minutes late," he said in a sharp voice.

"That's specific." She looked around and saw no clock. He wasn't wearing a watch. One of his things, she imagined.

"What happened to *'I'll be on time, boss'*?"

"I wanted to look around town, and it's not like you do a lot of lunch business."

Duncan swept his hand out to indicate the customers.

"Well, how was I supposed to know?"

"Table four's order is up," he snapped as Doyle walked out of the kitchen.

Echo got to work without delay. Thank goodness the customers were a lot friendlier than her boss. They were a little distant—they didn't treat her as if she were one of their own—but they weren't outwardly rude the way Brigid had been when Echo had mentioned her name.

A couple of them called her *love*, and she did not chastise them. Their intent seemed to be cordial enough. Duncan hadn't called her *love* since she'd told him not to. If he called her anything at all it was Raintree. On his lips, her surname sounded like a curse.

The early lunch crowd was all male, but just after noon three women came in together. It was obvious that they were here to see her. One of the three was Brigid, the woman who'd sold Echo her green sweater before getting all snippy. The way the women glared at her, with interest and more than a touch of antagonism... apparently they didn't get a lot of new people in Cloughban. Apparently they didn't want new people.

It didn't take any special abilities to tell that these

ladies didn't like her. Gideon kept insisting she was a powerful empath, but Echo had fought that curse tooth and nail. Endure the feelings of those around her as well as her own? Experience their hate, love, heartbreak and fear as if it was her own? No, thanks. Whenever she felt that ability drift to the surface, she did her best to beat it down.

As she was cleaning up a recently vacated booth, she heard one woman say to Brigid, "I asked Rye about hiring Shay a few months back, and he said he wasn't busy enough to take on a waitress. Apparently this Echo has special skills that my Shay doesn't possess."

The innuendo was so blatant it couldn't even be called innuendo. It was an out-and-out insult. Echo considered setting the woman straight, but Duncan insisted that she learn discipline. She supposed letting something like that slide was the height of discipline. She'd show him.

While the women waited for their food to be prepared, Echo managed to stay busy elsewhere. She chatted with a couple of customers, and cleaned tables that didn't really need to be cleaned. When it was ready, she delivered thick vegetable soup and ham and cheese sandwiches to the table. She managed to keep a smile on her face, a smile that was not returned. She even nodded to Brigid, an acknowledgment that they had met. Echo was no fool. The tight T-shirt had been intended to appeal to Duncan's male customers. It only seemed to piss the women off.

It was odd. Yesterday, right after she'd arrived, everything in town had seemed so bright. The flowers, the shop windows, the people. Brigid wore a nice outfit she'd surely gotten at her own shop, but it was a drab gray green. The other two were dressed plainly; they wore little or no makeup, and but for plain wedding rings they wore no jewelry, either. If there were Children of the Corn nearby, she was looking at their mothers.

The wind picked up. Echo heard it howling around the building, rattling the door, as she placed a fresh pitcher of water on the table. The wind whistled, danced and howled. The wooden sign that read Drunken Stone, a sign that hung outside near the entrance, clanked loudly against the side of the building. One of the women jumped. The other two ignored the howl and whistle of the wind. Maybe it was normal, for Cloughban. She hadn't been here long enough to know.

They ate, but did not linger afterward. The woman who had mentioned "her Shay" gave Echo one last glare as she walked out the door and into the wind, which caught her dark hair and made it stand straight up for one weird moment.

When the last of the lunchtime customers had left, Echo sat at the bar and faced Duncan. Again.

"Sorry I was late," she said with sincerity. "It won't happen again."

"I'll believe that when I see it."

She couldn't very well argue with him. She *had* been late.

There was so much she wanted to know about the man before her. The questions that filled her head as she looked at him were all personal. *Are you married, boss? Got a girlfriend? I didn't see a gym on my way into town, so how do you keep those muscles? I see Romany in you and I know the Irish are not fans of tinkers, so how did you get here?*

None of those were wise questions, so she said simply, "Tell me about Cloughban."

His response was immediate and rather cool. "Why?"

"I know it's home for you, but to me Cloughban is entirely different from anywhere I've ever lived. It's so far off the beaten path I had a hard time finding it. I kept getting turned around." She couldn't keep looking into his eyes, which were so dark and deep and angry they made her shiver. "I know there are farms nearby— I saw a ton of sheep on the way in—but…why does anyone live here? Why live so far away from everything?"

"You don't see the charm?" Again, his sarcasm.

"Don't get me wrong. It's nice enough, in a *'I want to remove myself from society'* kind of way, but where's the nightlife? What do the people of Cloughban do for fun?"

"Fun?" he asked, as if the concept were a foreign one.

"Music, theater, sports. Good heavens, Duncan, I haven't even found a hint of Wi-Fi anywhere in town." She'd walked around town all morning with her cell phone set to Wi-Fi and held high above her head as she watched for a flicker of a connection. Nada.

"Ah, the internet. I've heard of that."

She gasped, shocked, then almost instantly realized he was pulling her leg. So he did have a sense of humor in there. Somewhere.

"I pretty much figured there would be no cell service here." If she'd planned this trip more carefully, she would've invested in a satellite phone. But she hadn't so she was off the grid, so to speak. "And as I said, no Wi-Fi."

He leaned against the bar, casual but still wound tight. "You live in a world of electronics. We don't. Instead of playing computer games, we play cards or board games. Instead of chatting with people online, we chat with actual living, breathing people. Face-to-face. For escapist entertainment we have books, and storytellers."

"Storytellers?"

"They tell the tales of fairies and leprechauns, of dark magic and light. Nevan is a quite talented *seana-chai*. Why do we have need of Wi-Fi?"

"In this day and age it's barbaric to be without it," she said softly.

Duncan smiled. He *did* have a nice smile. Among other attributes. Her heart did a little extraexcited pitter-pat. Wait, no, that was not just her heart.

Damn, this was bad. Why couldn't he be an old white-haired man with stooped shoulders and yellow teeth? Why couldn't Nevan be the local wizard? She'd never be tempted to just sit and look at *him*.

"What about music?" she asked.

"There's music in church on Sunday morning, and on occasion the schoolchildren will put on a show."

She'd seen the quaint two-room schoolhouse as she'd driven into town. Judging by the size of the building and the number of people she'd seen out and about, there probably wouldn't be much more than a dozen children in that school. How good could they be?

Music was essential to life. It was a way to express joy and sorrow. The right song at the right time had the power to lift her spirits even on the worst day. She couldn't live without it, and didn't want to try. Whether listening or singing herself, she *needed* music.

Gathering her courage, she said, "I sing."

Duncan was not impressed. "Many people do. Crazy old Tully sings all the time. He can't carry a tune, though, so don't encourage him."

He wasn't going to make this easy for her. Why had she expected that he would? Everything about Duncan was difficult. "That's not what I mean," she said. "Is there a guitar in this town?"

"Of course there is."

There was no "of course" about it. She could take nothing for granted here.

Echo felt as if she was definitely experiencing some of the worst days of her life. A difficult and reluctant teacher. An imaginary little girl. No Wi-Fi! She needed music. It was the one thing she was good at that was normal, that required no magic. When she sang she had nothing to hide from the world.

"Tonight, instead of just waiting tables, how about you let me sing for your customers?"

For the first time since she'd met him, Duncan looked genuinely surprised. "Why?"

She leaned slightly over the bar, excited in a way she hadn't been in quite a while. "Trust me, boss."

He leaned toward her. Holy crappola, he smelled like fresh-cut grass and spring rain and *man*. Why did he have to smell good? Why couldn't he stink?

His voice was emotionless as he asked, "When you have a job that includes singing, do you show up on time?"

"Always."

"Then we have a deal." He offered his hand for a shake, and she took it. They shook once, then quickly released. Echo's hand continued to tingle long after he'd let it go. She could still feel his touch as she stepped outside. Must be a wizard thing, she decided as she headed back toward her rented room, a couple of fresh Drunken Stone T-shirts clutched in her hand.

She was almost there when she realized that the wind had died down. It was actually quite a lovely day. Cool, but sunny and clear. She'd teased Duncan about living here, and she did feel as if she'd lost a limb without her phone, but there were moments when she very clearly saw the appeal. It was almost like stepping back in time to the fifties or the sixties. She didn't have to worry about email or phone messages, and she hadn't even turned on the small television in her room.

There was one problem, though. Her cousins would have a fit if she just disappeared without a word. The last thing she needed was Gideon, Mercy, and Dante searching for her. They were busy with their own families, their own hectic lives, but eventually they *would* miss her. She'd be easy enough to follow to a certain point, through the plane ticket and car rental, and she had no doubt that they could find her here if they tried.

She did not want her cousins and Duncan to come face-to-face with her in the middle. No way. Not ever. Her family could and would find her if they put their minds to it. She'd told them she wanted to be on her own for a while, so there was no reason for them to search for her right away, but still…maybe she should make sure.

Echo decided she'd change clothes and then head into town for a few postcards and stamps. She didn't need to say much. A simple "I'm fine, need some time alone" should do the trick.

* * *

Rye sat in the rear booth Nevan and his pals usually occupied for a good part of the day, his legs thrust beneath the table. Even they were gone. Echo and Doyle wouldn't be back for a couple of hours; he had the place to himself.

He grasped the small, warm stone in his hand and closed his eyes, and there she was. Echo, a picture in his mind. A picture as clear as if she truly stood before him. She'd changed clothes. She wore jeans still, but now she wore boots and a loose-fitting long-sleeved purple shirt instead of a Drunken Stone T-shirt and comfortable tennis shoes. She smiled at the young man who sold her three postcards. He was smitten. She had no idea.

The smile was real, even though the pain of her gift tormented her. He'd seen her suffer; he knew she was tormented by the visions. Visions that commanded her, when it should be the other way around. Waking nightmares that tore at her very soul. He should not want to help her, should not care. But he did.

He'd tried to help Sybil, hadn't he? He'd seen her suffering and had done everything he could to save her. That attempt to help had ended so very badly... No, he could not let his mind go there, could not relive failures of the past. This time would be different. There would be no personal involvement.

If he failed, if she died, he would be able to move on without feeling as if the entire world had been ripped apart beneath his feet.

So why was he watching her? Why did he sit in a dark corner and use his abilities to spy on her as she engaged in perfectly ordinary activities? She sat at an empty table outside the coffee shop, took a pen from her purse and began to write on the postcards. Three short notes.

Her activities were ordinary—there was nothing for him to be alarmed about—but he did not stop watching, did not release the stone and clear his mind of her even though he knew he should. Echo was nothing like Sybil, not in looks or in temperament. She wasn't like his last student, either, an eager young man who'd wanted much more than he'd initially revealed.

Echo was an open book; she hid nothing from him.

Everyone in Cloughban knew what he was; they knew what he could do. Some of it, anyway. No one knew all, though he was certain a few suspected. Most of them were not entirely normal themselves, though no others had earned the designation *wizard*. Touched with magic, they had been drawn here as his ancestors had been. Some stayed for a year or two and moved on. Others were lifelong residents. A few came just for a few weeks, curious or needing a short refuge.

Echo asked why anyone would live here, and he had not been able to give her a truthful answer. *Here, I am with my kind. Here, I am safe from prying eyes.* And most importantly, *Here, I feed on the power of the stones.*

He never should've agreed to help her, never should've allowed himself to get caught up in her troubles. It was not too late to remedy that mistake, no matter what Cassidy had told her. Very little in this life was written in stone. *He* was in charge. He could and would change what was, perhaps, meant to be.

All he had to do was tell Echo he'd changed his mind about helping and send her away. All he had to do was look her in the eye and say, "No." Sounded simple enough, but as he watched her from a distance, he wondered if it would be that easy.

Chapter 6

Postcards mailed, Echo walked back toward the Quinlan house. She wondered if she had time for a nap. No, if she overslept and was late for work again, Duncan would kill her!

The white clapboard bed-and-breakfast was as charming as everything else in Cloughban, outside and in. It was well maintained, in spite of its obvious age. The porch, the lace curtains in the downstairs windows, the plain furnishings—everything was spotless. The kitchen was small but functional, as was the dining room. Mrs. Quinlan—there was never any mention of a Mr. Quinlan and Echo didn't feel she knew her landlady well enough to ask—slept in the single downstairs bedroom, while upstairs there were three bedrooms and a shared bath for her paying customers. At the moment, only two of those rooms were occupied. Since Echo and Maisy kept very different hours, they didn't see each other often. Just as well. As far as Echo could see, Maisy had preferred having the second floor to herself.

Maybe she disliked sharing a bathroom.

Maybe she was like those women who'd come into the pub simply to glare at the new woman in town. Maisy was very pretty, tall and dark-haired and definitely a D-cup, so Echo didn't see how she could see one more female in the mix as a threat, but…they were definitely *not* becoming friends.

There were several shelves of books in the downstairs parlor. As she passed by, Echo thought that maybe she'd grab one of those and read awhile. Then again, maybe she'd turn on the television in her room and see if it picked up more than one or two stations.

But, oh, a nap sounded so good. She still hadn't adjusted to the time change.

Echo passed on the book, deciding to check first to see if there was anything on the television. She ran up the stairs, more energetic than she should be, all things considered, and threw open the door to her room. It wasn't locked. What did she have to safeguard?

The first thing she noticed was that her bed had been neatly made. The next thing she saw was a manila envelope propped on her pillow. Maybe Maeve had dropped off the recipe for her scones, which Echo had praised that very morning.

She snatched the envelope off the bed, plopped down in the faded blue wing chair by the window and removed the contents.

Her heart nearly stopped. The single sheet in the envelope was *not* a recipe.

It was a recent photograph of her parents.

Echo had accepted a long time ago—somewhere around the age of nine—that her mother and father were useless in a crisis. They were not great parents and never had been. A child had never been in their plans. They liked to travel, to party at any opportunity. Her father's gifts had never been very strong. He could read minds, when he worked at it. Her mother had been a stray—an independent, Duncan called them—who had the occasional bit of insight into what was to come.

Maybe it wasn't fair to say they were useless. They did love her. Difficult as they were, she'd never doubted that. But they had never really known what to do with a daughter who had nightmares about disasters, a daughter who woke screaming in the night. A daughter who was much more powerful than they had ever been or could ever hope to be.

She knew the photo was recent because her mother's haircut—shared in an email a few weeks back—was new. It looked as if they were in Paris. Yes, that was definitely Paris.

In the photo, the eyes of both her parents had been crossed out, messily and completely, with a ballpoint pen.

Her hands began to shake, her breath would not come. This was a blatant threat to their lives, she understood that much, but why here and why now? Who even knew she was here?

She'd just sent postcards to her cousins insisting that all was well. Postcards they wouldn't receive for days. Maybe weeks, considering where they'd been mailed from. Now this.

For a few long seconds she sat there, horrifying picture grasped in her hands, heart beating so hard she could feel it pounding against her chest as if it wanted to escape. She didn't know what to do. She didn't know who to turn to. One word came to mind, as she began to recover from the shock.

Duncan.

Not only was Echo not late, she was more than an hour early. And she was not dressed for work. She was dressed as she had been that afternoon as she'd wandered about town with that easy smile on her face. For a moment Rye thought she'd shown up early to demand that they begin their lessons. That would be the time to tell her that he'd changed his mind.

No, that wasn't why she was here. Something was wrong. Her face was oddly pale; her hands shook. He wondered if she'd had another vision—or was about to—and then she shook a manila envelope in his direction and said, "I don't know what to do."

She sat in the nearest chair, her legs giving out from under her, and held the envelope up for him to take.

Rye walked slowly toward her. He'd spent the past hour trying to decide how to tell her that he'd made a mistake and she had to go. Now. Tonight. He couldn't afford to care about her troubles, and he sure as hell didn't want to be her knight in shining armor. He was the last man in the world to fill those shoes.

He grabbed the envelope and removed the single sheet inside. It was easy enough to tell that the attractive older woman in the picture was Echo's mother. They favored quite a bit.

"It was on my bed," she said. "Just…sitting there. I thought it was a recipe." She took a couple of deep, too-fast breaths. He worried she was on the verge of hyperventilating. "It's a threat to my parents, right? My cell phone is worthless here. I dug it out of my bag instinctively, then just stared at it for a moment. I can't call anyone, can't send an email or…or…" Her eyes widened. "Police. Are there police here? A constable? A…an inspector?"

"Of course, but…"

She stood, seemingly a bit stronger now that she had a plan. He didn't dare to tell her that the single constable in Cloughban wouldn't know what to do, wouldn't care, wouldn't help at all.

"I have to go," she said. "That's all there is to it. When I get to the next town over I'll call my mom's cell, and I'll call Dante, too. Maybe Gideon. Definitely Gideon." Mercy? No, Mercy was too far away to get immediately involved, though it was possible one or both of her brothers would call her. "I'm not that far from Paris, I can get there in…"

Rye placed his hands on her shoulders. A few hours ago he would've been relieved to hear those words. *I have to go.* He'd had the same thoughts all afternoon. Yes, Echo Raintree had to go. Out of his life, away from Cloughban. Away from Cassidy. Dammit.

"You're not going anywhere." Against his new plans, against his better judgment.

"But I…"

"I have a phone, a landline. You can use it to call whoever you need to call."

"Okay, thank you." She looked up at him, eyes wide, lips full and far too tempting. "I'll do that, but then I have to go."

He knew that was a bad idea. With magic and without, he knew that no matter how unwise it was for her to stay, leaving would be worse. Dammit, she was going to turn his life upside down.

"You're going to stay here," he insisted. "We're not finished."

She shook her head.

His temper got the best of him and he snapped, "You can't tell me the entire Raintree clan can't protect two of their own from whatever or whoever threatens them."

"Oh!" Echo's green eyes shone. Her tense shoulders dropped a little as she relaxed. "If they're on Sanctuary land they'll be fine. Maybe they can take over my old job for a while."

"Your old job?"

She grimaced. "I was keeper of the Raintree Sanctuary."

In his experience, she did not have the discipline to be the keeper of anything. She was a roamer, a butterfly. A princess, not a queen. "You were replaced?"

She wrinkled her nose. "I quit last year and left a few months ago. Dante was very unhappy, but others have filled in since then. My parents can be next in line."

She relaxed; she smiled. "They won't like it, but they'll be safe there." He could almost see her body unwinding. "Everyone else I care about can more than take care of themselves."

Of course they could. *Raintree.*

On occasion Rye had to remind himself that Echo was no normal woman. No lost and mildly gifted stray looking for others like herself, no independent in need of his assistance.

Doyle arrived early tonight, too. He sauntered through the front door, squinted as his eyes adjusted

to the dimness of the pub, smiled when he saw Echo.
His shoulders squared. Holy God, the woman was trouble. Doyle had been a perfectly steady and reliable employee since coming to town eight months ago. The man was nearing thirty, as Echo was. He was handsome enough to have caught the interest of a handful of women in town, ordinary enough not to cause a stir. Like most of the others in Cloughban, Doyle was different. Telekinesis was his gift. Rye had caught him moving pots about the kitchen a time or two, but he didn't like anyone to watch. Once, when Rye had walked in and caught Doyle playing—or practicing—several pots had wobbled in the air and then hit the floor at once. The stones fed Doyle's gifts, as they fed those of the other independents—strays—in town.

Echo nodded in Doyle's direction. "I have a couple of phone calls to make, but when I'm done can I get a bowl of soup and some brown bread? I think I'm getting addicted to your brown bread."

Doyle beamed. "Aye, lass. I'll get to it."

"Thanks."

Again, she looked up at Rye. "What are you scowling at, boss?"

"I'm not scowling. This way to the phone." He gestured with one hand and she stood. For a moment, a second or two, she stood too close. He could feel her body heat, smell her shampoo, sense the tremendous energy that rolled off her very fine body. She held her breath, and so did he.

Powers he'd tamped down for years shimmered. They danced. A part of himself that he'd buried deep—for good reason—took a breath as it tried to come to life. It took all his control to push it back down again.

He could not afford to allow the wizard he had once been to return. The stones that fed his power, that made Cloughban such a special place, also allowed him to control what he was. What he had once been.

Echo would not like what he had once been.

Walking behind her he pushed down the urge to brush her soft blond hair aside and kiss her neck. For comfort. For her and for himself. Just because he damned well wanted to know what that tempting neck tasted like.

He had no prophetic gifts; he did not know what the future held. But he knew that, like it or not, he wasn't going to get rid of her anytime soon.

In years past Echo had played for smaller crowds, but not often. She'd admit that in the early days her all-girl band had been, well, a little rough when it came to hitting all the right notes. That had changed with time, but in those first few months they hadn't been able to draw much of a crowd beyond drunk guys who thought it would be hot to hook up with a bass player or a drummer. The band had gotten better and had eventually built a following, but it had taken time.

She'd never performed alone, not until now.

Tonight less than a dozen warm bodies were scattered about the pub. The size of the crowd was a little disappointing. Of course, it was a weeknight. Maybe weekends were livelier.

At least those who were present seemed to like what they were hearing. She didn't have to call on her weak and unwanted empathic abilities to see that. Several customers in the room smiled, a few tapped their feet or patted fingers on a table in time to the music. They all faced the stage and listened.

For tonight Echo sang ballads, love songs, a couple of sappy songs she'd written herself. To really rock out she needed a band behind her. Drums, a bass guitar, an electric piano and amplifiers. At least two *big* amplifiers. One woman and one acoustic guitar made for a quieter, gentler form of entertainment.

What would happen if she had an episode while she was on the postage-stamp-size stage in the Drunken Stone? She hadn't had to worry about that before, when the visions had only come in her dreams. She hadn't dared to sing in public since her powers had shifted and she never knew when she might be affected. Driving was risk enough, though she'd always told herself she could sense a vision coming on in time to pull to the side of the road. Maybe.

Now, however, she did worry. A little. How was she supposed to live her life if Duncan couldn't help her manage this? Not for the first time, she wondered why his method of ridding her of the ability was so dangerous.

Sometimes she liked to imagine the life she would live without the visions. The people she could meet, the things she could do. No more worry about others finding out who she was and what she could do. No more hiding. It would be worth any risk to live that life.

Echo loved to play the guitar; she loved to sing. The fact that her fingers had already begun to hurt were a clear indication that it had been too long. She'd lost her calluses.

Tonight there were no visions. There was just music and laughter and applause. Even Duncan seemed to enjoy her performance. Doyle came out of the kitchen a time or two to wait tables and lean against the bar to listen to her. He liked her a little, she knew, but he wasn't her type. He was a nice guy. She'd never really gone for nice guys.

That was going to have to change. If she could manage a normal life without visions, without being called a prophet ever again, she'd eventually need a nice guy. The normal package—marriage, commitment, the whole wonderfully humdrum deal—didn't work with the kind of bad boy she was usually attracted to.

Her mind went to her current family. Gideon was in charge of getting her parents to Sanctuary, and she had no doubt about his abilities to do so. The phone call had been tense, to say the least. He'd asked too many questions she couldn't answer.

He'd been pissed to find out where she was; at least he didn't know why she was here.

Halfway through her set, Maisy—the librarian the landlady had been so sure would be a great friend—came in with her good friend Shay. They were both pretty girls. Maisy had very dark brown hair; Shay's was thick and a rich auburn. Dressed in their best—tight sweaters and short skirts and boots—they drew a lot of attention as they walked in.

It took no special powers to realize that neither of these women would ever be a friend to Echo. She got a sharp glance from both girls, then they gave their full piranha-like attention to the bar and the two men there.

Shay had her sights set firmly on Duncan; Maisy smiled coyly at Doyle. The poor guys didn't stand a chance...

Outside the pub, the wind howled with a sudden

burst. A few heads turned toward the rattling door. Echo continued to play without a hitch; this was a song she knew well.

Shay leaned over the counter, all but thrusting her breasts at Duncan. Hers were not as impressive as Maisy's, but she didn't have a boyish figure, either. Echo couldn't care less, but really, did the woman have no shame?

The wind picked up and the old building creaked. The wind howled so loudly it drowned out a couple of words of her song. Everyone looked up and back; the door rattled as if an invisible hand was shaking it, trying desperately to get in.

This was a weird town, and Echo had to wonder if someone in the pub, or outside it, was responsible for the sudden wind. Someone who had a gift for manipulating the weather. Someone who could bring the wind and the rain.

Duncan caught her eye, and a voice—*his* voice—whispered in her head.

That someone is you, love.

Chapter 7

"I don't control the weather," Echo said succinctly when she and Rye were finally alone. She'd been about to burst with questions for the past two hours, but she'd held it in until everyone else had left.

"There was little bleedin' control involved, I'll grant you that." She'd come to him in order to master the visions she did not want, and it was clear that she fought natural empathic abilities, as well. Now this? What other surprises were hidden deep in that seemingly delicate body?

The guitar she'd borrowed from him lay abandoned on the small stage; all the customers, as well as Doyle, had gone home. As they'd left, a few had whispered that a fierce storm might be coming.

They were not entirely wrong.

"You were upset to see Maisy flirting with Doyle, I expect, and that…"

"I was not!" Echo snapped defensively.

No, it had not been Doyle. Rye had seen into her mind clearly enough to know better, but she didn't need to know everything he saw or sensed. He didn't like how easily he slipped into her mind, how oddly near her thoughts were to his. The ability to see so much wasn't normal for him, not now. Even before, such connections had been all but impossible.

"Something upset you, and the wind came," he said. "Was it a missed note? An unexpected thought of your parents?"

She leaned back, pursed her lips and then said, "I did think about my parents and wonder how long it would take Gideon to get them to Sanctuary."

"That was likely it, then."

Echo seemed to relax a little. "Maybe there was just a perfectly normal shift in the weather," she argued.

"Wishful thinking, love." The endearment slipped out. *Love.* Maybe she was so upset she'd miss it. "There was nothing normal about that change in the wind."

She narrowed one eye. The expression was likely meant to be fearsome, but it was not. There was not a fearsome bone in her fine body. "By the way, speaking of *not normal*…stay out of my head!"

He remained calm. "You invited me in, or I could not have been there."

"Did not."

Rye leaned back in his chair, thrusting his legs out and trying for a casual pose. He felt anything but relaxed. "You have a gift for song."

"Don't change the subject."

"I'm not. It's time we started your lessons, properly." The sooner it was done, the sooner he could send her away with a clear conscience. "You have a gift for song," he said again, "as you have a gift for other things."

This time, she remained silent.

"Do you burst spontaneously into song without warning? While in the market, or on the street, or sitting in church, do you begin to sing without control?"

She looked confused, and perhaps a little insulted. "Of course not."

He edged forward, placed his elbows on the table between them, and lowered his voice. "It is the same."

She did not hesitate to respond with heat. "It is not at all the…"

"It is the same," he whispered. "As you learn to play the guitar, to hit a certain note with that lovely voice of yours, to sing the right words in the correct sequence. It is very much the same."

She was quiet as she considered his words. "You make it sound so easy."

"No, love, it is not at all easy. Neither is it impossible.

"You are more capable than you realize," he added.

Echo Raintree was beautiful and she possessed incredible talents, but she did not give off an aura of strength. No one would ever see her coming and be afraid. She did not, could not, instill fear with a glance. She was a pretty girl, always lost, always searching for answers. But he saw the strength within her, trapped. Hiding, even from herself.

She fought her strength, denied it. That denial was why she was here now. It was why she was late on occasion, why she ran from the truth of who she was. All her life she'd made light of her abilities, as she'd tried to tamp them down. The result was the mess that sat before him. Echo was definitely a beautiful, out-of-control mess. In order to move on, she would have to not only accept her great abilities, she would have to embrace them.

"I don't feel capable at all," she said. "I feel weak and as if my entire life is out of my control. Not just the visions, but…everything."

She needed a teacher; he had no choice but to become one, for her. One more time. One final student. "The strength is in you. Find it."

Unexpectedly, she reached out a hand and cupped his cheek. The darkness he had buried deep leaped; his body responded to that simple touch. He instinctively jerked away from her touch.

She leaned back, moved away from him. "Sorry. I…" She stood, grabbed her sweater and purse and headed for the exit. "Sometimes I'm a complete moron."

He heard the unspoken end of that thought as she walked through that door without looking back.

Where men are concerned.

It was her day off. She could very easily get into her rental car and drive to a bigger town where she could buy a nice meal, see a movie, shop in a store where she didn't get the evil eye and—miracle of miracles—pick up a cell signal and Wi-Fi on her phone!

Instead, Echo left the boardinghouse and her rental car behind and started walking. Down the road a bit, then easily over a low stone fence and into a green field.

She'd heard that Ireland was an amazing green. The

Emerald Isle. It was the kind of visual that couldn't be explained in mere words. Even pictures didn't do it justice. She walked until the boardinghouse was well behind her, allowing her mind to wander as she moved farther away from Cloughban.

It did wander. To songs and visions, to her family and to friends she hadn't seen in a very long time. It even wandered to Ryder Duncan a time or two. Those annoying thoughts she attempted to push aside, but they always came back.

Duncan was necessary, nothing more. The fact that he was gorgeous and had those great, dark eyes, that he sometimes made her heart beat faster than it should, those were simple distractions. Nothing more.

And, if she were being honest, not so simple.

After she'd been walking twenty minutes or so a strange, thick fog moved in. It carpeted the green fields, hid what might be over the next knoll from her curious eyes.

There were a few odd cottages here and there. Beyond the few primary streets of the village, there were no neighborhoods. No subdivisions. Just small cottages spaced randomly, as if someone had sprinkled them across the countryside with a casual wave of their hand. All the houses she saw looked as if they'd been built a hundred years ago, or more.

In the distance she caught a glimpse of something unexpected. Stones. Lots of them. A few more steps and a shift of the fog and she realized it was—or had been—a structure of some kind. As she drew closer she realized that what she'd spotted had once been a castle. A small castle, but still…a castle. The fog danced around the base of the stones, thick and white. Not much of the castle was left, but a large part of what had once been a tower remained standing. Not very sturdily, but still standing.

What little girl didn't dream of being a princess in a castle? She had, long ago. She'd had her share of plastic tiaras and scratchy princess dresses.

It wasn't until years later that she'd decided being queen would be much better. Queens answered to no one. They commanded; they did what they wanted to do when they wanted. If a queen ordered a princess to dance until she dropped, the princess would do so.

Wishes aside, she had always been a princess. She danced to a tune that was not her own, and always had.

Echo stopped for a long moment; she stared at the picture before her. Green grass and ancient gray stone, nothing and no one for miles around. This was the Ireland she had always dreamed of. She had the unexpected thought that she could live here. She could stay in this quiet and beautiful place.

No, beautiful as it was, it was not *her* place.

"Hello."

Echo recognized that voice, and then she caught sight of a head of red, curling hair coming out of the fog.

"Cassidy!" Echo said, surprised and pleased. The child was not a hallucination. At least, she didn't think so...

"You found the fairy fort," the redheaded girl said as she drew closer, her figure moving out of the fog and into the light. "Be careful or one might try to hitch a ride home with you."

Echo smiled. "Fairies. This castle is their fort?"

"Don't be silly. The fort is over there." Cassidy

pointed to a slightly raised mound not far from the ruins.

"And these…" Oh, she could hardly say it! "Fairies. They're a problem?"

"They're usually quiet and well behaved, as long as you don't disturb them."

It took Echo a moment to realize the child was serious. "I will do my best. What are you doing here?"

"I came to see you, of course."

Echo glanced around her. True, the fog was thick but…where had the child come from? "How did you know I would be here?"

"I just know things," Cassidy said in a matter-of-fact voice, and then she dipped her chin and looked up at Echo with eyes too old for one so young. "So do you, sometimes."

If Cassidy was a hallucination, she wouldn't feel solid to the touch. Echo took a step toward the girl, intent on placing a hand on her shoulder. Just to be sure. Girl? Ghost? Pure imagination?

Cassidy smiled and took a step back. "He likes you. He likes you a lot."

"Who likes me?"

The little girl giggled, and then said, "You know who."

"I don't…" Echo began. She was almost close enough to touch the child. Almost there. She reached out, slowly, so as not to alarm the kid. Up close Cassidy looked real. She appeared to be solid.

Just as before, Cassidy disappeared without warning. Poof. Gone.

"Dammit!" Echo stomped her foot on the lush, green grass. Then she turned and looked toward the fairy fort. She'd always put fairies in the same classification as the Easter Bunny. Pure fantasy. But there was definitely something odd going on here. Was it possible…?

She shook her head and turned away. No. She would not go there! She'd seen a lot of inexplicable things in her life; she knew magic existed. Magic those who were not a part of her world would dismiss without a second thought. Ghosts, premonitions, elements that could be manipulated with a wave of the hand. Again, she looked toward the mound. She drew the line at fairies. And leprechauns.

At that moment a gentle breeze kicked up. Tall grass around the fairy fort danced as the wind whistled around what was left of the castle.

"No way." Echo turned and headed back toward town. She had a long walk ahead of her, a long walk in which she'd have time to think, and to talk herself out of what she'd seen and heard. A nap, that's what she needed. A nice long nap.

Strange or not, this was a beautiful place. An enchanted land. She'd never seen grass so green or fog so thick. She'd never seen a child—or an adult, for that matter—appear and disappear at will.

As the village ahead came into view, Echo wished she'd had time to ask Cassidy again, "Who likes me?"

It rained for three days straight. Echo couldn't help but wonder if it was her fault. Her mood was definitely gloomy, and if Duncan was right and she'd discovered a new unwanted power in Cloughban…great. Just what she didn't need. She wanted to dampen—or even better, get rid of—the powers she possessed, not pick up another one she didn't know how to control.

The weather was so persistently wet she braved her way to Brigid's shop and bought a dark green raincoat and matching waterproof boots. While the shop owner didn't refuse to sell merchandise to her, she also wasn't the friendly, welcoming woman she'd been before Echo had spoken her name.

She wanted to ask the woman straight out what had happened. Why the change in attitude? But as curious as she was, she didn't see the point. Brigid didn't like Echo. Her friends didn't, either. If she was going to stay here maybe she'd feel compelled to find out what had happened and try to address the issue. But she was temporary here, and it didn't matter.

The rain didn't keep customers out of Duncan's pub. With raincoats and galoshes and umbrellas, they came. Sometimes they came for the beer—and the cider, which Echo much preferred. They gathered to talk, to share stories of their lives.

Sometimes they came to hear her sing.

Her sets were short, the crowds were small. But she sang, and the music soothed her in a way nothing else could. She sang love songs and sad songs, a little country, a little folk, a little new-age stuff. Normally Echo loved to channel Joan Jett, but not without a band behind her. So she settled for the softer stuff.

It was that softer side that was getting a little fixated on Ryder Duncan. *Rye*, most of his friends and customers called him. It was more than his good looks that made him interesting. He had secrets, probably lots of them. Men like him always did. Why no girlfriend? Every single woman in town flirted with him, some more outrageously than others. A few of the married women were just as bold. He kept his distance from them all. He smiled politely; he was never rude—to anyone but her, at least—but there was always a part of himself that he held back.

When she looked hard enough she could almost see the shield he'd built around himself, the shield that kept all those women at a distance. Not just the women, she realized as she watched him speak to a young man who was seated at the bar. His energy was contained, separate, as if he lived in another world and simply observed this one. Why?

Had his heart been broken so badly he didn't dare to love again? Did he have a heart at all?

She needed to stop thinking about Ryder Duncan as anything other than a teacher. For the past several rainy days he had been trying to instruct her in the quiet afternoons when they had the pub to themselves for a couple of hours. He worked with her on learning how to recognize when a vision was coming and how to control it. He insisted that she master the ability instead of allowing it to master her. That sounded good, in theory.

For three days of rain and moping and daydreaming about a slightly surly pub owner, there had been no episodes. There had been no opportunity to practice what she was trying to learn.

Control.

It would help if she actually thought control was possible.

Gideon controlled his abilities, to a certain extent. So did Dante. If not, they'd live in the midst of complete chaos. Their abilities were potentially dangerous. Dante and his fire, Gideon and his lightning. She could not imagine what their lives would be like if their abilities ruled them, rather than the other way around.

Just that afternoon Duncan had asked her, "Are your royal cousins better than you? Stronger? More capable of control?"

When she'd hesitated he'd answered for her.

"No, they are not."

She wished she could believe him.

Echo was about to start the final song of the set when a warning tickle in the back of her brain caught her attention. A niggling feeling, the kind you get when you sense that someone is watching. But this was different. It was deeper; it was a part of her.

It was the warning Duncan had been telling her to keep watch for. A vision was coming, and she did not want that to happen in front of the handful of customers that remained in the pub. Duncan would be able to explain it away, she imagined, whisking her away and telling everyone she had a medical condition, but she needed to learn to handle this on her own. That's why she was here!

It took great effort, but she smiled, set the guitar aside and said good-night. Her fingers trembled; her vision began to turn gray at the edges, taking away her peripheral vision. Her knees went weak. She eased down off the stage carefully, watching her step. One step, then another. *Please, please, not yet.* She headed for the door that opened on the stairway that would lead to the room where Duncan slept. It was her closest escape route—her only chance of getting away from prying eyes before the vision took her.

She heard voices behind her as she placed her hand on the doorknob. They seemed far away, and might as well have been spoken in a foreign language. A few words reached her brain. *Strange girl. Guitar. Another ale. Raintree...*

If she could just get to the bed. Shoot, she'd be satisfied just to make it beyond this door...

And she did. Barely.

Echo closed the door behind her, took two steps—difficult steps, as her legs now felt like lead and her knees shook—and dropped to the stairs. There was just enough control in her fall to keep her from hurting herself.

Forehead resting on one wooden step, hands pressed to another, she closed her eyes and let the vision come. Instead of fighting it, instead of trying to force it down and back, she embraced the scene playing in her head. It was beyond hard to embrace the very thing she'd spent a lifetime fighting, but she took a deep breath and allowed herself to go there, to live in the moment.

Fire, again. God, she hated fire most of all. The heat, the way her lungs burned, the air being sucked away...

But this time there was some semblance of discipline, a sense that she was amid the flames and at the same time not, as if she were having a vivid dream. She made herself survey the scene as if she were truly distanced from it.

She stood in a building—a warehouse, by the looks of it—engulfed in flames. She was at the center; she saw it all. Fire licked at the walls and danced on the ceiling. White-hot fire climbed and danced as if it were a living thing. It looked to her as if the entire building was made of wood that begged to be kindling. The ceilings were high. The walls were awash with graffiti, garish colors in an otherwise colorless place.

In the distance, she heard a faint scream. Who was calling? Where were they? Was she too late again? There was a small explosion, and heat washed over her in a wave that almost threw her to the ground. For a few seconds she had managed to stay in control, but now she could not breathe. She was going to burn; she was going to die here, along with the person she was meant to save...

Suddenly she was not alone. Duncan stood beside her, stoic as ever. Judging by the expression on his face and the easy way he breathed, he was not at all alarmed.

"You're not really near the fire," he said calmly. "You cannot feel the heat."

She knew he was right, but with each second that passed it seemed more real. "I *can* feel it."

He took her shoulders in his big hands and turned her about so she faced him. They were rarely so close. She had to tilt her head back to see his eyes. Reflections of flames danced there.

"Where are we?" he asked sharply. "*When* are we?"

"I don't know..."

Instead of being frustrated with her failure, he remained calm. "You do, love. It's there." He tapped her forehead with one finger. "It's here."

She closed her eyes and took a deep breath. The air she took into her lungs was cool, fresh, not at all heated. She smelled Duncan, not the fire and smoke that would not, could not, harm her. His scent was pleasant; it was his and his alone. He smelled like man and wood polish and grass. He smelled a little like the beer he served but, as far as she could tell, never consumed.

Again, in the distance, that scream. It sounded like a child.

"You can't do the boy any good if you panic." Finally, he began to show a hint of frustration. Just a hint. *"Where. When?"*

Echo took a deep breath of cool, Duncan-scented air, and with it she drew on his calmness. She searched her own mind deeper than she had before. She wasn't in the warehouse; the fire did not threaten her. She was a watcher, sent here by whatever force had gifted or cursed her with this ability.

"Atlanta," she said. "A Peachtree…something."

"Peachtree what, love?" Duncan whispered.

She came up with an address, could see the street sign and the numbers on the old building. The boy should not be here. There was a skateboard…

"When?"

Again, she went to that new place in her head. It was harder than coming up with an address, much harder, but when she saw the time she laughed. "Not yet. Duncan, the fire has not started yet!"

In an instant the vision disappeared, on a flash of flame and a fading scream. Echo opened her eyes to find that she was still on the stairway. Duncan was beside her, one arm wrapped protectively around her. A wonderfully heavy arm was draped around her waist. A comforting hand pressed against her back. She turned her head; his face was right there and she was so happy…she kissed him.

It was a kiss of joy, a way of celebrating a bit of new-found control and the fact that this time she was not too late. But it *was* a kiss, and as kisses sometimes do, it changed quickly.

Echo was far from a stranger to kisses. Friendly and passionate, impulsively and well-planned...she had been kissed. But this kiss with Duncan swept her away in an instant. He tasted so good; their mouths fit together so well. She forgot fire, she forgot the constant rain; she forgot who she was and why she was here. Only for an instant, but it was an instant that shook her to her core.

Duncan's shield didn't come down, not entirely, but it shimmered. It was weakened. Weakened by her and the kiss he had not expected. She felt that, too.

As a first kiss, it was unplanned but stellar. Heaven above, it was amazing. He smelled good. Their mouths fit together without even a hint of awkwardness. Their bodies aligned perfectly, and if she had her way this moment would never end.

It was Duncan who pulled away, who broke the short but passionate kiss with a curse she could not understand. Gaelic, she supposed. She only knew it was a curse because of his tone.

He cursed, but he did not move away. His body remained close to hers; he held her, still.

When Duncan had joined her he'd closed the door behind him, the door between the stairway and the pub and the people there. Though there were many people close, she and her boss, her teacher, were effectively alone. She could relax here, for a moment or two. She did not have to jump up and make excuses, did not have to explain away what had happened. Not the vision or the kiss.

"Thank you," she said. For the help, for the training, for unexpectedly coming into the vision with her, something she had not known was possible. And yes, for the kiss. In spite of his scowl, she grinned. "I have a phone call to make." She jumped up and ran up the stairs to his room; this was a call she'd prefer to make in private.

She was dialing when she glanced up and out the window and realized that the rain had stopped and the moon shone brightly in a cloudless sky.

Chapter 8

Having realized some real success, Echo approached her next lesson with a renewed purpose. If she could help people, if she could save lives instead of simply watching people suffer and die, then she had no right to wish her abilities away. Duncan seemed to understand that she was determined to be a better student.

He locked the pub doors, front and back. Instead of sitting at a table for their lesson, as he normally did, he moved a few tables aside, clearing the center of the big room. She'd meditated and worked on her focus, and they'd discussed her past troubles and tried to identify clues she'd missed, clues that might help her to identify and improve her gifts.

Looking back, she admitted there had been signs she'd missed. She'd been so determined to deny the visions, she'd blocked all the clues.

A part of her still longed to be normal, but who was she kidding? That wasn't meant to be. She was Raintree.

Echo and her teacher, a man she was much too attracted to for her own good, especially after that kiss, stood face-to-face in the space he'd cleared for this lesson. He stood so close she had to tip her head back in order to look him in the eye. Those eyes were so dark, so intense, she held her breath for a long moment. He would barely have to move in order to put his mouth on hers again.

"Why are we here?" she asked when he remained silent and still for too long.

"You came to me, Raintree. Have you changed your mind?"

Echo shook her head. She didn't mean here in Cloughban; she meant here in the center of the pub. But she didn't argue. She knew damn well he hadn't cleared the floor for a dance.

"Listen," he whispered.

Not to him, she knew that, so she didn't respond. He'd get to the point eventually. He always did.

"There's energy everywhere. Inside us, around us. Between us."

Oh, yes, there was definitely energy between them...

"Don't get distracted," he admonished, as if he'd read her mind. Again.

"You are not a carnival fortune-teller," he continued. "There is no ace up your sleeve, no con man's tricks in your repertoire. You, Echo Raintree, are connected to the energy in this world in a way few, if any, will ever know. You are an oracle, a prophet. A miracle."

"I don't understand what this..."

"Accept who you are, here and now. See and feel the energy around us, and accept yourself not as a small part of it but as its master."

"I'm not the master of anything," she whispered.

"You are," he said. "Whether you like it or not, you are. The question is, will you accept who you are or will you deny it until the uncontrolled energy that's flowing into your body destroys you?"

What choice did she have? None.

Duncan rotated his head as if working a crick out of his neck. He closed his eyes. The muscles in his arms and in his neck visibly tensed.

And Echo was assaulted. Under normal circumstances, she'd dismiss the sudden sensations as nerves or maybe an illness coming on. Her stomach clenched. The hairs on her arms stood up and danced. The assault continued; it grew stronger. Yes, this was what a coming vision felt like.

"Energy," Duncan said. "You can allow it to assault you or you can take control."

"How?"

"Shield yourself. Use your own energy to repel mine."

She tried. Goodness knows she'd been taught how to protect herself against negative energies, but it had never felt like this. She was under attack.

"Try harder," Duncan insisted.

Instead of arguing—her first impulse—Echo did. She tried harder. She strengthened her shield, imagined it thicker, stronger. Impenetrable.

She didn't say a word when she no longer felt the distress of the energies Duncan was sending her way, but he knew. Almost immediately he said, "Good. Now, allow a small amount of the energy in."

"I just managed to block it out."

"You're not controlling the energies, though, you're just protecting yourself."

That was the point, right? Echo took a deep breath. No, simple protection was not the point. Not anymore.

She tried to allow a small stream of energy in, but soon her shields fell and she was once again awash in amazing streams of force that Duncan sent her way.

The attack stopped, and he took a step back. "Not bad," he said in a lowered voice. "But we still have a lot of work to do. We'll try again tomorrow."

Tomorrow. She would be here tomorrow, and the next day, and the next. Why did that knowledge bring a smile to her face?

Rye fingered the leather cord that peeked out from his collar. After a moment he made an adjustment, pushing the cord beneath his shirt so it didn't show. The blessed stone at his throat and the leather cuff on his right wrist never came off. They couldn't. He could fashion a charmed amulet for Echo, but he knew her cousins had tried that and charms hadn't proven sufficient.

Besides, he didn't want her to depend on charms and spells to deal with her abilities. She had to learn. Acceptance had to be step one. Her constant fight against who and what she was had made it impossible for her to take charge.

He knew very well what he was, what he could be.

If he was going to teach control, perhaps he should find some of his own. He didn't possess nearly enough to deal with Echo Raintree, day in and day out. To watch her, to touch her, to step into visions with her so she would not be alone. The kiss had been a colossal mistake, one he dared not repeat.

She'd be here soon for yet another afternoon lesson. After an hour, maybe an hour and a half at most, they would both be spent. He taught, she learned. They both worked very hard to ignore the attraction that sparked between them. Her ability to shield herself was improving quickly, but she still had trouble controlling the energy around her.

He should've sent Echo away when he could have. That first day, he should've stood his ground and sent her packing. Not only did he now care about her more than he should, she'd been touched by the power of the stones. He had to finish the job, or she'd leave in worse shape than she'd been when she'd arrived. They *had* made progress, as her last vision proved.

She'd called her cousin in North Carolina, Gideon, the one who was a cop. Gideon made calls of his own and had saved a young man who'd snuck into an abandoned building to practice his skateboarding skills just minutes before a quickly spreading electrical fire broke out.

Rye hadn't told Echo about the stones, and if he had any choice he wouldn't. They were tempting. Intoxicating. Powerful. And the last thing he needed was a parade of power-hungry Raintrees marching through Cloughban. Taking her there would be a last resort.

He had not told her about Cassidy, either, and as far as he knew they'd not had another encounter. Just as well. The Raintree *could not* know about his daughter.

For the past five days the sun had shone in Cloughban. Echo had not had another vision, not sleeping or waking. Considering how they'd been progressing, she was surprised. Pleased, but surprised.

In addition to working on her ability to control energies, their lessons consisted of honing her concentration. Through meditation—something at which she did not excel—and mental exercises, they practiced. Only through mastery of her mind and body could she ever hope to control her gifts.

One of the most important things for her to accept would be that she could not save everyone. People died every day. She could have vision after vision and not save them all. As she honed her skills her predictions would become more selective.

It had already begun. Perhaps the skateboard boy was destined to do something important with his life. That or an as-yet-to-be-conceived son or daughter or grandchild had an important role to fill in future events. It was impossible to know why he had been chosen, why her vision had led to a second chance for that child. That was something else she'd have to accept—a lack of answers to the many questions still to come.

She had a lot of questions. He heard them, whispers from her mind to his, even though she had not yet found the courage to ask them aloud. She would, in time. *You're supposed to be so powerful; why have I never seen a demonstration? Why do you stay here, in the middle of nowhere? What is it with this town, anyway?* And the one he picked up on almost constantly. *Are you going to kiss me again?*

He'd just as soon send her on her way before he had to answer any of those questions.

* * *

She'd grabbed a scone and two cups of strong tea before leaving the boardinghouse, and enjoyed a walk through town. It looked to be another sunny day. Wasn't it supposed to rain all the time in Ireland? Wasn't that why the grass was so green? Maybe Duncan was right and it was all her fault. She was happy, so the sun shone.

She was happy.

It had been such a long time since Echo had been truly happy that she was almost giddy with it. She didn't even think much about the threat to her parents. Did that make her a bad daughter? No. She knew they were safe on Sanctuary land. Gideon wouldn't let any harm come to them.

Besides, given the way some of the women in town mooned over Duncan, the warning had probably come from some besotted female who saw the American newcomer as a threat. Would it have been all that hard to find a photo of her parents on the internet and do the rest? It did show an amazing bit of commitment that hinted at a serious bunny-boiling-on-the-stove mental issue, but she could think of no other reason for anyone to threaten her.

There had been no hint of danger since that one.

As she walked past the shop where she'd bought her green sweater and the newer raincoat and boots, she experienced a distinct chill. Could Brigid be the one who'd left the disturbing picture? Had she reacted in the extreme because she'd instantly seen Echo as a threat? She was really too old for Duncan. The clerk wasn't old enough to be his mother, but she was certainly old enough to be his mother's slightly younger sister.

Duncan had been teaching her to listen to her instincts rather than fighting them, to accept them as a natural part of herself. It hadn't been easy; she was constantly afraid of another crippling vision. But as she walked into the town square she attempted to let loose the empathic abilities that both Duncan and Gideon insisted she possessed in spades. She opened herself up to the energies around her. Good and bad, strong and weak.

As always, the square was perfectly put together. Flowers bloomed, everything was clean and fresh, every shop window sparkled. Scents from the bakery filled the air, and a few residents who were already out and about nodded and said hello. Echo took a deep breath and opened herself in a way she had always been afraid to do. She reached for energy instead of denying it. She embraced her magic.

She was instantly—but gently—overwhelmed.

Why had she never seen this before? Cloughban was no ordinary town. It wasn't just Duncan who was special. She was surrounded by strays. *Independents.* Most were not very powerful; some had nothing more than what most would call good instincts, or extraordinary good luck. But there were a few, a handful, who were quite gifted.

Mind readers, telekinetics, healers. Shifters! She had never met one, though she'd heard of a distant cousin who had that ability. Fire control, water manipulation... *mind* manipulation.

Cloughban wasn't all that different from the Raintree Sanctuary. These people had been called here, each and every one of them. They had been drawn together, called to a place where their kind could live in peace.

Cassidy, that enchanting little girl, was one of them.

Echo pursed her lips and frowned. She looked around, trying to assign an ability to those villagers she could see. It didn't work that way, not for her at least. The energies swirled and danced, much like the flames she'd seen in her last vision, but she could not single out where those energies belonged.

She was fascinated, but she was also puzzled. Strays didn't congregate, they didn't gather in clusters, didn't populate small towns. At least, she'd never heard of such a thing.

She had one last, strong sense of being surrounded by powerful forces before she purposely shut down.

But not quite soon enough. One last thought filled her head, a truth that would not be denied. Many of these people had come to Cloughban because Ryder Duncan was here. He was their leader, their Dranir as much as Dante had ever been for the Raintree clan.

How had they kept this place a secret for so long?

She should tell someone. Dante, maybe. Mercy? Gideon for sure. In the next instant she knew she wouldn't tell anyone. No one here was a threat to the Raintree clan. These people wanted to live in peace, and she could appreciate that in a way few could. The threat to her parents finally made sense, in a way. Anyone who wanted to be left alone was now a suspect. She was Raintree. Someone, possibly several someones, was afraid she'd bring trouble to their quiet little town.

As she turned toward the pub she experienced a flash of warning, a hint of darkness. Cloughban was not a dark place, but something evil lived here. Her protective shields went up instantly to keep that darkness from touching her. The empathy was new, and when she opened herself she was much too vulnerable. When she reached out again, she did so cautiously.

And got nothing. Whatever evil she'd sensed was gone. No, not gone. That evil hid from her. Whoever possessed that darkness realized she'd touched it, however briefly.

This charming village was a lot weirder than she'd first thought. Weird, but not dangerous. Wherever a number of people gathered, there was some sort of darkness. She'd sensed much more light around her than dark. Besides, Duncan wouldn't let anyone or anything hurt her.

She stopped, glancing back toward the pub. Where had that thought come from? She had no illusions about Ryder Duncan. He might like her well enough, he might kiss like an angel, he might even call her *love* on occasion—an endearment which was no different from a casual *honey* or *dear* or *hey, you*. He was not her protector.

Echo shook her head and continued on. She needed some soap and deodorant, and maybe a chocolate bar. She could learn to seriously love Irish chocolate. The pharmacy was small but well stocked. It had become a regular stop for Echo on her walks into town. With a shopping basket in hand she took her time walking up and down the aisles. She wasn't alone. Two other women carried their own small baskets, and filled them with necessities and luxuries. Like the chocolate. These women did not scorn her the way Brigid had. They even nodded and said hello.

Soon she had everything she needed in her basket. As she approached the counter to pay, her stomach roiled and her vision dimmed. Colors, bright almost to the point of being blinding, danced behind her eyes. The sensation didn't last long, but it was unpleasant. She felt as if a powerful wave of something she could not identify had washed over and through her.

Echo reached for a sturdy shelf and steadied herself as the colors went away and her vision returned. She closed her eyes, hoping for the last bit of nausea to pass. It did, and she felt fine again. Completely normal.

She shook her head and continued on. Well, that was strange! She hoped she hadn't eaten something bad. The odd distress had passed quickly and by the time she stood at the counter with euros in hand, all was well. Nevan walked into the pharmacy. He smiled widely and nodded. If he'd been wearing a hat he surely would've tipped it in her direction.

When Echo walked back onto the square, she shaded her eyes for a moment and smiled widely at the scene before her. What a perfect little town, what an enchanted place. She dropped her hand and headed for the pub with a purposeful walk. Then something struck her.

Hadn't she sensed something bad here not so long ago? Something wrong? Something…dark?

Ridiculous. Cloughban was an ordinary place, the people were ordinary people, and as much as she liked it here, she could not stay much longer.

I've been here long enough. The thought wafted through her head almost as if it wasn't her own but was a whisper from elsewhere. *What a boring town, time to get back home.*

"Ha," she said as she walked into the pub a full fifteen minutes before her appointed time. "I'm early."

Duncan stood behind the bar. It was amazing how

much she liked to look at him, how pleasant it was to simply stare and admire. There was much to admire. Had she just been thinking about leaving Cloughban? No. Not yet. The thoughts of leaving town flew out of her mind as quickly as they had entered.

"Second time this week," he said. "Are you ill?"

Echo remembered the bout of nausea in the pharmacy, then dismissed it. "No, I'm fine." More than fine, really. As she looked at Duncan one thought was foremost in her mind. *When are you going to kiss me again?*

When are you going to kiss me again?

The answer to that unasked question should be *never*. But damn, there was something irresistible about Echo Raintree. Rye was no longer certain he could finish what he'd begun without throwing her across the nearest table and...

Her expression changed; she took a step back. She even uttered a low, "Whoa. Too fast."

Rye instantly threw up a mental wall; dammit, he had to keep the woman out of his brain! She blinked, shook her head, and he realized that the image they'd shared had happened so quickly, so unexpectedly, that she actually believed the thought was her own.

Instead of being horrified, she actually gave in to a small, secret smile that spoke volumes. She wanted him as much as he wanted her. The only difference was, she had no idea how dangerous a deepening connection between them might be. For her.

As powerful as she was—and lack of control aside, she was quite powerful—she could be more. The weather power that revealed her mood, her ability to see into his mind, her clear empathic abilities. If he didn't know better he'd think she was like him. A sponge. A receptor.

A dangerous creature.

The two of them together could rule the world. Or burn it down around them.

"Echo…" Should he send her away or embrace her? Teach or shun? Pull her to him or make sure there were always thousands of miles between them?

Doyle burst through the front door, startling Rye, and Echo, too. Echo glanced at her coworker, obviously annoyed to be interrupted. Annoyed and relieved.

"I hear the town council called a meeting for tonight," Doyle said as he slipped off his coat.

Rye gave his full attention to the cook. It was probably a good thing they'd been interrupted, and still…he was hardly grateful for it. "Yes, I was informed earlier."

"What's up?" Doyle asked, then he glanced Echo's way and winked at her.

Rye was being perfectly honest when he said, "I'm not sure." He should be more curious. The town council rarely called unscheduled meetings.

Doyle laughed as he headed for the kitchen. "Shouldn't you know?"

"I suppose I should, but I don't." He could guess, though. There was a Raintree in town, and she appeared to be settling in.

"You're a poor excuse for a mayor," Doyle teased as he disappeared through swinging doors that separated the main room from the kitchen.

Echo blinked. She withdrew from him, more than a little. "Mayor?"

Chapter 9

Duncan sat across the table from her, looking grumpy. He was more than a little annoyed that she hadn't learned to bring on a vision of the future at will.

"I can't force it, *Mayor* Duncan." And she wouldn't want to. The goal—her purpose in coming here—was fewer episodes, not more. She didn't want to learn how to bring them on; she just wanted to control the ones that were going to come whether she liked it or not.

"Let's get out of here." Duncan stood, grabbed her hand and pulled her to her feet. He didn't head for the front entrance, but to the rear door. It opened onto a perfectly ordinary alleyway, she knew. Now and then he made her take out the trash. Around the corner there sat a small, rusty-red car that had seen better days. If Duncan ever left town, maybe that was the car he drove. Did he ever leave town? Shoot, did he ever leave the pub?

Apparently so. He walked around the car, then turned down a narrow street. He continued to hold her hand.

The air was not as cool as it had been earlier that morning. It was perfect. Cool but not cold, sun shining, an occasional gentle breeze. They passed a man working in his garden. Nevan, she saw as he lifted his head and then his hand. When she'd first seen him she'd thought him the ugliest man she'd ever seen, but now...not so much. He was a lovely man, not pretty or handsome in any way, but kind and funny. She waved back. So did Duncan.

He still did not release her hand.

The village was so small, once they'd walked beyond two rows of houses they were, for all intents and purposes, out of town. She had walked this route before, on that afternoon she'd found castle ruins and a fairy fort.

Duncan didn't lead her in the exact same direction she'd taken that day. Instead, he walked a bit more to the west, though he didn't go far before stopping and sitting on a gentle green knoll. She sat beside him, and instantly realized why he'd chosen this spot.

The view was like one from a picture postcard. This was the Ireland so many tourists longed to see, but rarely did. The grass was a brilliant green, the sky clear and bright. In the distance a sprinkling of thatched-roof cottages sat. There was no rhyme or reason to the way they were organized, not that she could tell.

She'd come here looking for help, and she'd found it. What she had not come here looking for, what she had not expected, were these intense moments of what could only be called peace. Peace at a bone-deep level. Complete, soul-brightening *peace*. The sensation never lasted long, but…it was enough. That sensation of peace was like a tonic, like finding beauty where you least expected it and being gently overwhelmed.

Echo now realized that she had never known true peace before coming to Cloughban.

Duncan finally released her hand. Reluctantly, it seemed. Maybe that sensed reluctance was wishful thinking on her part. Maybe he'd only taken her hand to make sure she followed obediently.

It hadn't taken him long to realize that obedience had never been her strong suit, she knew that much.

She looked at him, studied his profile for a moment and then she asked, "What do you want?"

He didn't dare to answer her question honestly. *I want you in my bed. I want you gone. I want my life not to be turned upside down by a woman I cannot ever have.*

For years he'd been perfectly happy to live single and alone. He had his pub, he had his daughter. It was foolish—and impossible—for him to want anything or anyone else.

"I needed to get out of the pub for a bit," he said simply. "It's a nice day. We might as well enjoy it."

Echo relaxed visibly, her shoulders easing. She smiled. "I had begun to think you never left the pub." She pointed to a cottage in the distance. "Is one of these houses yours, or do you live above the business?"

No matter how much he liked her, he couldn't let her in. Couldn't trust her, couldn't invite her to be a part of his life. Not even a small one.

"Where do *you* live?" he asked. "When you're not

traveling the world in search of wizards, where do you lay your head?"

She looked at him, obviously realizing he'd changed the subject. Bless her, she let it slide. "All over. I lay my head in a small apartment in Wilmington, North Carolina. In a big house on Raintree Sanctuary land. In the guest room in Gideon's house on the beach. With friends, when I need it."

"Which one of those felt most like home to you?" He wanted to be able to picture her somewhere specific after she left. Why? He could not say. Echo on the beach, in the mountains, in a small room in a crowded building...

She turned her head, looked away, and he knew what her answer would be. Did everyone read her so well, or only him?

"None," she whispered. "I guess that's what I've been searching for all this time. A place that truly feels like home." She shook off the mood and looked to him. "Is the pub truly home for you?"

"Cloughban is home," he said, attempting to be honest with her without saying too much.

"It's good, to know where you belong." She bit her bottom lip, continued to look away from him. Did she think he'd see too much in those green eyes? "Do you believe my problems will be easier to solve when I find my place in the world? Or do I have to find this control you insist I need before I can discover home?"

He didn't answer. He didn't know how.

Echo was beyond annoyed. Every resident of Cloughban above the age of fifteen was packed into the Drunken Stone, but *she* wasn't welcome.

She'd enjoyed her afternoon walk with Duncan. It had been easy, relaxing. Afterward they'd returned to the pub. She felt as if something had happened between them, but she couldn't put her finger on what exactly. He hadn't kissed her again, and he hadn't held her hand on their walk back to the pub. Right before they reached the pub's rear entrance he'd told her—rather abruptly, she thought—that he'd see her tomorrow. Normally she'd be thrilled with an unexpected night to herself, but this time, today, she didn't *want* the night off. She wanted to know what the residents of Cloughban talked about at a town meeting.

Why did she think it might be her?

She had the house to herself. Her landlady and the only other resident were both down the street at the meeting. It was not her imagination that Maisy had smirked at Echo as she'd walked out the door. As a nonresident, she was not welcome at their town meeting. What the hell could they have to hide? What sort of politics might go on here that would require secrecy? Was banning an observer from their town meeting even legal?

Echo, whose entire life could be classified as weird, decided Cloughban had to be the weirdest place on earth. Almost impossible to find, no cell service, no Wi-Fi, Children of the Corn…though come to think of it, the kids she'd actually seen around town seemed pretty normal. Some of their parents, not so much.

She hadn't seen Cassidy since that day she'd run across the tumbled stones of what had once been a castle. And a fairy fort. To be honest she only rarely thought about the child, as if their two meetings had been no more than a dream. Their first meeting had been the day Duncan had changed his mind about taking her on as a student. Echo had been desperate, panicked, had suffered a horrible vision. It had been such a long day and such a strange encounter, she could almost believe the child was a figment of her imagination. Or maybe a ghost like the ones Gideon saw. She'd seemed so real at the time.

When they'd met at the castle…her mind had been drifting. She'd been vulnerable.

If she had dormant empathic powers and maybe even a way to affect the weather with her moods, could there be another unexplained ability? Like manifesting a dream out of thin air? Dammit, she'd come here looking for less magic in her life, not more!

Having the house to herself should've led to going to bed early, or watching TV, or raiding the kitchen. Instead of indulging in any of those things, Echo found herself nervously rummaging around the parlor, scanning the bookshelves for something to read.

While there were a few fairly new—as in less than twenty years old—mysteries on the shelf, most of the books were ancient. Leather bound and clothbound, spines cracked and fading, pages yellowing but surprisingly sturdy. Echo removed a couple of history books, leafed through carefully, then returned the books to their proper places. As she leafed through she noted dates and names that meant nothing to her, political references and legal opinions. Yawn. Nothing caught her fancy.

Until she deciphered a faded, almost-illegible title on the spine of an old, thin book. *The History of Cloughban.* She squinted at the author's name. Alsaindar *Duncan.*

That answered, in part, her question about why

Duncan—*her* Duncan—lived here. It was home. His ancestors came from Cloughban. There was a blood connection. Roots.

She very carefully removed the book from the shelf. It was heavier than she'd expected. With easy fingers, she opened the book to the title page.

The History of Cloughban by Alsaindar Duncan. Beneath the title was a drawing of a big, standing rock, a stone that pointed toward the sky. She touched the page, readied to turn it wondering what she'd find. For some reason this book excited her. Her mouth went dry, her stomach flipped and her heart rate increased. Silly of her to react this way. It was just a book. She started to flip that first page...

The door flew open and a child—perhaps twelve years old or so—came rushing into the room. His reddish brown hair was shaggy and mussed, and his face was flushed. He'd been running. Slick as could be, he reached up and snagged the book from her hand.

"You'll not be needing this now, miss," he said breathlessly.

And then he was gone, the front door slamming behind him.

What the...?

She felt a bit ill, as if she'd eaten something bad, but she recognized the sensation as...wrong. Unnatural. Magical. She could see the book in her head, could *see* that title page. And then it started to fade away and she knew that in a moment the memory would be gone.

Her heart pounded with a new and disturbing realization. This had happened before. Recently. In the town square. No, in the pharmacy. Someone was messing with her memories. Or at least they were trying to.

Control. Duncan had done his best to teach her to harness that control. She did so now. Echo closed her eyes and concentrated, as he had taught her. All this time she'd thought the lessons had been wasted, that she was getting no stronger, but as she reached for control she realized that was not true.

She *would not* forget the book or the boy. She pictured them both as if they were still in the room; she fought to hold on to what had just happened. Her knees wobbled and her mind spun with the effort it took to keep that memory…and then the threat was gone, and the memory remained hers.

She did not bother to try to control the cold wind as she left the house and walked toward the Drunken Stone. They couldn't keep her out. They couldn't mess with her memories. Someone would, by God, explain to her what was going on!

Echo expected that her entrance would cause a commotion, but she was wrong. Every solemn face in the room was turned to the door before she opened it. They'd been waiting for her. Not a word was spoken until Nevan, the gnome, spoke from his usual seat at the corner table.

"Told you so!"

There was a hush on the heels of Nevan's statement, but it didn't last long. Voices rose, some angry, others merely confused. Rye demanded calm. He called for everyone to settle down, but his voice was not loud enough. A few men moved closer to Echo. They were not a threat, not yet, but like it or not a threat was coming. Rye left his post behind the bar—no one was drinking tonight—and jumped onto the small stage. This time when he demanded quiet, the crowd obeyed.

It would be a waste of time to run Echo out of the pub before continuing with the meeting. She'd see; she'd know. Every day she grew stronger. He should've sent her away that first day, should've ignored Cassidy's prediction and his need to make sure the Raintree had not come for her, but he had not and now it was too late. He cared about her. Their instructions were not done; he could not dismiss the threat she seemed to have forgotten about; he did not trust these people, his people, not to harm her. They were protective. Of their home, their lives, the stones—of Cassidy.

"I know what some of you think." He locked his gaze on a confused Echo. "You think the Raintree woman has come for one of us, that she will bring more of her clan here and destroy this…this…" There was no better word. "This sanctuary. You're wrong. Echo is not our enemy. She's one of us, for a short time. She has come here for the peace Cloughban can offer those like us. Nothing more, nothing less. I believe that to be true. No, I *know* it."

One kiss, a shared visual or two…it wasn't much, but he and Echo were connected in a way he had not expected. As he'd faced a crowd tonight—half of them angry, the other half merely confused—he'd come to the unwelcome realization that he would protect her at all costs.

Almost all costs.

"The meeting is over," he declared. "Your worries are for nothing, I promise."

That was a hollow promise, as empty as the freshly washed glasses that hung behind the bar. Life was worry, and had been since his child had come into this world.

It took several minutes, but the crowd did disperse. Most of the townsfolk walked around and well clear of Echo, who moved forward slowly until she stood stock-still in the middle of the room. She stared at him even as Nevan, the last to leave, gave her a comforting pat on the shoulder and muttered, "I tried to help you, lass. You're on your own now."

When they were finally alone, she said, "I believe some explanations are in order."

"Can it wait until tomorrow?"

The expression on her face was one of frustration and anger, and those emotions came through in her voice. "No, I don't think it can."

He wanted more time to think, time to prepare his words carefully. "It's a long story, and it's getting late."

She wasn't going to budge. He added determination to the list of easily read expressions on her pretty face. "Take your time. I've got all night."

He left the stage, walked silently toward her.

"First of all, what the hell is the deal with the book I found…"

Rye lifted one hand and the book, which had been sitting on Nevan's table, flew into his hand. Echo gasped, and her eyes—greener than ever on this night—went wide. She knew he was a wizard, knew he had powers. But he had been very careful not to use them in front of her, until now.

"There are secrets here you are not meant to know."

"Then why am I here?" Her expression softened a bit. "Very little in life can be written off to coincidence, you know it as well as I do. Do you believe it's simple coincidence that I traveled halfway around the world to find you?"

No. No, he did not. "That is the question of the hour, isn't it?"

Rye stopped when he was so close to Echo that he could smell her, feel her body heat. He'd wanted her since she'd walked into his pub. He'd dreamed of her, fantasized about having her even though he knew...

Echo shook her head. "Let's take this slowly, one thing at a time." She pointed. "That's just a history book that was, as far as I can tell, written by one of your ancestors. Why on earth would it be snatched from my hand as if it contained the secrets of the universe? Secrets I am not to be privy to apparently."

"It's complicated."

Anger flared to life again. "No shit, Sherlock!" She took a deep, calming breath. "Give me something. Throw me a bone, tell me...tell me...tell me *something*."

Something. Maybe he could talk his way around this by sharing a small detail, or two. "My family have always been guardians, of a sort."

"Guardians of *what*?" she asked, frustrated.

Like it or not, the time to tell her about the stone circle would come soon enough. Not tonight. If he had his way he would never tell her about Cassidy. "Cloughban. You know it's a different kind of place. You know the people here are not ordinary. They are...like me. Like you. They're afraid you'll ruin what we've found here. Peace. A place we can be ourselves. A home for many strays."

"Independents." She looked up at him, wondering,

confused, wanting something more. "Nothing about my life has ever been ordinary," she whispered.

"Or mine," he confessed.

"This morning, in town…" She wrinkled her nose and closed her eyes. "I swear, there was something. Something I can't quite put my finger on." She opened her eyes and looked directly into his. "I do remember thinking that you would never let anything or anyone hurt me."

A thought much too much like his own.

The pub was quiet; they were alone. The attraction that had always danced between them intensified. There was power here, a power he had tried very hard to ignore.

Rye cupped Echo's cheek in his hand. "You cannot stay here, not forever."

"I know that. This is not my home."

"No, it's not. And I suspect some of the people here will not make the coming days easy for you."

Her expression was relaxed now, soft and tempting. "My life has never been easy, either."

Easy. Who had an easy life? Not him, not his daughter…not the woman who stood before him. Life was not meant to be easy. "You should probably leave tomorrow."

"I probably should." She drifted closer to him, rested her cheek against his chest. "But easy or not, I'm not finished here. I know it to the depths of my soul."

He threaded his fingers through her hair, held her close.

No, she was not finished with him, and like it or not he was not finished with her.

Chapter 10

The kiss was not like the first. It was deeper, more profound. It was a kiss to wipe away the rest of the world. While Duncan held her, while he pressed his lips to hers, Echo didn't think about being a poor excuse for a prophet, stolen memories, villagers who didn't want her here, magic.

This was real. She wanted Duncan and he wanted her. His arms encircled her and held her close, so close she could feel the evidence of his arousal pressing against her. If the kiss didn't tell her well enough that he wanted her, that did.

She wanted him here...now. On the bar, on a table, on the floor...

"No," he whispered as he pulled his mouth from hers.

No? *No?* Not the word she wanted to hear.

"Not here," he whispered.

Not here was not the same as a flat out no. *Not here* she could accept. "You've been peeking into my head again," she said without anger.

"Sometimes I can't help but see." He kissed her again, quickly. Urgently. "Please tell me you're..."

She didn't give him time to finish. "On the pill. Yes." Not that she'd had any need for birth control in a very long time. Two things kept her taking the pill. One, she was optimistic. She wanted a man in her life, and if the right one fell into her lap—so to speak—she wanted to be prepared. Two, she didn't want children. Not ever. Any child of hers would be Raintree. Any child she brought into this world would have some kind of ability. Maybe it would be something lovely and manageable, a true gift. Then again, maybe a child of hers would be tortured, as she had been.

Duncan swept her off her feet. It wasn't the first time he'd carried her. It wasn't even the second time. This was, however, by far the most pleasant. She draped her arms around his neck as he carried her to the back of the room and up the stairs. Quickly. With purpose.

"I think I wanted you the first time I walked into your pub," she said. "I didn't want to want you. You were so annoying." She did something she'd wanted to do since that first day. She ran her fingers through his hair. "You were annoying and prickly," she said without heat.

"While you have always been a ray of sunshine," he countered with humor.

It was a valid argument, but at this moment she really didn't want to discuss her persistent distress.

"Why did we wait so long?" she asked. So many

wasted days, so many lonely nights, when she could've been, *should've* been, here.

He carried her into his dark bedroom. Moonlight streamed through the window, lighting it just enough.

When Duncan put Echo on her feet he did so gently, as if he was afraid she might break. She was no sooner standing on her own than he began to undress her. Shirt over her head, bra unsnapped and discarded with a flick of his hand. That done, he stopped to lavish attention on her breasts, touching, kissing, sucking, until her knees went weak.

She loved the way he touched her, the way he made her feel a part of something more. Something better than she'd realized was possible.

Enough, she thought. *I will come before either of us is completely undressed.*

And this is bad because...

"Get out of my head," she said without anger. "I want tonight to be..." What she'd always wanted, what she'd craved all her life. "Ordinary. Normal. Just your body and mine."

He didn't whisper in her ear or in her mind. Instead, he finished the job of undressing her, placed her in the center of his bed and very quickly removed his own clothing.

He looked fine clothed, but naked he was magnificent. Hard, muscled, just a little bit hairy. He did not remove the stone at his neck or the leather band on his wrist, but she supposed that was hardly necessary.

As he came toward her, moonlight lit his chest and she saw the jagged, ugly scar there, much too close to his heart. It hurt her to know that he had been hurt; she was saddened to know that he'd suffered such pain.

She'd have to ask him about that scar later. At the moment she had more important things on her mind, and she did not want to be distracted by pains of the past.

Bodies entangled as if they had been made for each other, he kissed her again. And again. He kissed her mouth, her throat, her breasts. Echo spread her thighs to cradle him there. Almost touching. *Almost.* She ached to have him inside her; she didn't want to wait another second. If he made her wait she was going to scream.

Then he was there, guiding himself into her, moving gently. Too gently. She'd waited for this for a long time. Forever. This was no time for trepidation, no time for second thoughts. She placed her mouth close to his ear, kissed the warm skin just beneath and then whispered, "More. Now."

He groaned and did as she asked, pushing deep, thrusting hard and fast until she shattered. She might be embarrassed about coming so fast if he hadn't been right behind her.

Next time would be slower. Next time they would savor their coming together. And yes, she knew without doubt that there would be a next time.

Now and then he called her *love*. She wanted to believe there was a kind of love between them. Temporary, unexpected, just two unattached people who understood each other finding and enjoying each other for a while. Could she call that love? Why not?

"That was amazing," she said. Not at all what she'd had in mind when she'd stormed across the street to confront him, but definitely amazing. She had forgotten everything while they'd made love. All her worries, all her questions…gone. Temporarily. Unpleasant thoughts had already begun to creep back into her head.

Duncan was rumored to be very powerful. He certainly had more abilities than she knew about. Was this a simple distraction? No, not simple, not simple at all, but still a distraction.

"Did you do something to me?"

"I believe I did," he said, his voice light. "If you've already forgotten, then I didn't do it very well."

"No, Duncan. I'm serious. Was there anything... unnatural...?"

He kissed her to silence her question, then pulled away slightly and said, "No magic was involved, at least not on my end of things. And if you're going to share my bed, perhaps you should call me Rye."

"Can't," she said with a sigh.

"Why not?"

"Rye is a bread. Come to think of it, Duncan is a doughnut. I really can't handle all those carbs." She pressed her body to his. Already she wanted him again. It was going to be a long night. "Can I call you Ryder?" It was the name she'd known him as before they'd met, a name no one else called him. At least, not that she'd ever heard.

"You can call me anything you'd like, love."

Love, again. She knew this wasn't the kind of love she was looking for. A forever, ordinary, romantic kind of love. But for tonight, it would do. It would more than do.

The Raintree woman should've left the pub long ago, should've returned to her room at the boardinghouse. Alone. Instead, she remained in the pub. More likely above stairs with Rye.

It was so unfair. Why had he never looked at her that

way? What did Echo have that she did not? She wasn't prettier, certainly wasn't sexier.

More powerful? Yes. For now.

Invulnerable?

No.

She hated her instructions to wait. Hated them! If she made Echo's death look like an accident, her body would be shipped home and no Raintree would ever come to Cloughban again. By the time they got suspicious and thought to do so it would be too late. Far too late.

Her last two calls to her employer—not the town council who paid her to keep up their pathetic library but the man who'd hired her to be a part of the first wave of his long-planned invasion—had gone unanswered. He should've at the very least seen that she'd called and call her back. Maybe he was on his way. Maybe he was already here, somewhere.

She knew he was close, and had been for a while. A couple of hours away, at most, and perhaps not even that far. Waiting had been difficult for him, but he'd insisted that everything be just right, including the time of year, the phase of the moon and—most important—the age of the girl. At the moment, she was prime.

Had he seen that a Raintree would arrive just as his plan was coming together? Again, maybe. He wasn't as powerful as he thought himself to be, but he planned to be much stronger very soon. She wasn't sure he'd get that chance. If she had her way he would not, but for now... for now she would continue to play the obedient soldier.

Maisy imagined herself comforting Rye when Echo

was dead. She imagined herself taking her place in his bed, making him do whatever she commanded.

Most of all, she imagined herself queen.

Echo slept sprawled across his bed. Naked, beautiful, sated...his, for now.

It was not long after dawn, hours before the pub would open, when Rye pulled on a pair of jeans and headed downstairs to make a pot of coffee. Sleeping with Echo had not been the smartest move he'd ever made, but he didn't regret it. It had been a long time, a very long time...

"Hello."

He jumped at the sound of Cassidy's voice, spun to face her. She stood near the bar, still dressed in her nightgown. The one her grandmother had made for her. It was old-fashioned and worn, and Cassidy swore it was the most comfortable nightgown ever. She would soon outgrow it. The hem hung well above her ankles. Last year it had almost touched the floor.

"Honey, I told you to stay out of sight while the Raintree woman is here."

"Echo." Cassidy smiled. "Her name is Echo, not 'the Raintree woman.' I like her. Is she going to be my new mother?"

"No." Echo could not stay here. It would be too dangerous—for him, for Cassidy, for every resident of Cloughban.

"Then why is she upstairs in your room?" Long red hair still tangled from sleep, Cassidy looked up as if she could see through the ceiling.

"She's a friend, that's all. A friend who isn't going to stay in Cloughban much longer."

"Oh. I like her, and I thought she might stay for a long time. But now I hope she leaves soon."

"Why?" Had Cassidy seen something? Had she sensed a danger?

Cassidy shrugged her shoulders. "I'm tired of staying home all the time. It's boring."

Rye relaxed. "Your grandmother takes good care of you."

"She does, but I miss my friends. I miss you, Da." She stuck out her tongue, then said, "I used to see you almost every day, for breakfast or for tea, or right after school. Now you're here all the time. You don't want Echo to know you even have a daughter."

"It's for your own good." He sounded like a father with those words.

"That's silly." Cassidy's face shifted, was suddenly older—much older—than her eleven years. She looked wiser, and far too powerful. She'd seen something, felt something, that made her thoughts shift. "It's okay to be the good guy, Da. You don't have to be alone. You don't have to be who you once were."

He wished, as he had many times in the past, that he could protect Cassidy from knowing who and what he had been. He wanted to protect her from the past, a past long before her birth. What he'd done…it was behind him, well behind, but he could not erase it.

Rye wanted to give his daughter a hug, but if he reached for her his arms would go through her as if she were made of mist. Cassidy was not here. She was in the cottage she and her grandmother called home. That cottage was not far from Cloughban, but it was far enough away to keep her safe.

"It won't be much longer, I promise."

"I really would like a new mother someday," Cassidy said, and then she was gone. She didn't fade away, she just disappeared.

He liked Echo more than he should. Last night had been great, and he was realist enough to accept that they weren't done.

But no matter how much he liked her, how much he wanted her, she couldn't stay.

If the Raintree found out about Cassidy, they would take her away. She was too powerful, too unpredictable. He had never known or even heard of anyone who could do the things Cassidy could do. They'd lock her away, study her or use her as a weapon. He didn't trust them; he didn't trust them at all.

And that meant he couldn't trust Echo. Much as he wanted to, he could not afford to trust her.

Chapter 11

Echo woke warm and happy, and sore. Holy cow, Duncan knew what he was doing in the bedroom.

Ryder, not Duncan. A name no one but she called him, a name that suited him. She liked the way it rolled off her tongue. *Ryder*.

She'd only been awake a few minutes when he came into the room with a tray. She sat up as he presented the tray for her inspection. Breakfast in bed. Eggs over easy, toasted brown bread, marmalade, both coffee and tea. No one had ever brought her breakfast in bed before!

"Hungry?" he asked.

"Starving." He placed the tray on the bed near her. She looked over and up to him. "You're wearing pants." She made that sound like the accusation it was. Damned if she didn't want him again.

"I make it a point not to cook naked." He sat on the edge of the bed. Close. Not close enough.

"I suppose you do have to protect yourself." For a moment she focused on the scar on his chest, a scar that looked nastier by morning light than it had by moonlight. She wanted to ask him about it, but not now. She also wanted to ask him about the amulet at his throat and the leather wristband, but she recognized both as being protective in nature. He had not removed either last night.

The real question was, what did a man like Ryder Duncan need to be protected from?

Echo took a cup of coffee and a piece of toast, leaning over the tray as she took a bite so as not to get crumbs in his bed. She wasn't shy about being naked in front of him. In fact, it felt like the most natural thing in the world. He didn't eat, but he did drink a cup of coffee. Maybe he'd eaten downstairs. Once she started eating, she realized that she really was starving.

When she was finished, she leaned away from the tray and asked, "So, do we have to keep this a secret? Do we have to pretend in front of everyone else?"

Ryder gave her question a few seconds of thought before responding. "No. Someone, probably several someones, would know, anyway."

Of course. "Because this is not an ordinary town."

"Not at all."

She should've seen it all along, should've felt it, but she had not. "Is everyone here…different?"

He hesitated. "Not everyone. There are a few spouses and children who are not gifted."

"The little girl I saw my first day here!" Echo sat up straighter, on alert. "I saw her again last week when I was walking, and…she told me about fairy forts." Both memories seemed dreamlike. Were they real? They seemed so, but something was off.

"Sometimes I actually forget about her, and that's not normal. The memory just fades away. It always comes back, though, like I'm remembering a dream or someone I haven't seen since I was a child."

Ryder didn't say anything, but his jaw got tighter, his eyes more distant.

"She told me I would stay," Echo continued. "I thought she was a delusion, a fantasy, because she just disappeared. I mean *literally disappeared*. Cassidy. She said her friends call her Cass but she prefers Cassidy." She looked up into a stony face. "Do you know her? Surely you know *everyone* around here, Mayor Duncan." She smiled. Ryder definitely did *not* fit her mental image of a small-town mayor.

His hesitation was minor, but she noticed. She noticed everything about him, and had since day one. His voice was perfectly even when he said, "Never heard of her, love. She probably was a delusion, as you say."

Ryder took the tray and moved it to the top of the dresser by the door. The tray out of the way, he kicked the door shut, gently but firmly, and then he removed his jeans to join her in the bed. The mattress dipped and creaked, and she rolled into him. It was the most natural thing in the world to drift together. He held her close; she held him. Just like that, she dismissed everything from her mind but Ryder.

"Do you know what I dreamed last night?" she whispered.

"No." His lips found her shoulder and rested there for a long moment.

She sighed in deep contentment. "Nothing. Nothing at all. It's been days since I had a vision, sleeping or awake."

"You've gone days before without a vision."

"Yes, but there's something different this time."

He threw one long leg over her hip, capturing her in the nicest way. "And what's that?"

She whispered, truthfully and with joy, "I am not afraid."

Walsh paced in his room, a too-small, too-shabby rented room, which was not much more than an hour from Cloughban. He didn't dare move any closer until it was time. Just a few more days, and he'd never be forced to sleep in such an ordinary place again. He'd have anything and everything he wanted. He was so close. Years of planning, and he was so close he could taste it.

Almost. Almost. It was a shame that Rye Duncan knew his face so well. Walsh wanted to watch every step of his plan; he wanted to be a part of it from beginning to end. When this was all over, would he have the ability to watch without being seen? To be invisible, or to shift into something—or someone—else? He could hardly wait to find out.

He'd be a part of it soon enough. The Raintree woman was a fly in the ointment, but she wasn't much of a worry. She was a girl of limited powers, despite her surname.

Just a girl, not an oracle to be feared.

The knock on his door should not have surprised him, but it did. His number-one soldier was early for their meeting.

Walsh invited the man in, but he shook his head and said, "Not here."

His older brother—half brother, and that half did make a difference—was a suspicious man. Walsh was careful, as well, but he wasn't paranoid. Still, until things were settled it was best to humor this man he had relied upon as the plan came together.

They walked around the building, into a deserted field. The grass that grew so high all but disguised a long-deserted famine graveyard. Walsh felt as if a ghost were walking up his spine, but his brother didn't seem to be bothered at all.

The man who walked in step beside him finally said, "I think we should move up the timeline. We need to move now, *tonight*."

Walsh tried to be patient, he truly did, but this man and the woman, they were not as reliable as he had initially thought them to be. When this was over... Well, when this was over he would need them still, for a while. But if all went well, he would not need them for very long. "No. We're not changing the plan now."

"Why not?"

Walsh had been very careful about what information he shared. He only had two soldiers in Cloughban. One was family. The other had shared his bed on several occasions. The others—those headed this way very soon—were pawns he had no qualms about sacrificing.

His brother was anxious. Until now, Walsh had kept much of his plan to himself. They were so close to success, so very close. Perhaps he could afford to explain why the wait had been necessary. It wouldn't do for things to be set into motion too soon.

The girl was of the proper age for optimum transference. He'd waited for this. He'd waited four long years. Four years of research, careful planning and waiting.

"The cycle of the moon must be just right for the incantation to work," Walsh explained. "The girl is the right age, and soon the moon will be full. Days, we are down to mere *days*."

"Days."

"On the three nights when the moon is fullest, the time to take her will be perfect. Be patient, brother. Our rewards will be great."

He would rule. His brother would be his right-hand man. His woman would have everything she'd ever wanted, and more.

And he would bring his mother's people, the once-powerful Ansara, back. When his army was strong enough, he'd wipe every Raintree off the planet.

Some might argue that he was not true Ansara, that they had been wiped out when the Raintree had defeated them, six years earlier. True, his mother had been adopted; she'd had no true Ansara blood in her veins. But in Walsh's heart the Ansara survived through him. He was the last, but he would soon rebuild what had once been a powerful clan.

The grass was waist-high where his brother came to a stop and turned to face him. "You have the incantation with you?"

"Of course." The words were few, the language ancient. But they were powerful words. Beyond powerful.

His brother smiled. It was a smile much like his own; it was their father's smile. Their father had been gone for years.

Walsh didn't see the knife until it was too late. The fact that his brother's hands were visible and empty and relaxed meant nothing. The blade appeared from behind him. It flew through thin air, twisting and turning, rising up to slice across Walsh's throat.

His last thought was, *This was not part of the plan...* and then...

Betrayal.

Echo climbed into her own bed, burrowed under the covers and closed her eyes. She was so exhausted she'd thought sleep would come instantly...but it didn't.

Her life had been a series of disasters. There had been good moments, too. Family, friends, making music. But disasters had always been a part of her life. She would willingly admit that more than a few of those had been of her own making. Other disasters had been seen and experienced through dreams and visions.

Her curse. Her gift.

Why did she never see anything nice of the future? Why did she never see happiness and joy?

She went to sleep on that thought, and dreamed.

She dreamed of green fields, fairy forts and children. Not her children, certainly, since she did not plan to have any of her own. Maybe these were her cousins' children.

No, Emma was not here, and neither was Maddy. She saw no sign of Dante's kids, or Mercy's. These children were...

Hers. Hers and Ryder's. There were blonde girls and dark-headed boys. They danced around some strange stones that glimmered with amazing energy. The fairies were there, sparkling like stars that had fallen near to the ground.

She didn't want kids, never had, and with good reason. But as she watched these children her heart filled with a love she had never imagined possible. These little people lit the world with a new light. She loved them with a bone-deep mother's love.

Echo realized she was in a dream. Not a vision, not a premonition, just a dream. In case there was some grain of truth here, she attempted to see…how many kids? There seemed to be a lot of them, but she couldn't tell. Maybe what she saw were the same children again and again. Children at different ages, at different stages of their lives.

Suddenly Ryder was with her. She couldn't see him but he stood behind her. She felt him there. As with the running children, that feeling was bone-deep. Love. Not infatuation, not lust. Love. She had never known such a deep love could be real.

His arms went around her; he pulled her back against his solid body, and she settled there.

He whispered in her ear. *This is a possible future. It is not set in stone, not a surety, just a possibility. There are many possibilities.*

His arms tightened around her. He picked her up, off her feet, and spun her around.

And she found herself facing a graveyard, looking at a row of headstones. Ryder Duncan was there.

So was Echo Raintree.

Chapter 12

Rye walked across deserted green fields. It was a path he'd walked many times in past years. Echo had gone back to her rented room to catch a nap between shifts. He had a million things to do, but he needed to see his daughter in the flesh.

The thatched-roof cottage that had been Cassidy's home for her entire life sat on an emerald-green hill an easy half hour's walk from Cloughban. The cottage was small but sturdy, a safe home for a very special girl and her grandmother.

When Cassidy was older and had better control over her abilities, maybe she and Bryna could move to town. Until then, until she'd made it safely through puberty, he didn't dare it. It was a risk enough to allow her to see anyone other than him and his mother-in-law, but he knew complete isolation would not be good for her.

She normally went to school, but had not been lately. Everyone in town was determined to protect Cassidy from the Raintree. His daughter had friends, but even though those friends all had gifts, they were not in the same class as Cassidy. Not even close. They were gifted. She was exceptional.

The villagers were also determined to protect the stones, which was the reason the book about Cloughban had been snatched from Echo's hand. It was a shared fear that the stones would be discovered. That others, gifted and not, would flock here in droves. That the roads would be widened to allow for buses filled with foreign visitors to gawk and stare, to touch and take photographs. The very idea was a nightmare to those who had found peace in this village.

The stones were sacred. They were not meant to be a tourist attraction.

Bryna knew he was coming; she always did. Rye got the evil eye as he walked through the front door. That was the norm, too. He couldn't blame her.

Cassidy ran toward him; she threw herself into his arms. "Da!" she said in an excited voice. "I've missed you."

Neither of them mentioned the early-morning visit. Bryna did not approve of Cassidy's out-of-body excursions. Neither did he—they were potentially dangerous—but that was a talk they'd have in private. Later.

Bryna didn't miss much, but her granddaughter had the ability to hide whatever she wished to hide.

Cassidy grinned at her grandmother without letting Rye go. "Da has a girlfriend. She's very pretty."

"It isn't polite to snoop into other people's thoughts," Bryna said sourly.

"But, Granny, sometimes I can't help it. Sometimes the thoughts just scream at me."

True, Rye thought as he watched the two of them interact. Echo's thoughts were so strong, so clear. Were his own the same? He hoped not.

Bryna's expression softened. "I know, *ma chroi*, but you must try."

Cassidy nodded and turned her attention back to Rye. "Can we go for a walk? Can we visit the stones?"

Rye nodded. "Fetch your jumper. It's nippy out."

Cassidy nodded and ran for her room, and that's when Bryna turned her hard attention on Rye.

"A girlfriend, eh?"

Their past had been difficult, that was inescapable, but love for Cassidy brought them together and kept them together. The past was the past; Cassidy was the future. "It's nothing serious," he said. "Just a fling."

Bryna scoffed. "Well, that's too bad. It's past time you moved on. Sybil's been gone nine years. That's long enough for you to be alone. More than long enough. A woman would be good for you, I imagine."

Anxious to change the subject, Rye said, "What about you? Your husband has been gone many more than nine years."

She almost smiled. The corners of her mouth twitched. "James McManus calls on me now and again, usually while Cassidy is at school." A snort followed that statement. "Which means I have not seen him lately. The Raintree lass has put a damper on my love life."

Love life? "He *calls* on you?"

Bryna lifted her chin. "That's all you need to know."

And more than he needed or wanted to know.

The conversation ended when Cassidy appeared, wearing sweater and boots and shouting, "Let's go, Da, let's go!"

Rye's heart swelled when he looked at his daughter. He had never known a love like it and never would again. She was his world, his reason for existing. She was also the reason Echo Raintree could not stay in Cloughban.

The thought of a coffee and pastry from the shop on the square drew Echo out of her rented room. She looked at the pub as she walked past and wondered what Ryder was doing at this moment. He should be taking a nap. She should be sleeping herself!

She'd tried to go back to sleep after she'd awakened from her disturbing dream, she really had, but her mind had been spinning and sleep would not come.

She was tempted to check the door to the pub to see if it was locked, maybe climb the stairs and slip into Ryder's bed...

No. It was not the time to be impulsive. She'd been impulsive all her life! This thing with Ryder was happening too fast, and she needed to think. Right now she was wrapped up in emotion, almost giddy with what she'd found. Emotion would only hold her for so long. Before this went any further, she needed to examine the pros and cons.

She did her very best to dismiss the dream she'd had. It had not been a premonition; it had not been a glimpse into the future. It had just been a normal, ordinary, particularly vivid dream. So, pros and cons in the real world...

She liked Ryder.

He lived in Ireland, which was a very long way from North Carolina.

They were definitely physically compatible.

He was a stray, and while she did not know the extent of his magic, she did understand that the normal life she craved couldn't possibly happen with him.

He kissed like an angel.

He was bossy and had no tolerance for employees who were, on occasion, late.

The sex was fantastic.

What if he wanted children?

Okay, now she was definitely getting ahead of herself. She blamed the dream. A dream of children in one future and her own headstone—beside Ryder's—in another. She still wasn't sure which aspect was more terrifying.

It was a nice day, sunny and warmer than she'd expected when she'd set out. What was she doing thinking about a future with Ryder Duncan? They'd had one very nice night. She'd needed that—the pleasure, the connection, the escape. Maybe that's all it was, all it would ever be. Physical. Fun. Sex for the sake of sex and nothing else. She really needed to get the thought that they might have a future out of her head before he peeked into it and saw too much. She didn't want to send him running. Not yet.

She ordered her coffee and a pastry that was about the size of a baby's head, collected her purchases with a smile and stepped out of the small shop to sit at an outdoor table. There were quite a few people out and about today, walking, shopping, visiting.

A number of the residents of Cloughban knew her. Most of them—maybe all—had been in the pub last night. Some had been in the pub a time or two to hear her sing. On this beautiful day, a few passersby nodded and said hello. Some just glared at her suspiciously as they passed.

She now knew that most of the residents of Cloughban were like her and her family. Special. Gifted. Cursed. She had seen little evidence of their gifts, but then they'd been hiding their true natures from her. They'd been protecting themselves, and this place.

One couple she'd never met before offered a hesitant "Good afternoon." They both had pronounced German accents. While most of the residents were obviously Irish, it occurred to her that the small town in the back of beyond, a place that should not be a mecca for international tourists given how difficult it had been to find, had a number of foreign residents. Bertrand was obviously French, and Michael's accent was more British than Irish. There were others, customers at the pub, who were definitely not originally from here.

Why had she never noticed this before?

Because someone instructed you, in an entirely magical way, not to.

The voice in the back of her head spoke the truth, and she knew it. Why? Why would the residents of Cloughban bother to hide so much from her? She was Raintree, magic was an everyday part of her life. She would never judge, or try to take advantage, or point and whisper...

The timing was terrible, but there it was—that tickle

at the back of her brain that warned her another vision was coming. She left her unfinished coffee and pastry sitting on the small round table and started walking toward the pub. After a few seconds she began to walk faster, then she jogged. Desperate, hurried, she caught a glimpse of herself in the boutique window, but did not look inside to see if Brigid was watching. It would be best if no one saw her and wondered what had her in such a rush.

If they knew what she was, would they judge? Take advantage? Point and whisper?

At the moment there was only one important question: Did she have time to make it to Ryder before she lost all control?

Her vision began to go gray around the edges. She could see the path ahead of her, and nothing more. She kept her eyes on the side of the building she hoped to—needed to—reach before it was too late. Jogging wasn't going to get her there soon enough. She began to run. Faster, harder. A month ago, she could not have made it this far; her lessons must be helping, at least a little.

By the time she reached the door to the Drunken Stone her body was more numb than not and she could barely see at all. She remained in control, for now, but barely. The entire world was going gray; there was no sound but the rush of blood through her veins.

She tugged hard, but the door was locked. She knocked, pounded, called Ryder's name. *Come on, Duncan*, she thought, trying to send him a message. *Wake up. Answer the damn door!*

She couldn't wait any longer, and she didn't want to collapse here, at the door. Someone might see, someone *would* see, and she was far too vulnerable while she was in the midst of a vision. Stumbling, she made her way around the corner, behind the far side of the building where she wouldn't be seen by those walking the square. Completely numb, entirely out of control, she sank to her knees and allowed the vision to take her.

Cold. It was so cold. Within the vision, she stood and looked around her. Front, back, all around. She didn't recognize where she was. Panic wouldn't help her now! Deep breath. Control.

She was in a field, Ireland green, she understood, even though in this world, in this time and place, it was night. She stopped, lifted her head and focused on the scene ahead. It continued to form, taking shape as she watched.

There were stones in the near-distance, stones that were tall and gray and powerful. Incredibly powerful. They were not haphazardly arranged, but formed a circle. An almost-perfect circle, she knew even though she saw the stones from the side, not from above. One of them, the largest stone, was the one she'd glimpsed in the pages of a very old book. A book she had not been allowed to read.

In the center of the circle of stones stood a dark figure. As the scene continued to unfold, it remained maddeningly unclear. She couldn't see a face, just a tall, dark, indistinct shape.

Mists danced and then converged, finally allowing her to see more. That dark form held a knife in one hand and a child in the other.

Cassidy.

Snow began to fall. Fat, white flakes that dropped silently from a cold sky as Echo began to run toward the stone circle. As in a nightmare, she ran as hard as she could but moved no closer. How could she help the child if she couldn't reach her? Ryder had joined her in a vision once; he'd helped her. Could she help this little girl here and now?

Hair wild, eyes unnaturally wide, Cassidy looked directly at Echo and said, in a whisper that sent a fog of warm breath into the cold air, "Save me."

For the first time ever, Echo felt herself being pulled out of the vision before she was ready to go. She fought to stay, to see more. To reach Cassidy. Where was she? When? Already she knew she was not too late. This had not happened, was not going to happen immediately. The event was so far out it might not happen at all if she did what needed to be done. How could she know which steps would lead to Cassidy's safety? What was she supposed to do?

Echo heard a new noise—quickly approaching footsteps—and realized she was no longer alone. She turned her head and there was Ryder, running, running, then screaming. Snow fell so fast and thick now it was like a curtain that threatened to hide the details of this vision from her.

Cassidy screamed, her high-pitched voice cutting through it all. "Da!"

Ryder ran hard, but he could not run fast enough. He lifted a hand to his throat, tore the leather cord so that the stone that always rested there flew away. Through the falling snow, the stone spun. It was gone. Ryder changed...

Echo's eyes popped open and there he was. Ryder Duncan in the flesh, leaning over her, calling her name. He looked worried. His hair was mussed and he was sweating and breathing heavily as if he'd been running as he had in her vision. Her breath came hard and fast, her heart was pounding, she was still cold—but her thoughts were focused on one truth.

He'd lied to her, more than once. He'd kept secrets. How many, she had no way of knowing.

As he helped her to her feet she pushed away her earlier, silly list of pros and cons. He tried to hold her close but she slipped away and said, without looking him in the eye, "You lied to me. Cassidy is your daughter."

Chapter 13

Echo refused to look directly at him. He reached for her, tried to gently force her to face him, but she slipped away. He'd been so scared to find her on the ground, shaking and moaning while caught in a vision. He'd been attempting to join her, as he had once before, when she'd opened her eyes.

Now she stood with her arms crossed and her back to him, her voice so soft he had to strain to her. She said, "Cassidy's in danger."

Rye's heart jumped in his chest. "What do you mean? I just left her." He spun around, ready to run back the way he'd come.

A gentle hand on his arm stilled him. He stopped, turned. She faced him now, but she was stoic, almost withdrawn. He tried to touch her mind, and found he could not. Because she was closed to him or because he had been shocked to hear her warning?

"Not now," she said. "It happens after the weather turns cold. In my... I was..." She shook her head as if to clear it. "It began to snow. There was a man...or a woman. I couldn't see clearly. Whoever the robed figure was, they had Cassidy trapped in the middle of a strange stone circle."

"Trapped? Trapped how?"

"She was being threatened with a knife."

It was his worst nightmare, that he wouldn't be able to protect her.

"She asked for my help, but I...I couldn't get to her." Echo took a deep, stilling breath and then she looked him straight in the eye. "Why didn't you tell me? I asked you specifically about Cassidy, and you told me you didn't know her. You let me think she was a product of my own imagination."

He'd done more than that. He'd tried to make her forget his daughter. He'd gone into her mind and tried to gently push all thoughts of Cassidy out of it. That particular spell hadn't taken. Because Echo was too strong or because Cassidy had interfered? She did like Echo, for some reason.

How could he explain that he'd been protecting his daughter from Echo's family? He didn't think they would harm her, but they were Raintree and they thought that when it came to those of their kind—the magically gifted—they had free rein. They might want to make her a part of their clan. They might want to study Cassidy; they'd almost surely want to take her away until they were sure she was no danger to them or to others. And if they determined that she was a danger...

His daughter was the magical equivalent of a nuclear bomb. In the wrong hands, she could do a lot of damage. What had happened to the last clan they'd deemed a threat? The Ansara had been wiped out. No, those who called themselves Ansara, who had the blood of that powerful family, had been either killed or *absorbed* into the Raintree clan.

"I see," Echo said in a lowered voice.

"Stop peeking into my head." Why could she see his thoughts when just now hers had been closed to him? His own panic, he supposed. Or else, as he'd suspected, she was now protecting herself from him.

"I can't help it," she said. "It's not all the time, thank goodness, but sometimes it's like you're inside my head whether I want you there or not. There have been times when it was pleasant enough to peek into your head, but...it hurts to hear so very clearly that you don't trust me."

"That's not true. I don't trust your *family*," he clarified.

"Same difference," she said, then she dropped her hand and walked away. She was headed for the boardinghouse, across the street and down a short distance. She didn't run, but there was purpose in her step.

If he didn't stop her she'd climb into her rental car and drive to the airport and be gone. In so many ways that would be for the best. He'd wished for her to go; he'd realized that his life would not be simple again until she was out of it.

In other ways, her leaving would be a terrible loss.

There were others here in Cloughban who could see

the future. None were as powerful as Echo, none were called prophet. Still, with their help and with the information he already had to go on he could save Cassidy without her.

But dammit, he didn't want to.

"Stop!" he said in a voice that would carry without being too commanding. He didn't follow her into the street, he didn't chase after her. He knew Echo well enough to understand that if he attempted to physically restrain her she'd just run farther and faster. "Don't leave. Stay."

She turned, but did not backtrack. Her expression was one of determination. There was no weakness there. No softness. No love.

"Don't get sentimental on me, Duncan. It was just sex. There are plenty of other women in Cloughban who would be more than happy to warm your bed. No wonder someone tried to scare me out of town by threatening my family. Someone saw this happening. They saw us. But there is no *us*, is there?"

"I'm not asking you to stay for me," Rye said, his voice rough. On a deep and undeniable level, he knew it had to be her. She was necessary; she was here in Cloughban for a reason. "I'm asking you to help me save my daughter."

Before coming to Cloughban she'd never tried to bring on a vision. It wasn't like she enjoyed them, or could control who or what she'd see. All her life she'd done everything possible to get rid of them, and there had never been any hint of control. What Ryder was asking her to do was impossible. Since she'd arrived he'd been trying to get her to purposely take a glimpse into the future. So far, she'd had no luck.

Of course, she'd also thought it was impossible for her to have a vision about an event that wouldn't take place for days or even weeks. It might be months before there was snow in Cloughban. Snow was not a usual occurrence in Ireland, though it wasn't impossible to get a few flakes, Ryder had said.

What she'd seen had been a full-on winter storm.

They sat at the back corner table, where the trio of old men normally sat. Ryder took her hand, and she grudgingly allowed him to have it.

"The reason you have such a problem controlling your abilities is simple enough, love."

"Don't call me *love*," she snapped. It was impossible to love someone you did not trust.

He sighed and continued. "Fear. Fear colors every vision you experience. Before, during and after, you are afraid. As a result, the visions rule you—you don't rule them."

"I can't…"

"No fear, Echo. *No fear*. You are in control. Past, present, future, you have the ability to see it all if you try. If you wish. If you embrace the visions without fear, then you will control them, not the other way around."

After all this time, didn't he understand her at all? "You wouldn't say that if you'd lived your entire life reliving disasters, seeing and feeling people suffer and die, never being strong enough or fast enough to save them."

He ignored her argument. He clasped her hand tight when she attempted to withdraw it from his. How was she supposed to run away when he held her so? She should not have turned. She should've gone on to the boardinghouse, packed her duffel bag and lit out without looking back.

But she had not.

"What do you wish to see?" Ryder asked. "Where do you want to go? Reach for it. I will help you."

Still weak from the vision of Cassidy, she closed her eyes. Danger was coming for Cassidy, but at this moment it was Ryder Duncan she wanted to see. Who was he, really? What did he hide from her, other than his daughter and a complete lack of trust?

She did as he asked; she reached for what she wanted with everything she had inside. Instead of fighting her gift she embraced it. For as long as she could remember, she'd approached her ability as if it were a separate entity from herself. A cancerous growth. A parasite. She now knew that wasn't true. It was as much a part of her as the color of her eyes or her love for music.

For a moment, at least, she ruled her gift instead of the other way around. Echo was, at long last, in control. She saw a door ahead, a door she wished to step through. She placed her hand on a cold doorknob. She turned it; she pushed the heavy door open so she could step into a room she had never seen before.

Instead of seeing the present or the future, she went back in time. A scene formed before her, much as the vision of Cassidy had such a short time ago.

Ryder hadn't changed much, but she could tell he was younger. Maybe not much more than twenty. Twenty-five. The scene before her was colorless, gray.

The images around Ryder were indistinct, while he remained crystal clear.

As was the knife in his hand and the woman he stabbed through the heart.

Chapter 14

Echo snatched her hand from his and slid out of the booth.

"I can explain," Rye said.

She wasn't surprised that he'd seen what she'd seen. Just like in the vision of the Atlanta fire, he'd been with her, observing.

"I bet you can," she said without slowing her stride. When she was near the door, she stopped, turning to face him. He wanted to chase her but he stayed seated because he knew if he stood she'd bolt from the pub. He didn't want this conversation to take place on the street, where others might hear. How did he look to her from that vantage point? Innocent? No. He wondered if she saw that he had no regrets.

"Who was she?" Echo asked. "Someone who was a threat to you?" *Someone like me?*

No, he had no regrets. Still looking her in the eye, still seated, he said, "She was my wife. Cassidy's mother. Her name was Sybil."

Echo went pale; she took a long step back so that her spine was pressed against the door. She was ready to make a run for it; she was terrified of him and he hated knowing he was the cause of the fear in her eyes. The past was the past, and he'd done his best to leave it there. Unexamined. Unexplained.

He'd never bothered to explain himself to anyone. Had thought he never would. Echo was just a distraction, a bit of fun. He had never fooled himself into thinking that they might have more. He was who he was, and she…she was Raintree. She was also, perhaps, his only chance to identify the threat to Cassidy before it was too late.

As he watched, Echo relaxed. He could see it, feel it. She didn't like what she'd seen—she'd been shocked by it—but she knew him. She accepted him in a way no one else ever had. After she'd taken a moment to think about what she'd seen, she was no longer afraid.

Maybe she should be.

"Did she give you that scar on your chest?" she asked. "Is that why you killed her?"

The truth. Nothing but the ugly truth. "Yes and no. She did stab me, minutes before I killed her, but that's not why I did what I did."

"Why, then?" He saw the flicker of hope in her eyes. She wanted to believe the best of him, but was having a difficult time of it. He couldn't blame her.

Rye stood slowly. He took a step toward Echo, one single long step. She didn't run. He didn't dare get too close, though. She was still uncertain. She wanted to believe in him, but she'd seen a bit of his past that he'd tried, for nine years, to deny. To forget.

"Do you remember how I told you that your powers could be removed but there would be a high price to pay?" He didn't give her a chance to respond. "After Cassidy was born, Sybil begged me to strip away her powers. She controlled fire, but like you she was afraid of her ability and sometimes it got out of control. When Cassidy was nine months old Sybil accidentally burned her. It was a small burn, but the baby screamed and then Sybil screamed." He still heard those screams in his nightmares. Both of them, a nightmare in stereo.

"We were both young, too young to be proper parents, but we did try. What had happened scared us. Terrified us, to be honest. I agreed to strip away Sybil's abilities. I knew it wouldn't be easy. I realized there were risks, but..." He looked at her; she had to know.

"I believed we had no choice, so I did as she asked. I did it for Cassidy, because a child deserves to have a mother who can hold her without fear of what might come of a close embrace." He had tried to shove the memory to the back of his mind, but it came roaring back in vivid detail. "We conducted the ceremony under the full moon, at the right time of night." And in the center of the stone circle, though he wasn't ready to tell her that much.

"It worked, the spell was successful. But as I warned you when you asked me to remove your abilities, there was a cost." A high cost, one he had never expected. "More than her powers were taken. After that night, Sybil was never the same. She no longer controlled fire. She could no longer hurt her child with a touch. But her personality was entirely different, and her memories were muddled. She knew me, but she didn't love me anymore. She was often confused about the smallest things, and the baby…"

He took a deep breath so he could continue. "Cassidy was always special. When she was less than a year old, her favorite toys would drift across the room into her arms. Music, lullabies, drifted out of thin air. Sometimes when she cried, it would rain. In the house." He had been so confused. So…young and lost and alone. To have a daughter who revealed her abilities so young, and so strongly, had turned his life upside down. "Sybil became jealous of the baby. She also missed her own abilities, felt empty without them." The combination had been a deadly one.

The truth. The dark truth he had tried for so long to shove to the back of his mind. "When Cassidy was two, Sybil attempted to take the child's powers for herself. The spell she found and attempted to use required the sacrificial death of her own daughter." He didn't tell her that he'd found them just in time, that Sybil had stabbed him when he'd interfered and then she'd gone for Cassidy.

He didn't tell Echo that he'd spun Sybil around and carried her into the next room of their small cottage before driving the knife through her heart, because he didn't want Cassidy to see her mother die that way. As close as he and Echo were, as easily as her thoughts touched his, perhaps he didn't have to. He tried so hard not to think about that night, not to remember the pain. Did she see?

"If I had to do it again, I would," he said so she would know that he had no regrets.

Echo walked toward him, and he knew her well

enough, saw into her strongly enough, to see that her anger and shock had faded. She was no longer afraid of him. She understood in a way no one else ever had. For that alone, he could love her.

She walked into his arms, tipped her face up and kissed him. Gently, tenderly. With love. Her fingers found the scar on his chest and she caressed it through the shirt he wore.

"You still don't trust me," she whispered.

"I don't trust anyone but my daughter," he said honestly.

His statement didn't anger her, didn't hurt her feelings. "I won't tell my cousins or anyone else about Cassidy, I promise you. And I won't tell them about the stones, either."

He grimaced. This was the price he paid for letting her into his heart, into his mind. "You saw them through me?"

"I did." She pressed a warm palm to his chest, directly over the scar. "There are many stone circles in the world. Yours is just one of them. It's a very powerful place. I suppose it's the reason so many gifted people live in Cloughban."

Why lie? She would know. "Yes."

"Do the stones feed your abilities?"

"Yes," he said, waiting for the next question. "They also help me with my own control. I know that sounds odd, that they can make my abilities stronger and at the same time allow me to find that control, but that's the way it's always been."

She leaned in, sharing her body heat, showing him in every way that her short-lived fear was gone. He liked having her there more than he should. No mat-

ter how close they were, no matter how connected...
she could not stay.

"What exactly are your abilities?" she asked. "You're
more than a teacher and a mayor. More than a barkeep
and a concerned father. What can you do?"

He sighed before looking deep into her amazing
green eyes. "Everything."

Everything? Impossible. That kind of power would
drive anyone insane. But it did explain why he was
called wizard, why people traveled from far and wide
for his instructions.

Ryder shook his head slowly. "Except out-of-body
travel. That's one thing Cassidy can do that I can't."

Out-of-body travel! That explained so much about
the two times she'd seen Cassidy. The girl had been
there in spirit only. Fascinating...

"The stone and the wristband you wear." Echo
waved a finger at her own throat. "They help?"

"They dampen."

Dante and Gideon had worn such talismans; they
had fashioned the same for her on more than one occasion. But she knew no one who wore dampening cures
constantly. It simply wasn't natural. The power of the
objects always—well, almost always—faded with time.

"In my vision, I saw you rip away the stone and
toss it aside."

"No," Ryder said sharply. He tensed along the length
of his body. "That was wrong. It had to be wrong."

She would admit that since the scene had taken her
so far in the future, nothing was certain. Still...

Her mind was spinning; this was almost too much information to take in. *Everything?* What did that mean?

"Last night," Echo began tentatively, "did you... Was it...?"

"Last night was just us."

She relaxed. No matter what had happened to this point, she believed him. "So you haven't used your woowoo on me?"

"I didn't say that."

She sighed and stepped away. As much as she loved being close to him, as much as she loved holding on, she couldn't let her emotions make her accept anything and everything. Crap!

"Explain, please."

He looked guiltier than he had as he'd explained how he'd killed his wife. "I've influenced you to forget a few things you've seen here. That's all."

"That's *all*?" Her feeling that something was off about this town, the way she had somehow missed the large number of foreigners, the way she occasionally forgot Cassidy. It all made sense now. He'd been poking around in her brain! That was unforgivable. "If you've been playing with my memories, how can I even know what's real?"

"My influence has been minor, I promise you."

Echo crossed her arms, adopting a pose that said, *Stay where you are, buster.* She needed to think about this. She didn't know many people who had the ability to push or remove thoughts from another's mind. It was a rare ability, and there was an unspoken rule about using that ability on friends and family.

She had the distinct feeling Ryder Duncan cared very little for unspoken rules. She calmed herself with the knowledge that he had been protecting his daughter.

His daughter and his home. Cassidy didn't need protection from her, but…he hadn't known that.

Echo allowed herself to relax a bit. If Ryder was right about what he could do, he could've made her leave Cloughban at any time. She would've climbed into her rental car and hit the road believing it was her own idea. He could've sent her away and wiped the memory of this place, and him, from her mind. But he hadn't.

"Don't worry," he said. "I'm all but dormant."

All but. That was nonspecific. And insufficient. He had enough power to join her in a vision, to affect her memories, to send the Cloughban history book flying into his hand. She wouldn't call that dormant, but those talismans were dampening something. *Everything,* he said. How was that possible?

"Why are you *'all but dormant'*?" she whispered.

For the first time since this strange conversation had begun, he looked angry. At her? At life? It was impossible to tell.

"Because I choose to be," he snapped. "The control you need, the mastery over your abilities, there's a reason some come to me to learn. I learned long ago that too much power is not a good thing. Not for me, and certainly not for my daughter. She needs a father, not a resident wizard so enamored of his own powers that he can't…"

"Can't what?" she asked when he faltered.

"Can't love. Not a child, not a woman. The old saying about absolute power corrupting absolutely? It can be true."

Was it true of Ryder? Had he been corrupted?

"Yes," he whispered.

"Get out of my head."

"I can't."

"Use your damned control! You keep telling me how easy it is, use it now!"

"I never said it was easy, and where you're concerned it's damned near impossible."

They couldn't be connected, not like this. He was everything she didn't want! Wanting him physically, enjoying each other in his bed, that was one thing. But to be connected, mind to mind, soul to soul... No. She would never be free of the magical world if she fell in love with a wizard who was damned mayor of a damned enchanted town filled with damned strays!

"Independents," he whispered.

She knew! Somehow the damned Raintree woman knew.

What was the old saying? It's better to ask forgiveness than to ask permission? She would make no more phone calls. She'd not ask for guidance. The time for action was now. Tonight.

Maisy collected her special knife from its hiding place at the back of her dresser drawer. She wadded up the ceremonial robe and stuffed it into an oversize purse. The robe wasn't necessary, but she liked it. When she'd tried it on she'd felt so powerful...so much more powerful than she'd ever been. Her abilities were annoyingly minor. Why have magical powers if they were going to be so insignificant she could barely qualify for a sideshow?

Her father had been able to control all the elements. With a wave of his hand he could control water, fire, earth and wind. Unfortunately, he'd married a woman with no magic at all. He'd spent most of his life hiding who and what he was from the woman he loved.

Maisy had been fifteen when her own abilities had come to life. She'd been shocked, though to be honest there wasn't much about her abilities to inspire fear or amazement. She could control water, to a minor degree. Dishwater in a sink, drinking water in a glass, a narrow stream if she worked very hard.

Bathwater.

After her mother had drowned in the bath, with a little help from Maisy, everything had changed. She'd thought without a mortal woman to influence her powerful father, they could travel the world. He could teach her, train her to be what he was. Powerful. It had worked, for a while. He had tried to train her, for a while.

Unfortunately, he'd eventually figured out what Maisy had done and had been horrified. She'd had no choice but to kill him, too. Her father had always preferred showers to baths, and she'd never been able to figure out how to drown someone in a shower, so she'd taken care of him with a knife. A knife she'd kept near her ever since. It was special. The knife had sentimental value.

After that, Maisy had been on her own for a time, and then she'd found Walsh. He was convinced they'd been drawn together by the powers of the universe, that like called to like. Maybe he was right. Like her, he was hungry for more than he had in his life. More power. More of everything. And he had a plan to get what he wanted.

She couldn't afford to be stopped on her way out of town. Once she had the enhanced powers it didn't matter what everyone knew. They'd all bow to her. Walsh intended to name his clan Ansara, after his mother's people. He intended to call others like him, like her, to Cloughban and take over the village and the surrounding land. People would come, of that she had no doubt. Would they care if they were led by a man who called himself Ansara or would they be satisfied with a woman named Payne? She doubted they would care at all. The Payne clan did have a certain ring to it. Why go back when it was possible to move forward instead?

Walsh intended to take the girl's power for himself, and she had allowed him to go on believing. Why would he think for a minute that she'd stand back and allow him to reap the benefits of this operation, when she'd been the one to do all the work? He wasn't *that* good in bed. No man was. Still, sleep with a man and he became gullible enough to believe anything he was told. That was her experience, anyway.

He couldn't come into Cloughban yet because too many people remembered him from his last visit. Years ago he'd come to Rye for help, as so many before him had done. Walsh had been born with some gifts, but like Maisy he wanted more. Much more. When he'd found out about the girl he'd instantly begun to wonder how he could use her.

It had taken him years to find the spell that would kill Cassidy Duncan and transfer all her powers to the one who wielded the knife. It had taken her just a few weeks to find that spell among his things. She'd searched his room while he slept—drugged just a little bit—and had finally discovered what she needed hidden under the false bottom of a dresser drawer.

He'd actually hidden the most powerful words she could imagine in his sock drawer. What a moron.

When this was over, Walsh Ansara would be answering to her, not the other way around. He could lick her boots and do her bidding, say "Yes, ma'am" when she passed along her instructions. She'd always wanted a lackey, or two. Or a hundred.

If Walsh didn't give her everything she asked for, she'd dispose of him with her newfound powers. She wouldn't need bathwater or a stream. She might rip his heart out or burn him alive. And then…oh, what a life she could have!

In Maisy's fantasies, Rye became the man he'd once been. Dark. Powerful. Heartless. Few here knew who he'd been, what he'd done, but she knew. Walsh knew, too, and he'd been foolish enough to share the information with her. Together she and Rye would rule Cloughban until the new Payne clan grew stronger—thanks to the stones, and thanks to her—and then they'd move beyond this small, insignificant town.

Walsh had used the Ansara name to call a few dark strays to him. His strays were nothing special, nothing at all to write home about. They were far from fierce. But they would do, for now.

Maisy dialed the sat phone again. Why hadn't Walsh been answering his phone? He had to be anxious; they were hours away from the end of his plan. Mere hours!

Chapter 15

Rye never closed the Drunken Stone on a weeknight, but tonight he hung a Closed Until Further Notice sign on the front door and locked it. He called Doyle and told him to take a couple weeks of paid leave. His chief cook and bottle washer didn't seem to mind taking an unexpected bit of time off, though he had sounded surprised.

Of course he was surprised. Everyone would be. Other than Sundays, he could not recall a time when he'd shut the doors to his business.

Alone with Echo, one kiss led to another. And another. They ended up in his bed. Their place. The only place he had known real peace in a very long time. She offered pleasure and comfort. She offered her body, her mind and her soul. Here, in the dark, they could forget everything for a few precious minutes.

He loved her. He couldn't tell her so, couldn't offer

her a life here. But he loved her. That was an unexpected awareness he fought hard to hide. He pushed it down, shoved it back. If she saw or sensed his feelings for her she was wise enough—or kind enough—not to mention them. Like him, she had to realize that their relationship, no matter how deep it might go, was temporary.

Curled in his arms, naked and sweating and sated, she sighed. All they had was now, this moment. It wouldn't last. He'd loved Sybil at one time, and look how that had turned out.

"I need a shower in the worst way," Echo said as she disengaged, slowly and reluctantly leaving him and heading for the small attached bathroom. She flipped on the light, illuminating herself. She was picture perfect, nude and shapely and relaxed.

Maybe she wanted some company in that shower.

He joined her under the hot water, scrubbed her back, let her scrub his. He hadn't had many really nice moments in the past few years. Hell, in his entire life. This was one. This was a moment to remember, a memory he'd call back after she was gone.

"I need to try to bring on another vision," Echo said. Water ran down her body, pooled at her feet. "I've never been able to do that, but I am stronger now, and the more we know about what's going to happen..." She shook her head. The tips of her hair were wet, her body gleamed. "I need to figure out how we can save Cassidy. There must be something we can do!"

Echo's vision of a danger to Cassidy was one of the future. He wanted to agree with her that, given the timeline, surely circumstances could be changed. If they could determine a date and a time, they could make sure Cassidy was properly protected. Nothing about the future was certain.

Snow. They wouldn't see snow for months, unless a freak weather system of some kind moved in. They rarely saw snow here at all.

A shiver walked up his spine. Echo smiled up at him. "If you help me..." she began, and then she went silent. Her smile faded away as she asked, "What's wrong?"

Echo had an untrained and uncontrollable effect on the weather. When she was sad, it rained. When she was happy the skies were clear blue.

Sometimes. Nothing about that particular power was defined. It was new and unpredictable.

Was it possible she could make it snow? What emotion would bring on that kind of weather?

"We have to go," he said, taking her hand and leading her from the shower.

"What's wrong?" she asked again.

Rye threw her a towel and began to dry his body with another. "It was cold, you said, there was snow. But was it a natural snow?"

Echo paled as she read his thoughts. She, too, dried her body vigorously. "Oh, hell, I don't know."

"In your vision, what was Cassidy wearing?"

Echo closed her eyes for a moment, thinking back, searching her memory. Her eyes popped open and she tossed her towel aside, rushing into the bedroom to grab her clothes and start pulling them on with efficiency. As Rye did the same, she described the dress his daughter had been wearing in the vision. Pink-and-yellow flowers, old-fashioned, short sleeves.

It was the same dress she'd been wearing when he'd left her.

* * *

Cassidy's first niggle of warning came too late. Her da had warned her, time and again, not to rely on the knowing. She might see things about other people, but when it came to herself and those she loved most dearly, there was a veil. Granny said no one on this earth was meant to know too much about their own path, not the good or the bad.

Someone knocked loudly. Cassidy, who had been reading in her room, stood slowly. She started to call out, "Don't answer!" but she was too late. Her grandmother opened the door.

Cassidy glanced at the window. She could escape by that route, perhaps, but then what? Whoever had come for her had Granny. Granny was old. She didn't have many powers, and she had none that would offer any self-defense. If the person who had come for Cassidy didn't find her, would they take their anger out on Granny?

By the time she decided to go out the window and get help, it was, again, too late. She'd hesitated too long! The door to Cassidy's room opened slowly. *Please be Granny. Please be Granny!* It was not Granny, of course. It was *her*. The woman standing there smiled.

Cassidy remained strong. Crying and begging would not help. Not with this one. She lifted her head and said, in an almost-even voice, "I did not expect you."

"Good." Maisy smiled. "I love the element of surprise. It makes life so much more interesting." Her eyes scanned the room, quickly, efficiently, and then she turned those scary eyes back on Cassidy. "Give me any trouble, and I'll kill your grandmother." She delivered the threat with that weird smile in place and an ordinary tone in her voice. As if she were saying, *I think you'd like this book.* "Then the people I'm working with will go after your friends. The brown-headed boy who always needs a haircut—you like him a lot, don't you?"

Brody! She wouldn't dare...no, she would. She would, without a second thought. Librarians were not supposed to be evil! It was just wrong.

"I won't give you any trouble," Cassidy said. If she was going to, it's not like she would tell. The librarian said she liked surprises...

"Good. Then the old woman should be fine."

"What about my da?" Cassidy asked.

"We won't hurt your da." Maisy stepped closer.

Instinctively, Cassidy leaned away. The librarian's shields dropped, and her aura changed. Black. There was so much black!

Leaning down, placing her face too close to Cassidy's, the librarian finished with, "Your da's going to become one of us."

They ran. Echo had immediately offered her car, but Ryder insisted the way the roads twisted around to get to the cottage, running—even walking—would be faster.

They ran. His legs were longer than hers so he pulled ahead easily, but she pumped her legs harder in an attempt to keep him in sight. More than once she offered a silent thanks to spin class. Maybe she should've gone to more...

They ran. Echo was too soon breathless, but she didn't stop. Ryder drew ahead of her, but he never left her sight.

She'd barely had time to be angry with Ryder for not

telling her the truth about Cassidy, but considering what she'd seen in the vision it was hard to blame him. He was a father protecting his daughter. She could argue that Cassidy didn't need to be protected from her or her Raintree family, but Ryder didn't know that.

She lost sight of him for a moment when he crested a small hill. What if she went over that hill and he was nowhere in sight? How would she know where to go? She topped the hill and there he was, farther ahead than he had been before. Lights from a small cottage glimmered directly before her. The front door stood wide-open. It was a nice enough evening, not too hot or too cold, but somehow she knew the open door was not normal.

Echo reached the cottage a few minutes after Ryder. He knelt beside a woman who was lying on the floor in an unnatural position. As she watched, he cradled her head and lifted it carefully. The woman was still alive, but a deep gash in her head was bleeding badly.

Ryder glanced back at Echo. She could see the pain in his eyes, the anger. "It was Maisy who took my daughter. Help me find her."

Maisy? The librarian? That was wrong on so many levels. Echo shook her head. "How can I do that?" It wasn't near cold enough to snow, and even if she could control the weather with her emotions, it was hardly a gift she'd honed.

Without rising, he offered his hand. She took it.

What she saw in his frantic and disjointed thoughts made her jerk away from him.

"Don't," she whispered.

"That's not what I asked you to see. Where's Cassidy? Where's my daughter!"

"I don't know."

"Is she safe?"

It was the older woman on the floor who said as she tried to sit up, "Cassidy is fine, for now. You will not see her again until the first night of the full moon. To-morrow night."

"I can't leave her with that woman for a full day!" Ryder shouted. The rafters shook, but the injured woman was unmoved.

"It does not matter what you do or say, you will not see her until that time." The woman grimaced. "Maisy will not harm her until then. She wants…she wants…" Pain and terror filled the woman's eyes. "She wants what Sybil wanted, and she is willing to do…the same."

Echo realized that this woman was Sybil's mother, Cassidy's grandmother. She cared for and loved the child her own daughter had tried to kill. She held the hand of the man who had killed that daughter.

The injured woman continued. "You must find a way to save Cassidy without…" Suspicious eyes cut to Echo. "Without doing what you think must be done."

"There's no need to talk in circles around me," Echo said. "I saw more than enough when I took Ryder's hand."

She didn't want to think about what she'd seen, what might be.

Ryder without control, without the talismans that kept him, as he said, dampened.

Without the stone at his neck and the leather band at his wrist, Ryder Duncan was a monster.

Chapter 16

Rye called Bryna's gentleman friend to collect and care for her. He refused to tell McManus anything about what had happened, and so did Bryna. Fortunately, the old man was accustomed to keeping secrets, and did not balk when others protected their own.

It was odd to see the man he normally knew as one of three friends who drank together and told bad jokes and argued about politics in this position. McManus held Bryna's hand. He comforted her, and did not press to know more as he helped her pack a small bag. He walked out the front door with that bag in one hand and Bryna's arm caught in the other.

There was no sound of an engine after they'd disappeared from view. They would walk. McManus's little cottage was not far away.

With Bryna in good hands, Rye was free to concentrate on his daughter and her kidnapper. Was Maisy working alone, or did she have an accomplice? Or two, or twenty? He didn't know what he was up against, and he did not dare ask anyone in Cloughban for help. He would have trusted Maisy, if Bryna hadn't told him what she'd done. Why hadn't he seen the danger for himself? What other truths hid from him?

He fingered the stone that lay heavy at his throat. Once he removed the talismans he'd know without doubt whom he could trust. He would see all.

Echo stood silently near the door. Poised to run? He couldn't blame her. This was not her mess, not her concern. Bryna and McManus were long gone when he finally looked squarely at her and said, "Go."

She shook her head. Stubborn woman.

"I don't need you," he insisted.

"Yes, you do."

He was going to have to be blunt with her. Could he lie well enough to fool her? He tried. "I don't want you here."

Again she answered softly, "Yes, you do."

He'd been so afraid of the Raintree coming in and taking his daughter, he'd missed the signs of betrayal under his nose. His own people. A Cloughban resident, someone he knew, had made his worst fear come true.

He didn't think for a moment that Maisy was working alone. She wasn't that smart, or that powerful.

If she took Cassidy's abilities, she'd be more than powerful enough.

"I have to stop her, no matter what. I will sacrifice myself." His voice was sharp when he added, "I will sacrifice you if I have to. If I think for even a moment that it will help to offer you up, I won't hesitate. You're

Raintree, after all. A prophet, and more. If they would take you in exchange for Cassidy, I would hand you over without a second thought."

Instead of running out the door as she should've, Echo walked toward him, took his hand and sat on the love seat. She drew him down beside her, and he let her. She was warm, soft, much calmer than he was.

It wasn't *her* daughter in the hands of a traitor.

"Of course you would," she said in an even voice. "I'd expect nothing less from a father who loves his child dearly."

"I should look for Cassidy tonight, no matter what Bryna says." He said the words, but he did not stand.

Echo's response was clear and too damn calm. "You won't find her."

He looked at her, this small, pretty, deceptively powerful woman who had come into his life and blown it apart. Everything in his life had been just fine, before she'd shown up. Was she a part of this?

You know I'm not.

Her words were clear. In his head, a whisper no one else could hear. He responded in kind.

I should do something. Anything.

She's fine. She's unharmed and she is not afraid. Cassidy is strong, like you.

You can't be sure.

I am.

With that the connection was broken. Echo leaned into him, placed her head on his shoulder.

Why couldn't he establish a mental connection with Cassidy the way he had with Echo? He could if he...

Echo's hand closed over his, drew it down from his throat and the stone there. He thought she would try to convince him that it wasn't necessary that he undo all he'd done. He thought she'd plead with him not to go to that dark place.

Instead, she simply whispered, "Not yet."

Echo had dozed on the love seat, curled against Ryder. She was almost positive he had not slept at all.

"Did you dream?" he asked as she came awake.

"Yes."

"Did you dream of Cassidy?" His voice was so stoic it was almost dead, and that scared her.

"I did, but I saw nothing new." Just another horrifying dream of snow and a sharp blade and Ryder becoming something dark. She could not make herself see anything beyond that point. Maybe because what had happened beyond that point had not yet been determined. She patted his hand, noting as she did that he continued to wear the leather wrist band. She glanced up. He wore the stone at his neck, as well. She didn't really need to look. When they were gone she would know it. She'd see and feel it. "You should sleep."

"No, I should not." He turned his head and looked down at her. "Go. Go now. Take your rental car and drive to Shannon, and get on the next plane to the States."

It was tempting. She'd be lying if she said it wasn't. The girl she had once been would've done just that without being told. She would've washed her hands of this family that wasn't hers, of this trouble that wasn't hers, and in a matter of hours she'd be on a plane headed out of here.

That girl had never known love. The woman she had become did. Funny, she'd always thought love would be all flowers and beauty and fun. Tra-la-la, love songs all around. Ha. So far, it was anything but.

"You need me here," she insisted.

"I don't need you or anyone else."

Her feelings should be hurt, but she understood Ryder's pain. More than that, she felt it. For once, experiencing the pain of another didn't make her want to run and hide. "Someone has to make it snow," she said lightly.

"I can make it snow, once I've…once I remove the talismans."

She experienced yet another pain. He should never have to make that decision, should never have to become someone he'd left behind years ago in order to save his child. That old Ryder…that wasn't a man she ever wanted to meet.

But saying that now wouldn't make things any better. She kissed Ryder on the cheek, surprising him, and then she released his hand and jumped up. "I hope there are eggs. That's pretty much all I know how to cook."

"I'm not hungry."

"You'll eat," she said confidently.

The kitchen was small but very well organized, and there were indeed eggs. Some kind of thin ham, too. She wished she knew how to make scones, but she didn't. Eggs and ham would have to do. Maybe there was some leftover bread she could toast. Echo didn't bother to look up when she realized Ryder had followed her into the kitchen. He stood in the doorway and watched her.

"Don't argue with me," she said. "In my vision it's snowing when you take that thing off. To my knowledge, I've never been wrong. Unless you can make it snow now, before you…" Change? Transform? Go dark? She wasn't sure what to call it. "Well, you know. Unless you can do it now, then I'll still be around to-night."

"My mother was a Gypsy."

Echo turned to face him then, and though it was hard, she smiled. "I know. I saw the look in you the day we met."

He did not look surprised. To be honest, his expression remained so blank it was impossible to tell if he felt anything at all. "My father took a lot of grief for marrying her, rather than one of their own, but I suppose he loved her. One of my earliest memories is of her teaching me a spell. I didn't have quite enough power to suit her, so she supplemented my mental powers through her own kind of magic. I could control all the elements by the time I was eight. The way her face lit up when I did something extraordinary…I lived for those moments.

"Unfortunately for her, I didn't remain a child who was willing to perform for his mother's approval. I studied on my own, and I grew stronger every day." He caught and held her eye. "I can shift into any animal, make you see and believe anything I wish you to see and believe. A little snow? All it would take is a snap of my fingers."

"What happened?"

"Why do you assume something happened?"

"Because if everything was hunky-dory, I doubt you would have gone to the bother to suppress all those abilities."

The moment of silence that followed that statement was almost palpable. He was deciding what to tell her, how much, how little. With a push she might be able to see for herself, but she wanted him to tell her. She wanted him to trust her.

Finally, he spoke. "You know the saying about absolute power corrupting absolutely?"

She nodded.

"It's true," he said in a lowered voice. "The people around you seem less than human, because they're so weak. It doesn't matter if someone gets hurt, and if someone dares to get in your way, you'll squash them like a bug. They won't be missed."

It was a bleak picture, one he painted too well. "Who died?"

"More than one," he whispered.

She turned to look at him, gave him her full attention. She should be horrified, but she was not. This was Ryder. He loved his daughter and would do anything for her. Echo was almost convinced that he loved her, too. Almost. He was not a man who could kill people because they got in his way.

"Tell me," she whispered. *Tell me everything.*

For a long moment he remained silent, and she thought he might not say another word. He was torn. Tormented. She could say, *Never mind*, or push him to go on, but instead she simply waited. He would get there in his own time, or he would not.

Finally, he spoke. "Before I married Sybil, I left Cloughban to work for a man who promised me money and power and women. Everything a young man wants and needs." Was that a smile? No, it was a grimace that offered her a glimpse of the man he had once been. "All I had to do was help him get rid of a few men who stood in his way. Bad men all, but that doesn't matter, does it? I killed them. We took their ill-gotten gains."

"How many?" she whispered.

"Three."

"How old were you?"

"Nineteen."

So young. So damned young. It was hard to imagine Ryder as a teenager. Even harder to see him as vulnerable and easy to manipulate. Obviously that's what had happened. She didn't expect that he'd been an angel, but he hadn't been a devil, either. He'd been twisted. Used.

"Where was your family?" Why hadn't they helped him? Saved him?

"My parents were both dead. I lived with my uncle, my father's brother." Ryder's jaw hardened, and so did his eyes. "He was never able to handle me. My uncle was not what you'd call a powerful man. He was an empath, but nowhere near as strong as you."

She nodded. He'd been basically alone. "What happened to this man who hired you?" she asked. "Where is he now?"

Ryder glanced down, then up again to look her in the eye. "I killed him. In all fairness, he was trying to kill me at the time."

"And since then…"

"I returned to Cloughban, determined to leave that life behind." Ryder was wound so tight, she suspected this story did not have a happy ending. "I came home and went to work for my uncle. He owned the pub back then. I tried to make up for the difficulties I had caused him. Most of all, I tried to leave all the darkness behind me and embrace a simpler life."

Out of all that, one word stood out. "Tried?"

Ryder shrugged, and again he looked away from her. "I was still...who I was. Drunk on power, able to do and have and be anything I wished to be. After a few months my uncle and I started fighting again. I was planning to leave Cloughban, to move to a place where no one knew me, where I could truly start over. But then I met Sybil and I stayed here for her. She was beautiful and funny, and she loved me. I thought I loved her, the way a young man will. I did love her, for a while."

She should not feel even an inkling of jealousy over a dead woman, but what Echo felt at that moment was definitely jealousy. He had loved her...

"That almost sounds like the end, but I'm pretty sure it's not."

His jaw tightened, his eyes went hard. Dark. "No, it was not the end. My uncle was the last of the Duncans, other than myself. He didn't like Sybil. Looking back, maybe he saw what she would become. We'll never know." His hands clenched into fists. Was it a trick of the light that the wide leather band on his right wrist shimmered? Maybe. Maybe not. "When I told him I was marrying her, we argued. He forbade the marriage. I shouted in indignant rage. His heart exploded in his chest as every lightbulb in the pub exploded."

She could see it too well, almost as if she'd been there. His uncle, the empath, had absorbed all that rage and it had killed him. "It was an accident."

"Was it? He wasn't like the others I'd killed. He wasn't a bad man who'd profited from the suffering of others. He was standing in the way of what I wanted, and he died. Sybil and I had planned to leave Cloughban, to travel after the marriage. This is no place for a powerful wizard. We were thinking London, maybe

Paris. With my powers we could make a fortune in no time, and if anyone got in my way...well, their hearts could explode, too."

Much as she cared for him now, she would not have liked the boy he had been. Ambitious, power hungry, willing to kill... "But you stayed."

"I had no choice. I was the last of the Duncans, destined to be keeper of the stones and leader of these people."

"And this?" She waved a finger at her own throat.

He touched the stone, which rested just beneath the collar of his gray shirt. "I made these talismans for myself the day Cassidy was born. I had tried for a while to simply keep my abilities in check, but all too often I was tempted to use them. They're like a drug. The more I use them, the more I want to use them. Why not? Why let such talent go to waste?"

Echo tried to keep her voice light, even while inside she felt anything but. "So, it was like walking to work when you had a Ferrari parked in your garage."

"I suppose."

She turned her back to Ryder and whipped the eggs vigorously, putting all her frustration and anger into working the eggs into a frothy mixture. She didn't want him to go dark, didn't want him to be without those protective talismans. But she'd seen it; she'd seen him become the man who was willing to kill.

She had to ask, "So, why not save Cassidy and then put the protective shields back on again?"

He didn't say anything until the long moment of silence intrigued her and she turned to face him again.

Then, while she was looking into his dark eyes, he told her the truth.

"I'm afraid I won't want to."

Chapter 17

The librarian was being very nice to her, but Cassidy wasn't fooled. Even though her ability to know what was coming didn't extend to herself, she understood that Maisy was not her friend. No matter how much she smiled her creepy smile.

Maisy had come to the school. She had visited at least once a week, smiling and talking about wonderful stories of adventure and family and animals. She'd recommended books from the town library, and Cassidy had loved some of those books! How could someone who loved books be evil? It didn't seem right. How had she fooled everyone? Someone should've known, but somehow she'd hidden all that black in her aura too well. The town librarian was like a villain out of one of the books she recommended.

In books, the good guys always won, but this was

real life, and Cassidy was not so sure that's how it would end.

Twice Cassidy had attempted to travel out of body to tell her da where she was, but Maisy must've put shields around the room to keep her contained. She could manage some defense if it came to that, but she was weakened here. She couldn't even read the librarian's mind, not even a little bit. Besides, Maisy said a friend had her grandmother and would kill her if she didn't cooperate. She'd also threatened her good friend Brody *specifically*. It was impossible to know if she was telling the truth or not, but Cassidy wouldn't gamble with her family or friends.

Her da had always warned her that not everyone in the world was her friend, that there were evil people out there who would love to use the powers she'd been born with for their own selfish reasons if they got the chance. Cassidy had always nodded and said she understood, but she hadn't, not really. Not until now.

Maisy brought her a hot ham sandwich and a glass of water at what must be lunchtime. Cassidy tried again to peek into the woman's mind, but like the room it was shielded. She pushed a bit and got nothing. So she simply asked, "What are you going to do to me?"

"Don't worry about it, dear," Maisy said in a weirdly friendly voice. "After tonight you won't have to worry about anything at all."

Well, that was good news... Wait, no, it wasn't!

Her da and Granny didn't think she remembered what her own mother had attempted so long ago. Even though Cassidy had only been two years old at the time, she did have a memory of that night. It was vague, pictures without words, but over time she'd come to understand.

Her mother had tried to kill her so she could take her abilities. A knife, a few powerful words. Blood spilled. She knew from the few occasions Granny had spoken about her daughter, Sybil, that at that time she'd not been right in the head. Duh. No mother who was right in the head would kill her own daughter, not for any reason.

Maisy, the librarian, was not her mother. Neither was she quite right in the head.

Echo tried to get Ryder to eat and sleep, but he would do neither. He did eat a few bites of egg early in the day, but he'd had to choke those down and did not care to try again. His worry poured from him in waves that almost knocked her down.

She felt his worry to the bone because she loved him. Maybe she had loved him all along, and that was why he'd been so damned annoying in those early days. She didn't want to fall in love with someone like him. Not just a man who possessed his own magic, but a man who was surrounded by it. Magic wasn't just a part of his life, it *was* his life.

As far as her dream man list went, he ticked none of the boxes. Well, the physical ones, yes—he was tall, dark and handsome—but in addition to his own abilities he had a daughter who was an extremely powerful child. Echo had decided a long time ago that she didn't want kids of her own. What if she was no better a parent than her own? What if her child suffered as she had suffered? She sure didn't want a hand in raising someone else's gifted child. Especially not one like Cassidy, who would need constant guidance.

Did that make her a bad person? She didn't think so. She had a list. Ryder and his daughter did not meet any of her requirements.

Except that he was beautiful and they were compatible in bed. And he made her heart beat fast and hard. She wanted to be with him, to be a part of his life. She wanted to take away his pain even if that meant taking it on herself. Dammit, love didn't pay any attention at all to her lists!

Even Cassidy was adorable, loving and sweet. It wasn't her fault she was special.

Echo had seen the darkness in Ryder when he'd invited her in and she'd touched his hand and his mind. When he was all powerful he cared for no one and nothing. He was ruthless. He was dangerous. He was a man who would do anything in order to get what he wanted.

Great. Another bad boy. All this time she'd planned to find herself a decent, nice man who didn't even believe in prophets.

Coming here had shown her a new side of herself, and she knew now that the abilities she possessed could not be denied. She couldn't wish or work them away. All she could hope for was to learn to control them.

She'd never wished for more magical abilities, but at this moment, she did. More than anything, she wanted to take away Ryder's pain.

He sat in the small living room, staring into space, staring at nothing and no one. She'd tried to bring on a vision, had tried to find Cassidy for him, but it wasn't working. The power she'd wished so hard to be rid of was being stubborn.

She sat beside him. His body stiffened. He withdrew from her physically and mentally. Echo was persistent. Some might call it stubborn, but she knew what she wanted and she wasn't going to back down. She leaned into Ryder and placed her hand on his chest.

What this moment called for was a rush of optimism. "When this is done, I think the three of us deserve a vacation," she said. "Where do you want to go?"

He didn't answer.

She wasn't about to give up so easily. "Where would Cassidy like to go?"

"Cassidy would like to go to Disney World," Ryder said in a lifeless voice.

"I haven't been in years. We should…"

"I can't take Cassidy away from Cloughban until she's older and in complete control of her abilities."

"Maybe you could bind her with talismans, as you've done for yourself. Just for a week or two. It could work."

"Maybe. Maybe not. You don't know what she's capable of." Ryder looked down at her. "You don't know what I'm capable of."

Now was not the time or place to tell him that she loved him. Later, when all was well. When Cassidy was safe and home again, when Maisy had been taken care of, one way or another. Did Ryder know? Did he feel her love? She tried to peek into his head, but could not. Not because there was nothing to see, but because he was hiding his thoughts from her.

Rye couldn't sleep. The day had passed so excruciatingly slowly he began to think that somehow time had stopped, that this was a nightmare from which he would never escape. His worst fears were coming to pass. Cassidy was in danger, and he couldn't help her.

But the minutes did tick past. He saw it in the clock, and in the movement of the sun. His time would come; he would be there for Cassidy. More than once he tried to send Echo away, but she refused to go.

He didn't want her to see what he would become in order to save his daughter. He didn't want her around if he couldn't manage to rein in the darkness once Cassidy was safe. What he had been, unleashed, might never be dampened again. Those powers had been bottled up so long, he did not know what to expect when the talismans were removed.

If he couldn't save his daughter, he knew he would never be right again. If she died, if Maisy succeeded, he would have no reason to return.

A time or two Echo had tried to peek into his mind, but he blocked her. It wasn't easy, but neither was it impossible. Eventually she stopped trying.

It was a warm day, all too slowly turning into a warm evening. It was far too warm for snow. Was it possible that Echo's vision—which had been much farther in the future than her normal episodes—was not entirely correct? That vision was all he had to go on. The stones, snow, Maisy and Cassidy at the center of it all.

Where would Echo be as he ran toward his daughter, tearing off the talismans as he raced through falling snow? Ahead of him? Behind him? She hadn't said. Maybe she didn't know.

He stood in the open doorway of the cottage and watched the sun set. Soon, but not soon enough, it would begin. And end.

He heard and felt Echo approach long before she placed a gentle hand on his back. "When it's done, come back to me."

He knew very well that she wasn't talking about a physical return.

"I don't know that I can." After being restrained for so long, would dampening that part of himself be possible? It wouldn't be easy. A part of him would rejoice at the return of power. A part of him would fight to remain, after being smothered for so long.

"Do it for Cassidy." She drifted closer. He felt her heat, felt her emotion. "Do it for me."

Darkness fell while they stood in the doorway waiting. Waiting. He knew what he had to do.

"I will do nothing for you, Raintree. I don't care for you at all," he said, his voice low and cold. "I never did."

She didn't believe him, not right away.

"You're pretty enough, you were handy, and to be honest when I need release it's best not to get involved with a local girl who might be foolish enough to think a night or two in my bed means something more. Face it, you needed to get laid as much as I did. Did you really think it was anything more than that?"

Her hand fell away.

He'd blocked his mind from her, but she was an empath. She'd sense his emotions no matter how hard he tried to hide them. So he thought of Sybil and how she'd tried to kill her own daughter. He thought of Maisy, and what he'd do to her when he got his hands on her. She was going to burn for taking Cassidy. She would suffer before she died.

He filled his heart with hate for those two women.

He embraced the darkness that was a part of him—long buried or not—until there was no love in his heart.

"You were convenient, Raintree. Pretty, willing and temporary." He turned to look at her. "For God's sake, go away."

She didn't say a word, but he felt the temps drop. She believed him. Cold air swirled around him, and around her, as her heart broke.

Beyond the doorway where they stood, side by side but no longer together, it began to snow.

Chapter 18

Echo walked away from the cottage. She walked, and then she ran. She wasn't wanted here. What an idiot she'd been! Thank goodness she hadn't told Ryder that she loved him. He probably would've laughed at her.

She'd been so sure he felt more, but…her empathic abilities were new. Maybe she had felt what he'd wanted her to feel so she'd…

Those thoughts had to go, before they stopped her in her tracks. Focus on the positive, if there was any. She'd accomplished all she'd come here to do. She had learned some control, could now recognize when a vision was coming. No more dropping to the ground without warning. She'd also learned some control within those visions. Maybe she'd no longer feel as if she were right there in the disaster, but could remain an observer. An observer who could help, if the timing was right.

That was all well and good, but it didn't make her feel any better.

She'd walked from the cottage Ryder had left, too, headed in another direction. Toward the stones, she assumed. She had not been brave enough to see if he glanced back toward her. He was focused on saving his daughter, as he should be.

Echo was freezing, and it was her own fault. She had brought on the cold, the snow. Snow and frozen rain fell in fits and starts. She hugged herself in an attempt to keep warm. Now she knew what emotion could bring on snow.

Heartbreak. Desolation. The complete loss of hope.

Cassidy popped into her path, not five feet ahead. Echo stumbled to a halt, her heart almost bursting out of her chest.

"Where are you going?" Cassidy asked harshly.

"Home, I guess."

"No!"

She wanted to hug the little girl, to offer some kind of comfort, but Cassidy wasn't really here. Not in body, anyway. Echo understood that much now. "Your father will save you."

"I know he will." Cassidy rolled her eyes in that maddening way young girls do. "But who's going to save *him*? That's your job. I can't do everything myself!"

For a moment, the snow stopped. The cold remained, but it was not so sharp and cutting. "Why didn't you come to us this way earlier? Why didn't you show yourself to your father? If you'd told us where you were…"

"I couldn't," Cassidy said, clearly exasperated. "Maisy had a spell on the room. I couldn't do *anything*."

"Where are you now?"

"Almost to the stones. Da's coming, I can feel him, but…I need you, too. I need you to save him, if you can, if you…"

And then Cassidy was gone, without warning. Without even finishing her sentence. That couldn't be good.

Echo had never been to the stone circle before, didn't even know what direction to take to get there. Ryder had headed east when he'd left the cottage, but that was not nearly specific enough. There were miles and miles of wide-open fields, and many gentle hills that hid what lay ahead.

Echo closed her eyes. She reached for the source of power, for Cassidy…for Ryder. When she opened her eyes she was surprised to see a trail of flickering lights low to the ground. Twinkling, dancing, yellow and blue and pink and lavender, they lit the way.

For a moment, Echo held her breath. Fairies? Oh, hell, no. Must be Cassidy's doing.

It didn't matter who—or what—lit the way. She had to find her way to the stones. To Ryder. Echo began to run. The flickering lights in her path broke apart as she ran through them, then flew ahead to keep the line going. As far as she could see, those twinkling lights lit her way.

Maybe Ryder didn't want her. Maybe he would never again be the man she'd fallen in love with.

But she was meant to be there, to help. To save him, if she could. If he would allow it.

Was she wasting her time trying to find him? There had been no love in Ryder when he'd left the cottage to save his daughter. No love, no hope at all. All she'd sensed from him was disdain for her and a dark determination. Still, she had to try. Cassidy needed all the help she could get. Echo ran, and once again snow began to fall.

The sight was just as Echo had described it. The stone circle, the snow, Maisy and Cassidy.

Maisy wore a dark ceremonial robe with a deep hood. She held a knife in her right hand. Cassidy was close to her, much too close. The knife was raised in the air, ready to swing.

He was not close enough, not yet.

Rye shouted; he roared as he stripped the leather cuff from his wrist. That was enough to wash him in a touch of forgotten power. It felt good, better than anything he could remember. He yanked the stone from his throat and tossed it aside, and the remainder of his long-locked-away powers returned. They rushed through him fast and sure. He'd been asleep for years, and now he was awake. He'd been sleepwalking; he'd been weak. He was weak no more.

Rye saw nothing but Maisy as he ran, moving faster than he should be able to. Seeing everything around and before him sharper, *clearer*, as if until now his life had been out of focus. She heard him, turned, smiled widely.

In the blink of an eye, he took on some of the powers of a panther. More speed, more lithe strength. His teeth became fangs, his hands claws. Maisy, who had been momentarily entranced, lost her smile. Perhaps she knew that he intended to rip her to pieces.

She turned and the knife she held swung down and into Cassidy.

No!

The knife swung not into Cassidy but *through* her. His daughter was playing out of body again. *Good girl.*

Maisy had no more time. Rye slammed into the evil woman at full force; he grabbed her arms and pushed her out of the circle and away from his daughter before knocking her to the ground. She landed on her back, hard, losing her breath for a moment. Once she'd recovered she looked up at him, wide-eyed and looking like a bleedin' librarian, not an evil witch.

How dare she threaten his daughter!

Prone, vulnerable, she dared to speak. "We could be good together, Rye. You and me, and Cassidy. We can be a family like no other. Look at you," she whispered. "Half animal, half man, all dark power and so, so beautiful."

He barely listened. The woman on the ground was nothing. She was no one. Without warning she swung the knife she continued to hold in one pale hand, aiming for his ankle, trying to bring him down.

She wasn't fast enough. Not nearly fast enough. With one swipe at her throat with a hand that still possessed the claws of the animal she'd admired, Maisy was dead. The knife she'd managed to hold on to all that time dropped to the ground. The silver soaked up the power of the nearby stones; the blade shimmered, it danced and then it went dark. Dead. As dead as the woman.

Rye resumed his complete human form with a minimum of effort. No more fangs, no more claws. The power he had reclaimed remained, rushing through his blood. For the first time in years, he felt alive.

The snow stopped, but flakes had gathered on Maisy's face and on her dark robe. Dead she looked... surprised.

He'd wanted her to suffer for what she'd done, but her death had come too quick, too easy. Not satisfied simply to kill the woman who had dared to threaten his daughter, Rye waved his fingers and sent a stream of white-hot flame at her body. Fire lit the night, illuminated the landscape before and around him. It took only seconds for the traitor to burn to ash.

With a twist of his hand he lifted the ash from the ground, creating a small whirlwind. He sent the dancing ash high, propelled it into the night sky until there was literally nothing left of Maisy.

Rye turned back to the circle. An alarmed Cassidy— not really Cassidy—disappeared.

Where was she? Close? Far? He knew she could manifest from a goodly distance, but she couldn't have gone too far. Maisy wouldn't have had her eyes off the prize for more than a few seconds. He returned to the center of the stone circle and turned about. Twice. His eyes scanned the shadows, the darkness. In an angry panic, he called her name. Nothing. No Cassidy.

He'd scared her; he'd revealed a part of himself that had been hidden for all her life. Taking a deep breath, reaching for calm, he commanded his daughter to show herself. Warily, she stepped out from behind the tallest stone.

"Da?" she asked, her voice trembling.

His daughter was so powerful, so amazingly special. Why had he kept her hidden away in this place? Together they could have anything, do anything. Money, power…what else was there worth having?

Love.

That thought was not his own.

He turned to watch Echo approach. He'd let his

guard down and she'd slipped into his head. Again. Raintree bitch. She made him weak. She wanted him to be the shell of a man he'd been for so many years. He'd never again limit himself that way. Why had he ever allowed himself to be so weak?

"I thought I told you to go," he growled.

"You did. I started to obey, I really did try. To be honest I've never been very good at obeying. I had to make sure Cassidy was all right."

With a power he'd all but forgotten racing through his blood, Rye realized that Echo was a threat. She was, perhaps, the only person who stood between him and everything the darkness wanted.

"She's fine, as you can see. Go."

"No."

"I'll rip out your throat," he said in a calm voice. "I've done that once tonight and now I have a taste for it. Will you die as quickly and easily as Maisy did?"

She should be terrified, but she was not. Echo looked past him; she looked to Cassidy. "Your granny is coming to get you."

"She's close. I see her," Cassidy said too softly.

"Run to meet her. I'll take care of your da."

Rye watched his daughter run away. She was scared of him, but that wouldn't last. When she realized what they could do together, what they could have...

Echo walked into the circle. She was powerful, too, but what she possessed was nothing next to him and his daughter. He could not allow her to get in his way.

"If you know what's good for you, you'll turn around," he warned.

"I've never been very good at knowing what's good for me, either." She smiled. Smiled!

"You asked me once, more than once, to take away your powers. I can do that, here and now." That act would wipe away who she was, perhaps even her memory of him and her idea that she should be here. It would remove any hint they were connected. The way the power was washing through him, he'd likely kill her in the process, or at the very least leave her brain-dead.

She walked up to him, placed a hand against his chest as she so often had. Her palm rested against the scar too near his heart.

Rye reminded himself that the last woman he'd loved had tried to kill him. Had almost succeeded. This one was as much of a threat as Sybil had been. Perhaps more of a threat.

"I can do it," he said. "I can take it all away."

She responded, still far too calm, "Whatever you think is best, love."

He placed the palm of his right hand against her temple.

His eyes were wrong, and she still couldn't see into his mind the way she once had. She felt his emotions, though, and they were strong. Hate, fear, ambition, lust and somewhere, buried deep, love. He'd done his best to deny that love earlier, but she saw it now. She felt it.

"I love you," Echo whispered.

"You're a fool."

"Am I? I don't think so, not anymore. I think maybe love is the only thing worth living for." And dying for, she supposed. Not that she wanted to die.

The hand that had been pressed to her temple dropped away.

"I'll show you what you think is love, Raintree."

Ryder was rough as he pulled her shirt over her head. She lifted her arms to assist him. "Sex, that's all it is. You could be replaced by any woman, and I could be replaced by any man. Did you really think there was more to it than that?"

"Yes." She knew there was more. "I love you."

"You fooled yourself into thinking you love the man I used to be."

"The man you still are."

He unfastened her jeans and pushed them down. She kicked off her shoes and stepped out of them.

She stood naked in the center of the stone circle that gave Cloughban—White Stone—its name. By day the stones themselves would be an ordinary gray, but by the light of the full moon they were gleaming white. She felt the energy in the stones, in the ground, in the air. It was good energy, white magic. The only darkness here was within Ryder.

"I love you," she said again.

"Stop saying that!"

"Why? They're just words, unless you give them meaning with your heart as I have." She leaned into Ryder, went up on her toes and kissed him gently.

He stiffened, but he did not move away.

The stone circle sat upon an unimpressive plot of land with a pond to the north and a field to the west. It was far from any cottage, and on this night it was far from prying eyes. Anyone touched with magic would sense the danger here. They would sense the danger Ryder had become and stay away. She was the only one around who didn't have the sense to flee.

Most people didn't realize that Stonehenge wasn't the only stone circle in the world. Not by a long shot. It was just the most well-known. The Cloughban stones were smaller, but the circle here was just as ancient and every bit as powerful.

The clouds that had brought the snow drifted away, broke up to reveal the dark sky above filled only with countless stars and a bright full moon.

Lightning danced on Ryder's fingertips, fire flickered along his arms and in a circle around their feet. The heart of a panther beat within his chest. He could rip her apart as he had Maisy, but he wouldn't. She believed that with all her heart.

"You might not admit yet that you love me, but you do want me."

He didn't deny it.

"I knew you were trouble from the moment I saw you." Echo kept her voice low, even though there was no one around to hear. "I walked into the pub, took one look at you and almost gave up then and there."

"You should have."

"I'm glad I didn't." She slipped her hand beneath his shirt, pushed it high, helped him remove it. Then she moved her hands to his jeans. He didn't fight her efforts. In fact, he helped.

Soon Ryder was as naked as she was. He laid her on the ground, roughly, but not as roughly as she'd thought he might.

"I love you," she whispered.

"You're a damned broken record," he growled. "This is not love." With that he was inside her, pushing, claiming. He moved fast and hard, without a hint of gentleness. She welcomed him, cradled him, offered softness and love where he believed there was none.

The breeze that washed over her was warm and

smelled of the ocean. *Impossible*. That was the scent of home…and a very real indication that *this* was now home. Ireland, Cloughban…Ryder.

"Deny it all you want, love," she said. "I'm yours. You're mine."

At that, he did slow. His entire body relaxed. Echo closed her eyes and tilted her head when he moved his mouth to her neck and kissed there. They were still one, still joined, but now there was more. He was as warm as she was. Warmer. The darkness was still there, but it stepped back. It faded. For her…just for her.

The world didn't stop, not entirely, but it slowed down. There was only him, and her, and the way they fit together. And pleasure. Oh, yes, there was pleasure, sharper and deeper than any she had ever known. When she tried to tell Ryder again that she loved him, the words were all but unintelligible.

She climaxed quickly, too quickly, screaming as she lost all control.

And then he came with her, and on the fading waves of her own climax visions not her own filled her swimming head.

Fire.

Illusion.

Lightning.

The snarl of an animal.

Darkness.

And beneath it all, light.

Chapter 19

He fought. In his mind, his heart, in the blood that rushed through his veins. Rye was at war with himself. A few minutes ago his life, his plans, had seemed so simple. All he needed was Cassidy. Together they would have anything and everything they wanted...

Now, still inside her, still a part of her, he wanted Echo, too. He wouldn't call this love; he didn't believe in love, but he did want her.

Naked, entangled in the center of the stones, he said, "Come with us. You, me, Cassidy... We can have it all."

She sighed; her warm chest rose and fell. "You're an idiot. You already have it all."

He shouldn't allow her to talk to him that way, but... he let the infraction slide. For now. So much had happened in such a short time. He was free. Cassidy was safe. Echo was here. His. Knowing who he was and what he'd done, she still offered herself to him. Body, heart and soul.

He rolled away. Touching her was a weakness. "We have nothing, not yet," he said. "In time, we can rule the world."

She laughed. Laughed! Then she rose and looked at him. Naked and beautiful in the moonlight, flushed with pleasure, she was tempting. Still. Again.

Her smile remained as she said, "You know, in comic books and movies villains always want to rule the world. But really, what do they expect to do with it once it's theirs? Ruling the world just sounds like a lot of trouble to me. One problem after another."

He pushed her down, pinned her wrists to the ground and asked harshly, "What do you want?"

In spite of her vulnerable position, she smiled at him with what she thought was love.

"Easy," she said. "I want you. I want music and, one day, I want babies. I didn't think I wanted kids at all. Even earlier today… But I've changed my mind. Life is so short, so fragile." She sighed and said again, "I want babies. I want to laugh and make love and occasionally just sit back to watch a particularly beautiful sunset. I normally miss the sunrise, but I'm sure they're beautiful, too. Maybe I can learn to get up early enough to see it now and then."

That was ridiculous. Small and unimaginative. "You can have anything."

Her smile faded. "Anything?"

"Yes!"

"Love me."

Rye rolled away and grabbed his pants. What she wanted was impossible.

"Well, you did say anything," she said as she reached for her own clothes.

Pants on, Rye sat in the center of the stone circle and closed his eyes. The darkness he had reclaimed remained, but it was touched with something new. Something he did not want. It was Echo and Cassidy; it was this place of white magic. What he felt, what interfered, was warmth in a cold world. He pushed the warmth down, shook it off as he might an annoying insect.

Echo was dressed when she said, her tone serious, "I suppose what you're experiencing now is very much like what a heroin addict goes through when they fall off the wagon. The rush is everything, and you don't want to give it up. You have to think about what you must sacrifice in order to keep on experiencing that rush."

Cassidy… There had been a time when he would've done anything for his daughter. And now Echo…

He couldn't love her. It would complicate everything.

"Like any addict," she continued, "I suspect this will lead to an early death for you if you don't…let it go."

"Most likely," he admitted.

"Lock the dark away," she whispered. "Give it up, put the darkness to sleep again." And then, once more, "I love you, Ryder."

He stood and ran.

Echo followed Ryder, running as fast as she could. It didn't take her long to realize where he was headed.

Perhaps he wasn't beyond hope, after all.

By the time she reached the cottage, he was already

inside. The front door stood open, so she walked in. Ran in. She wasn't sure what she would find.

On the far end of the living area, Cassidy stood with her grandmother on one side and James McManus on the other. All three looked terrified.

Cassidy's eyes jumped to Echo, and she said, in a child's terrified voice, "That is not my da!"

"Of course I'm your da," Ryder said without emotion.

Cassidy shook her head, and again she looked to Echo for help. "He's still in there, but he's weak. He's fighting, fighting." She took a deep breath. This little girl who could see so much, do so much...she was scared. "The curse is trying to take over, and if it does..."

"God help us all," McManus said in a lowered voice.

Ryder lifted a hand and began to wave it in the older man's direction, but when Cassidy threw herself in front of McManus, Ryder's hand dropped. Slowly. Echo found hope in that instinctive decision. The man she loved would not hurt his daughter.

"There's no curse," he said, flexing the fingers of his right hand as if he wondered why he'd lowered it.

Cassidy argued, "There *is* a curse. Echo sees it, too. Don't you? Please tell me you see it."

Echo walked around Ryder, studying him, wondering what Cassidy saw in him that she had not. The abilities she'd tried so hard to bury drifted to the surface, and with some effort she suddenly saw—sensed, felt—what the child had seen right away.

The powers Ryder had been born with were there, but they were buried deep beneath unnatural abilities that had been poured into him a very long time ago.

Poured by his mother, who Ryder had admitted gave him more magic than he'd been born with. She had not taught her young son, Echo realized, she'd changed him. The magic she'd worked hadn't been good or healing. Instead, it was as if she had cursed him. She'd forced this darkness upon him. He hadn't been made to carry that much power and so it had warped him. Perhaps she'd thought she was doing him a favor...

Some favor. She'd made her son a Jekyll and Hyde. Had his soul been in constant battle since then? Light against dark—innate abilities fighting against a powerful curse.

She had so often thought of her own abilities as a curse, but this...this was a true curse.

Echo placed a hand on Ryder's arm hoping for more insight, but he quickly shook her off. He turned dark eyes to her, and she saw the battle. Another being, a dark one, had been created when his mother had cursed him. Had she realized what she was doing?

"Curses can be broken," she whispered. Ryder wouldn't need talismans to hold back the curse, not if it was removed entirely. That was the only good she saw in this, the only positive development. He had not been born with dark magic; it had been forced upon him.

"What if I don't want this particular curse broken, Raintree?"

She placed her hand on his arm again, and this time she wouldn't allow him to shake her off. "My name is Echo, and you love me."

The smile he gave her was cruel. "No, I don't."

He said he didn't love her, but after that initial attempt at distancing himself from her—which she'd handled easily—he didn't move away or push her back.

Something within him liked her touch. Still holding his arm, she closed her eyes and tried to concentrate, tried to identify more. When? How? What could she do to help? She gave it everything she had, but it was not enough.

Until Cassidy took her free hand and squeezed.

At the child's touch, power rushed into Echo. It was the kind of power that could easily knock a woman off her feet, but Echo remained standing. She was strong; she was determined. Ryder's arm was cold and hard beneath one palm; Cassidy's warm, soft hand was in the other. Cassidy's touch fed Echo. It empowered her.

Images filled Echo's head, while a sharp pain filled her heart. She saw beyond the darkness and strength she'd found before in the man she loved. She saw a boy, the boy Ryder had once been. Hair too long, eyes too dark and filled with pain…she would have recognized him anywhere. Anytime.

He had not asked for this, had not sought it.

Yes, the curse could be broken, but only Ryder's mother, the woman who had cast the dark spell, knew how. And she was long dead.

She didn't have to tell Ryder what she saw. He slipped into her head the way he sometimes did, but more completely than before. It would be difficult to hide anything from him now. She was going to have to try…

"Even if I wanted to go back to the man I was, and I do not, it's impossible."

"Maybe not," Echo said as she dropped her hand and stepped away from Ryder. Cassidy's hand remained in hers. She gave the child's small hand a little squeeze, an offer of comfort, of hope.

Ryder closed his eyes. She could see the struggle in him. "I can't..."

"You can!" she insisted.

He opened his eyes and looked at her, and in a flash she saw a hint of the man she loved. For a split second she saw who he was, who he might one day be again. It was not too late.

"I can't," he said again, but then he added, "Not yet. Maisy wasn't working alone. This isn't over. I need every advantage I have..."

"This is not an advantage!" she argued.

He would not be swayed. "Look into the future, Raintree prophet," he said in an unkind tone, and the man she'd glimpsed was once again gone. "I can't save Cassidy if I'm weak."

"You're not weak," she argued.

"Look, if you can. If you have honed your powers at all while you've been here, you'll see and know, as I do, that without this curse the men who are coming to Cloughban will win." This time he took her hand, and he squeezed tight. Too tight. She thought her bones might break if he continued to squeeze so hard.

She did see, and for a moment her heart stopped. They were gone. They were supposed to be gone! She knew who was coming for Cloughban, who was coming for the stones and the power, for the sanctuary. A name popped into her head as if it were a flashing neon sign, and in that instant she knew who was coming for Cassidy.

As Ryder released her hand, she stepped back and gasped, "Ansara."

Rye walked slowly back toward town. Echo was in his wake, silent—for once—but refusing to give up.

He'd told her to stay at the cottage with Cassidy and the others, but she'd refused. Refused to stay behind, refused to be protected. Why did he care if she was protected or not?

He'd placed a spell on the cottage and the people inside, hiding them from prying eyes, keeping them safe. He didn't care about the others, but deep inside he did care about his daughter. Not because she was his daughter, his blood, his child, but because she was so incredibly powerful she might one day be of use to him.

Echo had thought the evil and power-hungry Ansara clan to be no more. Foolish. One had survived. Over the years that single surviving Ansara had brought strays into the fold. Strays like Maisy. They'd begun to build a new clan, one independent at a time. What sorts of promises had been made? Power, certainly. Money. Revenge. Possessing Cloughban would be the final step. They'd have the stones, the magic, the people. And Cassidy. No matter what, they could not have Cassidy.

He could simply take his daughter and go. Screw the town and the people in it. The Ansara could have them.

But a part of him, the weak part he could not yet shake, still cared. With his old powers coming back and trying to take control, he felt like two very different people occupying the same body. He'd managed a balance before, but his dark side had been sleeping so long it was stronger than before. More determined to survive. To win.

That part of him was angry, and determined not to be denied again.

The back of the pub was in sight when Echo said, "Two days."

"I'm aware," he snapped.

"In two days the Ansara will march into Cloughban and if we don't do something they'll take it."

"Go, then. Get into your rental car, drive to the airport and go home."

"No," she said softly.

"Why not? This is not your battle to fight!"

"It is my battle, dammit! Do you think I like it? Do you think I like admitting that this is home now? I don't, but it is." She didn't sound happy about the fact. "All my life I've searched for home. Not Raintree home, not Gideon's home, not a place to crash for a while. *My* home. And finally, I find it on the other side of the world. No Wi-Fi, no Walmart, no movie theater or bowling alley or…hell, anything!"

"Then go," he said again. "Find another home, one with your bleedin' Wi-Fi."

She sighed. He did not turn to look at her.

"It doesn't work that way, and you know it." Her voice was slightly calmer than it had been. "Besides, faults aside, this is the most beautiful and peaceful place I've ever been."

Rye snorted. "Peaceful?"

"Well, normally. Maybe not this week, but…all in all. The important thing is, I belong here. I feel like I've spent my entire life taking one small step after another for the specific purpose of finding Cloughban. And you," she added in a more determined voice.

He needed to be just as determined as she was. Colder. Surer. "This is not your home, and what we have is nothing more than lust."

"Bullshit!" she said as she ran forward to pull up alongside him. "Empath here, remember? A part of you does love me."

She was silent for a few moments after that. Silent and thoughtful. Finally she said, "Two days is not enough time."

"To get ready for the Ansara?"

She didn't answer, not out loud, but he heard her thoughts more clearly than ever.

To make you love me. Jerk.

Chapter 20

Ryder didn't invite her into the pub, but he didn't push her away when she followed him inside, either. Empathic abilities were not required to see that he was a man at war with himself, that since removing the protective talismans he'd been light and evil wrapped in one package.

Her Ryder was a father, a lover, a leader and protector. He was what he had been born to be—a guardian. Guardian of the stones, of his child, of Cloughban… even of her.

He was also a killer. Ryder had killed years ago, and he'd killed again tonight. Did it matter that those lives he'd taken had been dark ones? She couldn't—wouldn't—say. She did understand that with his own darkness flowing free again he was power hungry and slightly sociopathic. *Slightly?* Who was she kidding…?

In spite of all that, there remained deep inside a part of him a man who was willing to do anything for those he loved. For her. For Cassidy. She looked at him with loving eyes and so easily saw the man he had been as well as the man he was now, at this moment. She saw the good and bad.

It sounded like a fairy tale, she realized that, but in her heart she was certain that love could save Ryder. No, not save. *Guide.* He was going to have to save himself. Love could push back the dark and feed the light. *Her* love. It wasn't enough that she loved him, he had to love her back.

Then they could handle the Ansara, and after that, the cure. The removal of the curse.

Unfortunately, Ryder was right about one thing. He needed every power he possessed to win in a battle against the coming invasion. Dark and light. The Ansara had never been known for fighting fair. She wished she could see more of the future, that she could bring on one of the visions she'd been trying so hard to shake for good.

As they climbed the stairs to his living quarters— she right behind him, he not looking back—Ryder told her, in the crudest terms possible, what he would do to her if she was foolish enough to crawl into bed with him. Her quick response was a simple "Fine." If she ran now, if she allowed him to scare her away, the man she loved would truly be lost.

And so would she. He needed her, but this was not a one-sided relationship. She needed him, too. All her life she'd been lost, in one way or another. She'd been dissatisfied with her lot in life, rootless, wandering. For as long as she could remember she'd been searching for a better place, a better life. Now she understood that her better life was here.

He didn't bother to switch on the light, but it wasn't necessary. Bright moonlight shone through the window. There were shadows here, but not complete darkness. She could see him; he could see her.

By the side of his bed, Echo calmly removed her clothes. All of them. Ryder, standing just a few feet away, watched closely. Eyes dark, hands clenched, he tensed. He remained at war with himself, a war that seemed to cause him physical pain as well as mental anguish. She supposed that would continue until one side or another won. Until he was her Ryder again, or…the other.

She wanted her Ryder back, no matter what the cost.

When she was naked she looked at him. And waited. Eyes never leaving her, he removed his own clothes methodically and tossed them aside. His body was fine, and even in the midst of crisis she could appreciate it. The length, the shape, the muscles, even the erection, which told her that no matter what he said he did want her. Physically, at least.

He took a few steps to join her, wrapped his strong arms around her and without warning threw her onto the bed. She bounced, and then surprised him with a laugh. There wasn't much light in the room, but there was enough for her to see the shifting emotions on his face.

"Maybe I don't want you anymore," he said. "I'm sick and tired of you and your problems and your cloying, needy obsession."

She ignored his words and pointed. "You don't *look* like you're tired of me."

"Any woman would do," he said as he crawled into the bed, spread her thighs and touched her.

"I don't think so," she whispered as he thrust into her.

His emotions battled even as he made love to her. She felt it all when he was inside her. Hot and cold, love and hate, power and loss. Most of all, she felt the pain this war within him brought to life. Not physical pain, but a pain of the soul. A pain of the heart. She soothed him with her body, with her hands in his hair, with the love he refused to acknowledge. Soon he slowed his movements, he relaxed. He flowed into and out of her in an almost dreamlike way that was more than she could bear. This was beauty amid darkness, pleasure amid pain. She didn't want it to end.

As long as they were together, truly together, the darkness could not win. She wouldn't allow it. Couldn't. In this place, in this time, joined body and soul, there was no room for evil. It was pushed aside, shoved into a small dark corner where it was forced to cower, to wait. For a while, at least, for a few precious minutes, he was *her* Ryder. A man who loved his family, his people and her.

Stay with me forever.

I don't know that I can...

As long as they could stay here, stay connected, remain one, he was safe. She was safe. But he began to move faster and so did she. Bodies ruled, not brains and hearts.

It had to end, her body and his insisted.

Echo was in the stone circle; she was in his bed; she was nowhere and everywhere. He filled her, stroked her, brought her to a beautiful edge where she stayed as long as she could. As long as her body would allow. She crested, cried out, held on while the orgasm racked her body. Ryder was right behind her.

And at the moment it was Ryder. *Her* Ryder.

"I still love you," she whispered.

"For God's sake, stop it."

"Stop loving you or just stop saying it?"

"Both." He rolled away.

"No on both counts," she said as she left the bed and headed for the bathroom. She cleaned herself with a warm washcloth, returned to the bed and crawled beneath the covers beside Ryder. When he turned away from her she curled up against his back searching for warmth and connection. Her fingers danced along his spine.

There would be no more snow, not on her account. It was time for her to be strong, to stick to her guns. She knew what she wanted, what she'd been searching for all her life, and she wasn't about to walk away.

"Go home," Ryder insisted in a low, gruff voice.

Echo answered honestly, and in a tone that left no room for argument.

"I am home."

How could Echo sleep with him knowing who he was? She knew very well what he had been and what he could be again. She'd seen it, had peeked inside his dark past. She saw, felt, even experienced, things even he had forgotten, and yet she remained here. She trusted him enough to sleep.

When Echo relaxed completely into his spine and settled into easy, even breathing, Rye moved away from her. Carefully, so as not to wake her. He should leave the bed, leave her be, get away from her influence. Instead, he settled in and watched.

She was beautiful. More than beautiful, she was the embodiment of good, of everything he was not. Echo was beautiful inside and out, an angel to his devil. Light to the dark that was trying so hard to win.

He'd been right to sense the danger when she'd first walked into his pub.

He watched her sleep for a while, then he nodded off himself. It was not a restful sleep. His dreams were vivid and disjointed, and they felt so damned real.

When he woke the sun had risen. Echo was awake, still naked, still beautiful. She was watching him as he had watched her last night for a while.

"If you tell me again that you love me, I'll break something."

She laughed and rolled out of bed. "In that case I'll restrain myself."

"Thank you."

"For now," she added. How could there be humor in her voice? Why was she not running from him? This was not her home to defend, not her family to protect. And yet she stayed.

As he watched her gather her clothes, Rye had the thought that when he and Cassidy left Cloughban, Echo could go with them. Cassidy would need a woman to take care of her. She was only eleven, after all, and there would be many difficult years before she was an adult and could get by on her own. During her early teenage years she'd become volatile and overly emotional, and her powers would be unpredictable. Help would be a good thing. Female help would be best.

Rye accepted that he needed his daughter with

him—she possessed so much power, and there was still more to come—but that didn't mean he wanted to be her caretaker. Echo would serve a real purpose, and it wasn't as if he didn't like having her in his bed.

It was the perfect plan. Echo could take care of Cassidy by day and him by night.

She wasn't shy about walking around the room naked. He got hard, watching her. Did she know what she was doing to him? Of course she did. Tease. She was using him, manipulating him. He'd show her, and this time he wouldn't be so gentle...

"Go," he said, fighting the darker urges.

"I told you, I'm not..." she began as she turned to face him. She stopped when she saw him. Her easy smile faded. Whether it was her empathic ability or simple female instinct, she recognized that at the moment he was more dark than light. "I could use a shower and a change of clothes," she said. "Maybe I'll run back to my room at the boardinghouse for a little while." She dressed quickly, more efficient than he'd ever seen her. "I have a phone call to make first. I'll use the phone in the kitchen, if that's okay with you."

"Just leave," he said, and then he turned his back to her.

He had another thought as the door to his room opened and closed. He should leave Cloughban on his own. Alone. A child and a woman would be too damn much trouble, no matter how powerful either of them might be.

Echo was a real danger to the man he needed to become.

Cassidy frowned into her porridge. That man who looked like her da but was really only part of her da

had done something to her. He'd said it was for her own
protection, but she couldn't travel out of body to check
on him and Echo.

She couldn't complain to her granny or to Mr. Mc-
Manus. Her grandmother had long ago forbidden her
to use that power. Granny said it was rude to pop in
on people unexpected and unannounced. She was also
afraid that at some point Cassidy might not be able to
return to herself, that she'd be stuck in two places unable to become one again. Cassidy knew that would
never happen, and at the moment she wasn't at all worried about being rude. This was different! This was
important!

"Don't worry, dear," Granny said from a short distance away. "Everything is going to be all right."

Cassidy looked up. Her granny did know some
things, but she didn't see all, not the way Cassidy did.
"You don't know that. I don't even know that!" She
should know, but there was a lot that had to happen
before she could be sure.

Sometimes the immediate future was set in stone,
but usually a series of decisions led to any outcome. It
was the reason so many visions of the future came right
before they happened. While some events to come were
meant to be, those instances were rare. The right decision at the right moment—or the wrong decision at the
wrong moment—could change everything.

Her da's protection spell had done more than take
away her ability to travel at will. All her powers were
dampened. Some were sleeping entirely. Was that a side
effect of the spell he'd cast to keep her from visiting,
or had he purposely bound her this way?

At the moment she knew only one thing with any

certainty: no one but Echo Raintree could save her da
from the curse that threatened him.

Showered and dressed, Echo walked toward the
town square with coffee and pastries on her mind. She
wasn't quite ready to return to Ryder. The expression
on his face as she'd left him a couple hours ago…that
look had scared her. What if her plan didn't work?

It had to work. She couldn't allow for failure. How
could she find so much in him and then lose him to a curse
that was more than thirty years old? Ryder's mother…
She knew women who had issues with their mothers-
in-law, but those mothers-in-law were usually alive.

Echo caught a glimpse of her reflection in the boutique window, and then she noted Brigid beyond. The
red-haired woman stared, *glared*, without trying to hide
her hatred.

No, not hatred, Echo realized. Fear.

Was Brigid in on the plan? Had she been working
with the Ansara all this time?

Forgetting her coffee and sweets for a moment,
Echo walked into the shop. A bell overhead heralded
her arrival, but it wasn't like her entrance was a surprise. Brigid continued to stare. The eyes were hard,
the mouth set, but yes—that was fear.

"Why?" Echo asked. "What are you afraid of?"

"I'm not afraid," Brigid snapped.

Echo pointed a waggling finger at her own head.
"Empath. Might not like it, might not want it, but don't
lie to me about your feelings."

Brigid took a small step back and lowered her eyes.

Echo sighed. It had not been her intention to cow
the woman! "I know more about this village than I did

on my first day here. A lot of things make sense to me now, but you—what are your abilities? Why did you go cold when I mentioned my name my first day here?"

Brigid lifted her head and looked bravely at Echo. "I'm a healer. Nothing spectacular like my grandmother, but I do have some skills. I also see glimpses of the future but that's not a strong power. It comes and goes."

"What was it?" she asked in a lowered voice. "What did you see?"

"I remember what Rye was like before. Before Cassidy, before…before Sybil." Brigid clasped her hands together. "When you said your name I saw that Rye return. Darker than before. More dangerous. I thought you'd come here to bring back the man he used to be." She lifted her chin, still afraid but reaching for bravery. "From what I hear, you've succeeded."

Echo shook her head. "I'm here to bring him from the darkness, not pull him into it."

"Why should I believe that?" Brigid snapped. "He's been fine for years. Years! He's a good mayor, a good father. A good friend to some. You show up and within weeks…" She shook her head. "Several in town felt the shift last night. Some of our most sensitive empaths felt the darkness return. Are you trying to convince me that it's not your fault?" Braver than she had been before, Brigid stepped around the counter.

"It's not my fault," Echo said in a calm voice. Brigid wasn't a bad person. She hadn't seen Echo as a romantic threat. She'd seen her as a threat to her friend. As many residents had. Shay. Those who glared. They hadn't hated her; they'd been afraid for Ryder.

"Did you try to scare me out of town?"

Brigid's expression of confusion was a genuine one. "No. Of course not!"

So, someone else had seen the threat, as Brigid had, and left that note. Or else it had been Maisy. Maisy, all along.

"If you want to know what happened, come to the pub tonight. Seven o'clock. Spread the word." After all, she and Ryder couldn't very well defeat the Ansara on their own.

"Why should I?" Brigid asked, her anger rising. "You're here, Rye has changed just as I saw that he would. Why should I or anyone else show up for your… your explanations."

"Because Ryder needs you. He needs you all."

Echo turned and walked toward the door, but Brigid stopped her with a short sentence.

"You're wrong."

Echo spun around. "He does need you, I swear. The others, too. I can't do this alone!"

"Not about that." Brigid was paler than before, and her eyes were wide and watery. "They're not who you think they are."

"Who's not who…?"

"I don't know," Brigid whispered.

Suddenly, Echo did.

Chapter 21

Rye glared into the crowd. These were his people. His friends, new and old. A few of them had known him all his life. Others were temporary residents of Cloughban, gifted independents looking for a place to rest for a year or two or ten. Tonight they were afraid of him. All of them were colored with fear. To the animal that rested inside him, they smelled of it.

They were right to be afraid.

But they were here, here at Echo's invitation. She'd told him they would come, that they knew he was changed but they still cared about him.

Fools, all.

If the dark side was in complete control, he wouldn't bother to warn the people of Cloughban about the planned Ansara attack. They were here, gathered as they had for so many town meetings, but that didn't mean he had to participate. There were enough psychics in the group to make sense of what was to come.

He could leave. Now, tonight. He'd take Cassidy—and maybe Echo—and go, leaving the village to be taken by the Ansara. Even if they knew what was coming, they wouldn't be able to put up much of a fight. He looked around from his perch on the stage. These were gentle people, people hiding from a world that didn't accept who and what they were. They were shopkeepers, farmers, wives and husbands and grandparents.

The pub was as full as it had ever been as night fell. The faces around him were solemn and afraid. The villagers were here, but no one came too near him. No one but Echo, who sat on the edge of the stage just a couple of feet away. She refused to acknowledge her fear, even though he felt it on and in her.

She wasn't afraid of him, she was afraid *for* him.

He explained as best he could, in as few words as possible. Ansara. The stones. This place. "The invaders will arrive tomorrow afternoon, likely near nightfall," he said in a calm voice. "I suspect they will bring weapons of magic as well as weapons of more ordinary destruction. We have to be prepared for anything."

He was silent as they talked among themselves for a few minutes. All of them were glad to have the opportunity to turn away, to look elsewhere for a while. When they looked at his face they saw the dark. Some saw more deeply than others.

No. They see both, and they are afraid for you.

Of me.

For you.

He looked at Echo while around him the townspeople talked about where to put the children and the elders who were unable to fight. They discussed defenses, weaponry, and arranged for the drugstore to be prepared to house the injured, while the two healers in the area treated them.

His anger got the best of him and he pushed into her head with, *Why are you still here?*

She remained calm. *You know why. I'd say it aloud but I don't want you to break anything. Or anyone.*

It was Maeve Quinlin who bravely approached Rye and asked, in a tremulous voice, "I must tell you, I'm worried about Maisy. I haven't seen her since yesterday afternoon. Do you think one of these Ansara persons abducted her?"

Rye felt no guilt when he answered, "Maisy is dead."

Maeve's shock was clear on her face. "Are you sure? What happened?"

The truth, always. He hadn't wanted to tell all, but it had been foolish of him to think this part of the truth could wait. "I killed her myself."

Many in the crowd gasped. A few edged toward the door.

He didn't owe anyone an explanation, but he needed these people to fight with him. For him. No, for themselves. "She was one of them," he said. "I caught her attempting to sacrifice my daughter."

"No!" Maeve said. "I don't believe that. Maisy was a good girl."

No one had any reason to believe him, not today, but they did believe Echo when she said, "I'm afraid it's true. I saw Maisy raise a knife to Cassidy. I'm sorry, Maeve, but she was not the woman you all believed her to be."

"Cassidy? Is she all right?" someone from the back of the room asked.

"She's fine," Echo said with a tempered smile. "Scared, but unharmed."

"What about McManus?" Nevan asked nervously. "He should be here."

It was Rye who answered before Echo could. "He's unharmed." Trapped in the cottage with Bryna and Cassidy, invisible to any eye but his own, but alive and kicking.

The question Rye had been waiting for came, again from a coward who was hidden by other bodies. "What happened to you?" It would not be difficult to reveal the person who asked that question, but Rye didn't bother. One brave soul had merely asked what everyone else was thinking.

"Some of you remember what I was like before," he said. "I'm back."

"It's temporary!" Echo interjected. "We'll remove the curse after we take care of...of...those who are coming."

"Curse?" Doyle asked.

Doyle hadn't been here before Cassidy was born. He had never seen the man Rye could be. There were few lifelong residents of Cloughban. People came and went. They got what they were coming for—peace or instruction or respite—and then they often moved on. But a few had known him all his life. They'd witnessed his dark power. Did they see that it was worse now for being denied for so long?

The true man he was—and perhaps could be again—rose to the surface for a moment. He looked to Doyle. It was an effort, but he forced the words out.

"If she can't remove the curse, kill me."

* * *

Echo ran everyone out of the pub and locked the door behind them. A solemn Doyle had been the last to leave. That done, she spun on Ryder.

"Kill you? Have you lost your mind?"

The man she loved, the man who would die to protect her and Cassidy and the people of this town, was no longer at the surface. "He can try. They can all try. You saw what I did to Maisy." Ryder—not Ryder—smirked. "Maybe he'll try to brain me with a flying pot."

She was not amused. "I told you, I have a plan," she said. "It might take some time…"

"We don't have time," he responded. "I suspect the heat of the battle that's coming will force out what's left of the man you want me to be." He narrowed his eyes. "You have done a remarkable job of shielding this plan from me. I can normally see your thoughts so well. What is it that you don't want me to know?"

Echo lifted her chin. She wanted to trust him, but… she couldn't. Not yet. "I'm not going to take the chance that your less-pleasant half will decide to put an end to it before I even get started."

"Not many people can hide anything from me."

He pushed, a little. Echo felt that push through her entire body. It was like fighting an ocean wave or a strong gust of wind on a stormy day. She pushed back, calling on every ounce of power she possessed. This had to work! It simply had to. She'd gladly share her idea with the man she loved, but if he knew would the other try to stop her?

It was surprisingly easy to think of the man before her as two separate beings. One was the man she loved, the man she would do anything for. The other had been created by the curse, and was doing his best to take over. For now, both men inhabited the same body, but that wouldn't last much longer. One would win. The other would die.

"Was it like this before?" she asked.

He knew exactly what it was she wanted to know. "Was I a Jekyll and Hyde?" She didn't like the smirk that followed. "Not always, but as I became stronger my presence became more clear to others. Most of the decisions he made were mine, not his own. I was weeks, perhaps even days, away from casting the other out when he put the restraints on me."

He took a few steps closer to her. "I was sleeping when he killed his wife, so don't believe for a moment that the man you think you love is an angel. He's far from it."

"He had no choice," she whispered.

"Didn't he?" The man she began to think of as Dark Ryder reached out to touch her cheek. "He liked it," he whispered. "He liked the rush of taking a life, the blood, the look in his wife's eyes as she left this earth. He'd grown tired of the woman who was, to be honest, a whiny bitch." Broad shoulders shrugged, eyes darkened. "She asked him to take away her abilities and he did, and then she went nuts because she didn't have her abilities. Just like a woman, never satisfied with what she has. She was a lot like you, and you're going to come to the same end."

"Ryder won't hurt me," she insisted in a low whisper.

"Not yet," he conceded. "But when I'm in complete control no one will be able to stop me. Soon the time will come for you to make a choice. Join Cassidy and me when we leave, or die." He leaned down and placed cold lips on her throat. She could back away, she could move, but she knew that her presence was the only thing keeping the man she loved awake.

His arms slipped around her; he held her close. Echo reached deep within herself, searching for every bit of magic she possessed. She needed to see into the future to know how to save him. And herself.

But the future was not yet set. It was fluid, ever shifting. She could see so many possibilities, dark and light, swirling together. In one future she was success-ful in casting out the darkness of the curse. Ryder, *her* Ryder, was saved. The intruders were defeated and Cloughban was once more a safe haven for those like her. Like Ryder and Cassidy and all the rest.

In another possible future she saved Ryder too soon. He faced the invaders weakened, lost. Those who called themselves Ansara but were not won and they both died ugly. She couldn't help but think of the tombstones in her dream.

In another possible future she made her move too late. She could not save her Ryder no matter how she tried. The darkness won, and while a battle raged around them he drove a knife through her heart with a smile on his face and left town while Cloughban burned.

One chance out of three. Not exactly as discourag-ing as the odds of winning the lottery, but she did wish they were more in her favor. She'd never been able to see her own future; that wasn't the way it worked. Was that why she had no clearer picture? Or was it simply that what was to come would not be set until they made the decisions that led to it? Either way, she was all but blinded to what might happen.

She wanted to tell someone, anyone, what Brigid had helped her to discern not long ago. Those who were coming were not Ansara; they had simply taken the name as their own. Maybe they'd chosen it because in the past the Ansara clan had had such a savage reputation. Did it matter? Would being called by a different name make them any less fearsome?

The people of this village needed to be afraid. They needed to be prepared for fearsome.

Echo knew she could go, as Ryder had suggested often in the past few hours. Without her here odds were Ryder would be happy to leave Cloughban to the invaders, take his daughter and start his own new life elsewhere. A life of dark magic, of decadence and excess. He would use his own dark powers as well as his gifted child to get what he wanted.

It was more than worry about Cassidy that made Echo accept that she could not leave.

Without Ryder, *her* Ryder, she didn't have a life worth going back to.

"Run," he whispered in her ear. Was that her Ryder talking, or was it the other? *Both.* An order or a plea? Had he managed a glimpse into the mind she was working so hard to shield from him?

She wrapped her arms around his neck and kissed the side of his neck. He was so cold, so hard. So lost. She whispered back, her lips near his ear.

"No."

Chapter 22

It was the clap of thunder that woke Rye from a deep sleep. He sat up in bed, and for a moment, a few precious seconds, he forgot where he was. He forgot who he was. All he remembered was Echo.

Everything that had happened in the past two days came rushing back, filling his head and his heart with pain.

Then the darkness he'd unleashed came rushing back, as well.

For the moment they shared the same mind, the same body. Two separate beings, two personalities, two distinct souls. Eventually one of them would have to go. He wasn't yet sure which one it would be.

Echo was curled up against his side. She should've run yesterday, when she'd had the chance. Now it was too late.

Again, a clap of thunder. Lightning flashed. The storm outside his window was not at all natural. He felt it deep down.

Had it begun? Echo had seen the Ansara attack happening by the light of day, and it was not yet dawn. Her visions were sometimes late, but she was—as far as he knew—never *wrong*.

She stirred with the third clap, and as he had she jumped up.

"He's here."

"Who's here?" It was annoying to have to ask. She'd done a good job of hiding her thoughts from him, protecting them in a way no one else had ever been able to do.

She narrowed her eyes as she looked at him. "Which one are you?"

He began to answer truthfully. Both. But she didn't wait for his response.

"Never mind," she said as she hopped from the bed and grabbed her clothes. She looked at him as she dressed quickly. "Even if you're mostly my Ryder at the moment, the other will also hear and know, and...not yet. Sorry." She threw open the door. "Soon, I promise!"

Echo ran out of the room and down the stairs. Rye dressed more slowly than she had before following her. He didn't know what she'd planned, but the energy of his surroundings had changed somehow. He felt a current flowing through him. Power. Electricity.

He found Echo standing in the middle of the street, in front of the pub. The sun had not yet risen, but he could not say the skies were dark. There was a blue cast to everything, and it spread as far as the eye could see.

The storm, which was unusual for the area, had drawn out others, as well. Those who lived along this main road were coming out of their homes to look to the east.

Blue lightning started near the ground and traveled up in powerful streams of electricity that lit the sky. Thunder followed, rumbling with unnatural power. It was beautiful and frightening and unnatural.

And Echo smiled.

A man was walking along the road, cursing and shooting sparks as he went. Rye would've known this man anywhere, even if Echo hadn't started running toward him with a joyfully shouted, "Gideon!"

"What the hell?" Gideon shouted as she drew closer to him. Electricity danced along his arms. He must've come straight from work. He'd left his suit jacket and tie behind somewhere, but wore black trousers and a white dress shirt, as well as his badge and gun. Her cousin was a homicide detective. A homicide detective who could talk to the ghosts of victims. That gave him a decided advantage.

He lit the early morning in an unnatural way, and she soon saw his wife, Hope, well behind him. She was no longer a detective—she stayed home with their two girls these days—but she wore a gun, too.

They must have come over on Dante's private jet and landed at a private airfield. That would explain their early arrival and the firearms. They had not come through customs...

Gideon snapped, "My rental car died two miles back. What the hell is going on here? I haven't been out of control like this since I was fourteen!"

She ignored the electrical sparks and threw herself

at him. The air around him buzzed. It tickled her all over, but she knew Gideon's powers would not hurt her. He would never allow it. She had never been so glad to see him! He was her best, last, *only* hope.

"There's a very strong stone circle in the area," she explained as she let him go and stepped back. "Like Stonehenge but...not Stonehenge."

Echo released her cousin and smiled at Hope.

Gideon's wife was not a member of any magical clan and she was not a stray. Unlike the rest of the family, she had no abilities at all. Well, she had abilities, just not supernatural ones. She was a whiz at keeping her husband and two magically gifted daughters on the straight and narrow.

Knowing what was causing the influx of energy helped Gideon to control the excess electricity that flowed through his body. Thunder and lightning ceased, but he retained an unnatural blue glow. She resisted telling him that he looked as if he'd eaten a neon sign for breakfast.

"We have an audience," he said, nodding his chin to indicate the growing crowd behind her.

Echo glanced over her shoulder. Sure enough, twenty or more villagers stood behind her. At least none of them carried pitchforks and torches.

"It's all right," she said, raising her voice so all could hear. "This is my cousin Gideon."

The murmur that followed was not one of relief. Like her, Gideon was Raintree. Until she'd come here, she'd had no idea her family was so intensely disliked by some strays. No, *disliked* was the wrong word. They were distrusted. That was going to have to change, and fast.

"Come on inside," she said, taking Gideon's arm as Hope drew up beside him. "We have some serious catching up to do."

Cassidy stood at her bedroom window and watched the lightning. Twice she had tried to leave the cottage, but her da's magic still kept her trapped here. She didn't like it. It was not good magic, not at all! Neither did Mr. McManus, who had complained for hours before finally falling asleep on the sofa.

Granny, on the other hand, was perfectly content to wait out whatever was happening. They were safe here. Nothing could touch them; they were invisible to the outside world. Cassidy could not relax, no matter how often her granny advised her to do just that. Too much was undecided. Maybe they were safe at the moment, but would they remain safe?

What if something happened to her da and they were trapped here forever? What would become of them? Would they starve? Go crazy? Would they simply fade away?

The lightning ceased, though in the distance where Cloughban stood a strange blue glow continued, as if a huge and unnatural light shone there. Eventually that faded, too.

She knew something bad was coming, and she wanted to help. She *could* help! If only her da would let her.

Her da but not her da.

The sky changed again, but this time it was the rising sun that lit the sky.

This was the day. Cloughban was about to be under siege.

And she'd never had the chance to warn her da or Echo that Maisy had not been the only spy in Clough-ban.

Gideon shook his head. Again. "I don't call spir-its back to earth. It's dangerous, for them and for us. When ghosts come to me it is their choice, not mine."

Echo tried to argue. "I know, but…"

"Once a spirit has moved on, it's extremely difficult for them to travel to us. And then, getting back where they're supposed to be is even harder. I will not trap a spirit here, not even to save your friend."

Friend. Ryder was so much more than a friend, but that argument wasn't going to sway Gideon.

After being introduced, Gideon and Ryder had parted as if they could not stand to be in the same room. Maybe they couldn't. She was more sensitive to energy than she'd ever been, and her cousin and the man she loved mixed like oil and water. Did Dark Ryder realize what a danger Gideon was to his existence?

Hope had gladly taken up Echo's offer of her bed in the boardinghouse. She and Gideon had had a long night, after an already long day. The girls were with their grandmother—Hope's mother—probably being spoiled horribly. Every little girl deserved to be spoiled now and then.

Echo lowered her voice as she made her argument. "Ryder's mother cast this…this curse on him, trying to make him more powerful. Maybe her intentions were good, maybe she was trying to help, but her spell al-most killed him." It very well could kill the man she loved. Today, tomorrow…he could not bear this for much longer.

Gideon attempted to be reasonable. "Why not just let me make another talisman to hold the powers in check?"

Echo shook her head. "We're beyond that." Well beyond. Dark Ryder would sleep no more. He would live and rule the body he possessed, or he would die. If he lived, the man she loved would disappear. The body would survive but the soul, the essence of him...that would be gone for good. "There's going to be an attack..." She'd explained this already.

Again, Gideon shook his head. "There can't possibly be enough of the Ansara left to mount an attack."

She explained what she'd discovered, that those who were coming were not true Ansara, but independents who had taken on that name. Like her, he didn't think that distinction made much of a difference.

"How many do you think it would take to run over this village?" This wasn't a mecca for the most powerful of strays. Most of the people here had just enough magic in their blood to make them different. Enough to make them long for others of their kind and the comfort of the stones.

His expression went dark. "Not many, if the people here are not prepared. But you're here and you have prepared them."

It was the change in Gideon's posture that told Echo Ryder had entered the room, coming through the door behind her. Her cousin was angry and suspicious. She could tell by the way his fingers curled that if Ryder made one wrong move he'd be on the receiving end of a powerful bolt of lightning.

That hand soon dropped.

"She's here," Gideon whispered.

Echo stood. "Ryder's mother? She came without being called?"

"Not exactly. She's been here all along. She's attached herself to her son." He frowned. "And she won't leave until I fix her mistakes. Great. Just great."

Rye had found himself in control long enough to allow Echo to duct tape him to a chair. Without his help an entire roll of duct tape wouldn't be enough to restrain his other half, but if he could hang on for a while longer it would suffice. He thought of his daughter; he thought of Echo sleeping in his bed. He fought for his very life, for Cassidy and for Echo.

Gideon Raintree looked like an insane man, pacing the room and talking to himself. More than once he ran his hands through his hair, making it stand on end at one point. He continued to occasionally glow blue and...hell, there was no other word for it. *Sparkle*. But he wasn't insane, and he wasn't talking to himself. He was carrying on a conversation with Rye's mother. The Gypsy who had cursed him before she died.

"Sorry is not good enough!" Gideon shouted to an empty space behind Rye. After a short pause he continued in a slightly lower voice. "Well, it was a curse, not a gift, and now see where we are."

Another pause, then, "Tell him yourself."

Echo had been watching, silent and pensive, as her cousin did his thing. Now she spoke up.

"Does she know how to remove it?"

Gideon looked at her. "Yes."

She took a deep breath. "Can it wait until after we take care of the attackers who are coming?"

Gideon threw his hands into the air, frustrated and angry. "Really?"

It was Rye who answered. "This town needs me. It needs the power this curse has given me if we're to win."

"What happens when the cursed part of you decides it might like being aligned with the invaders? What happens when you switch sides in the middle of the battle?"

Rye wanted to argue that wouldn't happen, but he couldn't. Not if he were being entirely honest. He didn't know what his dark side might do.

If Gideon removed the curse, and with it Rye's enhanced abilities, could they still win the battle?

Did he want to take the chance that he might turn on his friends and neighbors, or worse, his family?

"Can you ask her if she also cursed my daughter?" From beyond the grave, or through him, somehow, but...anything was possible.

Gideon shook his head. "No. Your mother saw a gifted child of her blood, and she thought it was you. She wanted to help you along, that's why she did what she did. But that child she saw wasn't you, it was her granddaughter." His head snapped to the side. "All these sorries are not making things any better!"

He waved a hand at Rye. "So, without the curse what are your abilities? What would you bring to the party?"

Rye answered honestly. "I don't know. I was so young when my mother started working with me...I don't know."

Again, Gideon looked into an empty space and listened for a moment, and then he mumbled, "Great. That's just great." He turned eyes a brilliant green, so much like Echo's, to Rye and said, "Nothing. According to your mother, without the curse you have no special abilities at all."

Chapter 23

"Do we dare to wait?" Echo asked. The word still echoed in her head. *Nothing.* All the talismans had done, for the past eleven years, was keep the curse in check. She'd been so sure she'd sensed his own... But no, not if the ghost was telling the truth. The abilities Ryder had called upon since Cassidy's birth were bits and pieces of his mother's curse seeping through.

Gideon shook his head. "I don't think we can afford to wait. How long do we have?"

"An hour, maybe two." The invaders were coming. They were moving closer and closer. She felt them coming, in a strange rush in her blood, in the small hairs on her arms standing up. She felt the shifting energies, and still she could not predict the outcome.

"If I don't do it now," Gideon said, "I might not get another chance."

Winning was almost a given, with Ryder at top form. If he were mortal? Without any power at all? Not so much. Echo said as much, mumbling under her breath as she weighed the pros and cons.

"Hey," Hope snapped. "Not having a woowoo power doesn't make a person helpless, you know. Jeez." Well rested after a nice, long nap in Echo's bed, she looked pumped and ready to fight. "I'll give him one of my guns."

Echo looked at Hope. "You brought more than one?"

"You said the *A*-word. Ansara. I would have brought an arsenal if I'd thought I could get away with it."

"I've never handled a firearm," Ryder said. "I don't think I have time to learn…"

His head was thrown back, his entire body tensed. Dark Ryder was fighting to the surface. The duct tape would not contain him much longer.

No matter what, her Ryder had to survive. To allow the dark into the world, to let the curse kill the man she loved and free the other…

Echo looked at Gideon. "Do it," she whispered. "Do it now. We won't have another chance."

Her track record as a prophet was less than stellar, but Gideon trusted her. He trusted her now.

Hope stood behind her husband, her gun drawn as he placed a glowing hand on Ryder's forehead. Echo wondered if it hurt, if there was heat in that hand, but Ryder didn't pull back or even flinch.

After a long moment Gideon looked at Echo. "She says you need to say the words. Because you love him, it has to be you." She saw the puzzlement in his eyes. He probably wondered if Ryder was another one of her crushes, a fling, an infatuation. Now was not the time to explain that this was so much more.

She had been prepared to watch, to step back and let Gideon fix what was broken, but that was not to be. Echo nodded, and in a low and soft voice she repeated the strange words her cousin directed her to say.

That's when Ryder screamed. He jerked his head around to look directly at her, to glare at her. She could see the pain in his eyes; she could feel it. Those dark eyes she had come to love were touched with Gideon's electricity as if the lightning lived there, inside him. Did it burn? Was it terrible?

"Help me," he whispered.

Instinctively, Echo stuttered, the strange words uncomfortable on her tongue. She hesitated, choked on the words. She hadn't realized that removing the curse would hurt him so. The pain was too much! There had to be another way! But Hope said in her no-nonsense voice, "It's a trick, Echo. I can see it from here."

Ryder snapped his head around and growled at Hope, who only adjusted her aim a bit.

The words Gideon whispered, words Echo repeated carefully, were Romany. Carpathian Romany. She didn't know the language, didn't even realize there were different variations, but listening, speaking each word carefully…she simply knew. This was Ryder's mother's language, a language of power. The language she had used to cast the curse and the one required to remove it.

Ryder truly was in pain, but it wasn't her Ryder, it was the other. It was the darkness created by a curse which had been cast to instill powers that never should have been. As she spoke the strange words, the darkness and the curse died. A little at a time. Her Ryder hurt, too, as something that had been a part of him for almost his entire life was ripped away.

Would he love her after? Would he be so changed that there was nothing left of the man she loved? He had warned her that removing her own powers would damage her forever. They had damaged his wife, Cassidy's mother, beyond repair. Was this the same?

No, the powers now being removed were not a part of him. They had been added, forced, poured into a soul unprepared for such magic.

He screamed, an unnatural scream that made every glass in the pub ring. One bottle of whiskey exploded. Then another. The chairs shook slightly, as if Cloughban were experiencing a minor earthquake.

Echo stuttered again and then she whispered, "I love you." Her words were too soft for anyone to hear over the screams, but Ryder heard somehow. He looked at her. Into her.

Save me.

That's what I'm trying to do.

You're killing me...

Would they still be able to communicate this way when he was stripped of the curse? All her life she'd wanted a normal man, a man with no magical abilities, but if they could no longer touch each other this way... she would miss it.

But there was no other way. She didn't want to ever peek into the mind of Dark Ryder, and she did not want him in her own mind. What could he, would he, do there if he had free rein?

No matter what the cost, they had to strip away the darkness. To see the man she loved entirely gone would break her heart. If the darkness won and her Ryder disappeared, it might snow in Cloughban until the end of time.

Gideon placed his free hand over Ryder's heart and directed Echo to say a few more words. She did.

Ryder's head snapped back. His body bucked and then he went still. His head rotated slowly and then dropped forward; his shoulders and arms went slack. Gideon backed away.

"Is it done?" Echo asked.

"I think so." Gideon looked at a far corner and nodded in acknowledgment of the ghost. "She won't leave until he wakes up and we know for sure."

Echo took a knife and began to cut away the duct tape that held Ryder.

"Shouldn't we wait until he wakes up and we know if the spell, you know, took?" Hope asked.

"No," Echo responded sharply. "We need him, dark or light." She lifted her head to look Gideon in the eye. "They're coming."

Rye opened his eyes slowly. Wiggled his fingers as the world around him came into focus. He felt hungover, only half-present. For a long moment, no one else in the pub realized he was awake. They were making plans, gathering others to fight with them.

He tried to listen in, attempted to peek into the minds of those around him. They could block him, and had, but if they didn't realize he was listening why would they bother?

He heard nothing. Saw nothing. He reached for a vision of the battle to come; he tried to identify the dark magic he knew was coming their way. Again, nothing. He lifted his hand and attempted to start a small fire on his palm, something which had, until now, been child's play.

Nothing.

Without the curse, he was no wizard. He wasn't even a mildly talented stray or a slightly gifted independent. He was an ordinary human, and in the coming battle he would serve no useful purpose at all.

Echo saw—or sensed—that he was awake and she ran to him. "Ryder, how do you feel? Are you…?"

He lifted his head and looked at her. She paled, and for a moment he believed she was disappointed to see that he was just a man. She'd fallen in love with a wizard and now he was *nothing*. In a town like Cloughban, he was less than nothing.

And then she whispered, "Thank God it's you." She leaned down and kissed him briefly, too briefly, taking him by surprise. That kiss was warmth in a cold world, a moment of peace and, yes, love.

"We don't have much time," she said as she pulled away from him. "They're coming, they're close. As far as I can see, there are only half a dozen of them or so. They still think they'll catch us unaware, which is foolish considering where they're headed, so I believe we'll be…"

"Echo," Rye interrupted. "I'm…" *Powerless, worthless, empty.*

She placed a hand on his shoulder. "I know."

He found a way to continue. "The spell I cast on the cottage, the one to hide and protect Cassidy."

She paled as she finished his thought for him. "It fell when we removed the curse."

Cassidy glanced out her bedroom window, bored with her book, bored with being stuck inside for so many hours. Days! Well, a day and a half. It seemed like longer. She had never realized how much she liked the freedom to come and go as she pleased, even when she didn't *physically* come and go.

The figure walking toward the cottage was one she knew well, though she had never seen him here in her home. He never came out to the cottage, never visited. She blinked. Strained to see. Why was he walking straight for the front door when he shouldn't be able to see the cottage at all?

At that moment he spotted her in the window. He smiled and waved.

Cassidy had never been able to see her own future, but that smile made her shiver. There was something wrong about it, something evil. It was like her da as he had been in the past couple of days, but without the influence of the good man he had always been deep down.

For a second, a horrifying second, the face coming toward her shifted into an ugly, skeleton-like image. Hollow eyes. Gruesome grin.

She ran from her room, into the main room where Granny sat with her friend. "Don't open the door!" she shouted, but it was too late.

Doyle didn't knock. He blew the door off its hinges with a burst of fire and walked inside through a puff of black smoke.

Rye ran. Echo had offered to come with him, but he'd refused her and taken off at full speed. There was no way she could catch up with him, even if she tried. Just as well. She'd be needed in town.

Had his mother cursed him because she'd realized

early on that he had no powers? What a disappointment he must've been, for her to take such steps. Had the curse affected him physically? Was that why Cassidy was so powerful?

Was she still powerful, or had her gifts disappeared with his own?

There was no way to be sure until he was with her again.

Within a matter of days he'd gone from a wizard so powerful his gifts had to be dampened, to the dark man he had once been, to an ordinary man who could not help his daughter or the woman he loved when they needed him. They should've left him as he was, dark and lost. At least then the people he loved, the only people in the world he cared about, would be safe.

But would they have been safe from him?

Suddenly Cassidy was beside him, running unnaturally fast in order to keep up with him. Cassidy, not in the flesh but traveling out of body. Her feet did not touch the ground. The wind created by their speed made her red curls fly back. Her presence was proof that his spell had indeed fallen.

"Doyle killed Mr. McManus!" she shouted. Tears streamed down her face. "He says he's going to kill Granny, too, if I don't…if I don't…" And then she was gone. As quickly as she'd appeared, she disappeared.

Doyle. For all Rye's so-called gifts, he had never seen it. Neither had Echo, or anyone else in town. His cook—much more than a cook apparently—must've called upon a powerful shielding charm or spell to last this long without anyone realizing what he was up to.

Rye ran faster, pushing himself to the limit, wishing

he had the powers of a wizard—dark or light—to help him save his daughter. He ran as fast as he could, but he had no idea if he was anywhere near fast enough.

Chapter 24

"They're here," Echo whispered as two long black SUVs raced into town. Maybe their prophet—if they had one—was as substandard as she was. As substandard as she had been, anyway, before taking lessons from Ryder. Didn't they know what they were up against? Didn't one of them see that they were riding into a town that was well prepared for their arrival?

Maybe they knew but didn't care. That was a scary thought.

Standing near the door to the pub, she tried to reach out to Ryder. *Where are you? How are you? What's happening? They're here.* Her efforts were wasted. Since Gideon had broken the curse, she'd been unable to touch Ryder's mind at all. She was effectively blind where he was concerned. Their connection was gone. She missed it, more than she'd imagined she could.

What did it matter at this moment? They had to survive this attack before she could worry about Ryder and Cassidy.

The people of Cloughban had varying gifts, and widely varying degrees of strength. Most were not very powerful. None were what could be called warriors. Warriors or not, all adults under the age of seventy were on the street, armed in one way or another. With sticks, swords, knives and flexed fingers, they were ready to fight for their home.

Echo was ready to fight, too.

Did the invaders want the independents, the stones or Cassidy? Odds were they wanted all three. There was power here, there was strength. For a clan looking to begin anew, there was likely no better place on the planet.

The people here were prepared to defend all. Themselves, the stones, a little girl like no other...

Hope had her gun and Gideon's, one in each hand. In this situation, Gideon didn't need a firearm. Blue lightning danced on his skin as he prepared.

The vehicles stopped, one after another. Doors opened simultaneously as six...no, *seven*...people stepped out. Three women, four men. All were dressed entirely in black. Three were wearing sunglasses, which had to be for effect only since clouds shielded the late afternoon sun. They carried swords and guns of their own. Echo saw no evidence of fire or lightning, but that could come once the fight began.

A tall brunette woman with a severely short hairstyle took the lead. She had to be close to six feet tall! One of the three wearing sunglasses, she was obviously in charge. The other six formed a flank behind her, marking her as their leader, but it was her demeanor, her fearlessness, that told Echo she was leading the pack.

"Seven against...fifty? Sixty?" The tall woman's smile was at odds with her words as she surveyed the crowd. "It seems the numbers are against us, but in this situation numbers mean nothing. Can we talk? You people don't know what you're fighting against." She raised her voice; it all but boomed down the street. "Become Ansara, join us. Be a part of resurrecting a powerful clan that was wrongly eliminated years ago." She turned her head slowly and pinned her eyes on Gideon. "By the Raintree. Have they come to take you, too? Please tell me you haven't all bought into their goody-goody facade."

The crowd was restless. They murmured to one another, they shuffled their feet and a few took uncertain steps back. There were doubts among them.

"They're not Ansara," Echo said in a voice loud enough for all to hear. "They're impostors." She took a deep breath. "Wannabes. They are no stronger, no more capable, than any one of you." She glanced around her. "Any one of *us*."

Shay stood next to her mother; they were dressed in plain, loose clothing that left them room to maneuver, and sturdy low-heeled boots that would allow them to run. And kick. They each held what could only be called a club. Hefty clubs, at that.

The girl who had been Maisy's friend, who had coveted Echo's job at the pub, who had made it clear that she didn't like the newcomer much, caught Echo's eye and nodded once. Echo had no idea what Shay's powers were, but at this moment it didn't matter. That nod was an acknowledgment. Soldier to soldier. *Let's kick some ass.*

As if he were in on the silent exchange—and perhaps he was—Nevan, who carried no weapon that Echo could see, raised his voice as he surveyed the crowd. "Avoid killing the bastards if you can. This is sacred land, and the spilling of blood will darken and weaken the stones. There's been enough blood spilled of late." Then he, too, nodded to Echo.

She took a deep breath and stepped forward, moving closer to the woman who led the attack. Echo was no leader, never had been. She'd always been content to be a soldier, not a general. A princess, not a queen. For the most part, she did as she was told. But in a way she had never expected, these were her people. They needed guidance, with Ryder changed. Changed and, more importantly, not here.

"Go while you can," Echo said in a commanding voice, facing the woman who seemed, at the moment, to stand a full foot taller than she.

Gideon lifted one hand and an alarming ball of lightning danced on his palm. It was a warning, nothing more.

"You've lost the day," Echo said, loudly enough for everyone on the street to hear. "The people of Cloughban have no wish to align with you or with the Raintree. They're independent and will remain so. Leave. No one has to die today."

Behind the leader, the other six prepared to do battle. Guns and swords were raised. She saw no evidence of powers among them. At least, none that could be used in a fight. Echo allowed her empathic abilities to come to life. She reached out, trying to ascertain what dangers these invaders would offer. Fire, lightning, balls of energy.

Nothing. This new clan was so weak they were all but powerless. No wonder they wanted the stones—and these people and Cassidy—so badly!

A short, dark-haired man standing behind and to the left of the tall woman fired the first shot. The bullet missed its intended mark—Gideon—and grazed the arm of the young man who had sold Echo ice cream and coffee on several occasions. He fell. The crowd swarmed forward.

Echo took one step forward, two, ready to engage the invaders. Like Gideon, she had the ability to produce a ball of energy that would disable any attacker. Before she could even produce a twinkling of energy, that newly identified feeling niggled at the back of her brain.

"No," she whispered, stopping her forward progress. Not now! She needed to fight, to play a part in saving this village that had become her home. An important part. These people were her friends and neighbors; she was a part of the community.

But she couldn't fight like this, no matter how much she wanted to do just that. She dropped her hand and backed away, moving closer to the pub, realizing she'd be trampled if she stayed in the street. She'd never been able to stop an oncoming vision.

Her knees gave out, and she sat with her back against the pub door. The people of Cloughban—Ryder's neighbors and friends, *her* neighbors and friends—defended their home with honor. Shay knew how to swing that club. She was stronger than she looked. Echo saw two of the townspeople go down, then watched as Maeve

Quinlan hit one of the men in black over the head with
an iron skillet. Brigid had kneeled to tend one of the
fallen, the boy who had been shot, and Nevan...Nevan
had lightning like Gideon. Echo smiled as the old man
began to glow, more green than blue but just as powerful and sparkly...and then she was gone.

Gideon hit the leader of the Ansara invaders in the
center of her chest with a bolt of lightning. Not enough
to kill her. *Probably* not enough to kill her. She flew
back and landed hard on the road, hitting the ground
with an oomph. Her sunglasses flew off. She stayed
down.

Echo was slumped on the sidewalk. Damned bad
timing for a vision. At least she'd had the good sense
to move out of the way before she'd been incapacitated.

As he fought, he kept one eye on Hope. She'd been
through this before, during the final battle between the
Raintree and the Ansara. As one of the invaders swung
his sword at an elderly man wielding a long stick, Hope
took aim and fired. A good shot, she hit what she'd
aimed at. The man in black's shoulder. The old man
gave a nod of appreciation in her direction before lifting his stick again and going to the aid of a friend.

Gideon stepped back, out of the midst of the fight.
His side was winning; the people defended themselves
well. There didn't have to be a massacre in order for
the people of Cloughban to win. This was a magical
place, thanks to the nearby stones Echo had told him
about. As the old man had warned, bloodshed here
would seep into the ground and touch the place with
a new and unwanted darkness. The people of Cloughban needed to win, had to win, and it was inevitable

that many would be wounded and some might die. But there could be no slaughter here.

Light fed good power; evil fed the dark. He could only imagine how bad it would be for the stones of Cloughban to be touched with evil.

One by one, the invaders went down easily. Wounded, not killed, they fell. A couple of them would recover, stand and fight again, but most just slunk away, edging toward their vehicles.

Watching, no longer participating, Gideon experienced a tickle of warning. The invaders were surrendering much too easily. It occurred to him that they could not have hoped to win. None of them, not one, fought with magic. No fire, no balls of energy, no lightning other than his own and the occasional burst of green lightning from the incredibly ugly old man. As battles went, this one was almost amusing. Almost.

The people who had come here to take this village were not trained fighters. They were dressed for the part, and they were armed, but once they began to fight they got in one another's way, tripped over their own feet. The people of Cloughban were not much better.

Gideon stepped back; he lifted a hand to call Hope to his side. The villagers were winning handily. They needed no Raintree assistance. Hope began to make her way toward him.

All but two of the invaders were down when Echo struggled to her feet. Unsteady, she leaned against the pub door as she called his name.

She tried to shout at him but her words were garbled and weak.

Gideon turned his back on the fight and stepped in her direction. "What?"

Her voice was louder as she said, "This is just a distraction. He's going for Cassidy!"

Hope called Gideon's name, a sharp warning, just as something hit the back of his head. He fell, he heard a gunshot and all went dark.

Bryna sat on the sofa next to her gentleman friend who, Rye was happy to see, was very much alive. After the initial attack McManus had been unconscious for a while. Cassidy had thought him dead, but he remained among the living.

For now.

Doyle. All this time, the traitor had been right under his nose. Rye hadn't seen the deception, hadn't even suspected. Echo hadn't seen it, either, which meant that Doyle's abilities were much more than an unsteady bit of telekinesis. Flying pots and an impressive gift for blocking. Judging by a lingering odor in the room and singe marks on the door, he also controlled fire, to some extent. An inborn gift or a one-time trick? It was impossible to know at this point.

Whatever gifts he possessed, they weren't enough to satisfy him. Doyle wanted Cassidy. He wanted her powers, the same amazing abilities Maisy had tried to take.

Rye stood in the center of the main room where he'd watched his daughter grow up. From an infant, to a toddler, to a curious child. Soon she would be a young woman. God above, she deserved to be a young woman. A grown woman. A mother to her own children one day. A grandmother who warned her own grandchild against using potentially dangerous magic.

He wanted to rush to her, to take her into his arms,

but he didn't dare to move while Doyle held a knife to Cassidy's slender, pale, *vulnerable* throat.

Curse or no curse, powerful or powerless, he was Cassidy's father; he loved her. He would do whatever was necessary to save her, even if it was the last thing he did.

"What do you want?" Rye asked. His voice was rough and unsteady. "Let her go, and I'll give you anything. Anything at all."

Doyle looked and sounded downright cocky as he answered, "My brother and I decided that we want what you have, and what you have can be had through her, thanks to a very old spell Walsh discovered."

Power. Magic. The ability to have anything his heart desired with a snap of his fingers. Doyle was not without considerable magic of his own, but he wanted more. He wanted it all.

"Brother?"

The man who held a knife to Cassidy's throat smiled. "You knew my brother well. You taught him, for a while. He was your last student, before Echo Raintree came along to revive your teaching career. That's why I had to be the one to come here, to make the arrangements on this end."

It took no magic for Rye to understand. His student Walsh, the one who had expressed an unhealthy interest in Cassidy and what she could do. Knowing that Walsh and Doyle were related he could see a minor resemblance. In the nose, in the shape of the mouth. He saw too late.

He had to keep Doyle occupied until he figured out a way to disarm him without hurting Cassidy. If he talked awhile, if his arm and hand relaxed. Would he be fast enough to move in and take that knife if Doyle got sloppy?

"You're Ansara?" Rye asked, taking a half step forward.

"Yes and no. Walsh, my late brother, could claim a tenuous connection through his mother," Doyle said with a weird hint of humor. "She died young, so my father, our father, took him in. We both secretly took the Ansara name a few years back. There's power in a name."

One word stuck with Rye, out of all that. "Late?"

Instead of relaxing, Doyle's grip on the knife tightened. "Walsh and I had a disagreement over how we should proceed here. I had to remove him from the equation."

So, Doyle had already killed—his own brother—and would not hesitate to do so again.

Rye lifted his hand, palm forward. He was ready to beg, to plead. He'd do anything...

Doyle shifted the knife he held on Cassidy so that it pressed against her skin. "Use any of your magic on me, and I'll kill her here and now."

Rye dropped his hand. For a long moment, he didn't respond. For all his abilities, Doyle didn't see that he had no powers? Cassidy knew—he could see it in her eyes—but she said nothing to give him away. They had even spoken of the curse...though Doyle had not been around to hear details of the curse or its removal.

"Tell me what you plan to do," Rye said. "This spell Walsh discovered...is it the same one Maisy attempted?"

Doyle nodded. "Ungrateful bitch. She knew Cassidy was meant for me, not for her. I'm glad you took care of her."

The dark man he had been had ripped out Maisy's throat and then set her on fire. Cassidy had been there, but how much had she seen? He prayed she had not seen much.

"Maisy is nothing but ash now," Rye said.

Doyle nodded his head. "Thanks for that."

"I don't understand." Rye took another small step forward. "What kind of spell is this exactly?"

Doyle noticed Rye's forward movement this time. He nodded his head and motioned for Rye to move back. Reluctantly, he did so.

When Rye had taken two steps back, Doyle answered his question. "The spell takes everything a person is, all abilities and strengths, and transfers it to another. In this instance, Cassidy's powers will transfer to me."

Rye's heart was pounding so hard Doyle had to be able to hear it. Everyone had to be able to hear. He had to stall; he had to find a way to stop Doyle before it was too late. "Maisy had a knife. A special knife. I took it. It's in my room above the pub."

"Blood has to be spilled," Doyle admitted, "but I don't need any special knife. Maisy just liked that one. I think it belonged to her father. Or a sister." He shrugged, as if Maisy and her knife were of no consequence. As if the words he spoke were just ordinary words.

"Blood," Rye repeated in a lowered voice.

"Yes, blood," Doyle said carelessly. "That doesn't mean Cassidy has to die. I don't have to take it all."

Cassidy's lips moved, but she made no sound. *Liar.*

"That's good to hear," Rye said, trying to hide his panic at Cassidy's silent, single word. "The stones... Does the spell have to take place there?"

"It's preferred," Doyle admitted. "Not necessary, but there is a better chance of success. It's more likely that all abilities will transfer if the words are spoken there." His eyes narrowed. "Don't think I won't kill her here and now if you give me any trouble. Wait, let me have the powers I need and when it's all done you can have her back. I can't say she'll be unharmed, but she will be alive."

Liar.

He had to stall, had to find a way to move Doyle away from Cassidy. With that knife at her throat, a sudden, impulsive attack was possible. Doyle might prefer to kill her in the stone circle, but he'd kill her here and now if he felt he had no choice.

Rye had never felt so helpless, had never wished so hard for the powers he'd taken for granted.

Doyle wanted power. He wanted it badly enough to kill his own brother, as well as an innocent child. He craved what the darker side of Rye had wanted.

Everything.

Rye asked as calmly as he could, "Why her? Why not me?"

Doyle smiled. "Nice try, boss. Let's face it, you have a lot of abilities and I wouldn't mind having them." The expression on his face said, *Maybe one day I will.* No, he didn't realize that Rye had lost his powers; he still had not seen that truth. "She's more powerful than you are. More powerful than anyone, I expect."

Rye had always understood that Cassidy's abilities would put her in danger, would make her attractive to those who wanted what she had. Power beyond imagining. He'd always thought he could keep her safe at least until adulthood. No child should be threatened like this, and Cassidy…she was a sweet girl, untainted, generous. Filled with love. He loved her. He would die for her if he had to.

"That's true, she is more powerful than I am," Rye said. "But the kind of power that flows through Cassidy's veins doesn't come without a price. There's the issue of control, the very real possibility that the magic will rule you instead of the other way around." He knew that too well, since it had almost happened to him.

"That's a problem I can handle," Doyle said, but Rye saw his doubts.

Now was the time. A shift in the conversation, a suggestion… "If you take my abilities you can keep her, control her and have it all. You can have everything."

"You're offering?" Doyle snapped.

Yes. Hell, yes. He'd do anything, so in the midst of lies and deceit he spoke the truth. "I love my daughter. Promise me you'll let her live, promise me you won't hurt her, and you'll get no fight from me."

Doyle hesitated. He shifted his feet almost nervously. One swipe of that knife and Cassidy would be gone. Just *gone*.

Rye snapped, "Have I used my powers to fight you?"

"No." Again, he saw Doyle's indecision. "But only because I have a knife to her throat."

True enough. If the move wouldn't put Cassidy in danger, he would have wrestled Doyle to the ground already. "Maybe I'm hoping that once you take all I am into yourself you'll love her as I do. Maybe I hope more of me than my magic will affect you. I want my daughter to live, to be taken care of. She can give you everything if only you care for her."

The knife at Cassidy's throat wavered, moving slightly away from her skin. "I've never seen much to speak of out of you. How do I know you have abilities I want?"

He'd been afraid this might happen. Doyle wanted a demonstration, and Rye was without magic. "You want the man I used to be. Ask anyone in Cloughban about the man I was a dozen years ago or so. I've kept my abilities dampened for a very long time with talismans. You saw them, the wristband and the stone at my throat. They're gone now." It was all gone. "Without those safeguards I can do anything Cassidy can, and more. My abilities are fully developed—they are not the gifts of a child. What power do you wish to see? I have them all."

One eyebrow rose slightly. "We'll start with something easy. Fire?"

The cold fireplace was instantly filled with flame.

"I have control of all the elements," Rye said. As if on cue, a strong wind whipped around the cottage, whistling, screaming like a wounded animal. It died suddenly and completely a moment later.

"Telekinesis?"

"Like you?" A lamp, a book and a cup of tea floated around the room so smoothly not a drop of the tea was spilled.

All three items returned to their proper places. Cassidy didn't twitch, didn't so much as wiggle her little finger. There was no way for Doyle to know that she'd been the one to provide the demonstrations.

The man who had been a valued employee for

eight months gave the idea some thought. Rye began to sweat. What if he turned down the offer? What if he still wanted Cassidy?

Without magic, could he save his daughter?

"We'll do it at the stone circle," Doyle finally said, edging toward the door. "If I don't like what I become after I kill you I'll continue as planned, with the girl."

At least he was no longer lying about his intentions. Someone would die in the stone circle, and Doyle would become a formidable force in the magical world.

"Fine." Rye followed.

He thought of Echo, wished he could reach out to her as he once had. But he was not the man she'd fallen in love with, and he was on his own.

At this moment, nothing mattered but Cassidy.

Chapter 25

Echo ran. Others had heard her words and followed, but they'd fallen far behind. She'd never run so fast. She'd never had reason to.

Gideon was hurt, but not seriously. She hadn't had time to stop and tend to him, not after what she'd seen in the vision that had taken place as the people of Cloughban had fought for their home. Brigid had nodded at Echo, had all but dismissed her as she knelt down to tend to Gideon's head. The final act of the last standing invading soldier—a short blonde with ears too big for her head—had been to conk Gideon on the back of the head with the iron skillet she'd taken from Maeve. Hope had stayed with her husband and the healer, and with an annoyed Maeve, who'd angrily snatched her skillet back from the wounded soldier. Gideon would be fine; he was being well cared for.

Echo's place was with Ryder and Cassidy. Now and forever. They were her family as much as Gideon. She'd traveled around the world to find them...

The attack on Cloughban had been nothing but a distraction. She'd seen it in her vision, a vision which had once again come too late. Doyle. Doyle! She had never suspected him, not for a moment. The attackers had distracted the entire town from the real purpose on this day. Taking Cassidy.

She saw everything now. The pieces of the puzzle had finally come together. When he'd hired the soldiers to attack Cloughban, Doyle had promised them the magic they lacked. Four of them possessed a minor ability, three were entirely without magic. He'd promised to make them all Ansara wizards in his new order, to make them his trusted council when he ruled the magical world. Lies, all lies.

Doyle was desperate to rebuild what had once been a powerful, and evil, clan. With himself as Dranir.

He wanted Cassidy, wanted her amazing abilities for himself, but in Echo's most recent vision it had not been Cassidy Doyle stabbed; it had been Ryder. The knife had slipped into his body. She'd felt his pain as if it were her own, had felt the warmth of his blood flowing out and down his body.

It started to snow again, fat flakes and icy bits of sleet falling in spurts. Around her, ahead of her, behind. She couldn't help it, couldn't stop it. The air turned frosty as big white flakes fell to the bright green grass and hung there for a moment before melting away.

She ran for what seemed like a very long time... had she missed it? Had she somehow passed the stone circle? The air turned colder, and the snow that fell did not melt away quickly. It clung to grass and rocks. Was she headed in the right direction? Was she *too late*? The sun had set. Soon it would be dark. She had no chance of finding Ryder and Cassidy once that happened.

Suddenly the way was lit with those sparkling lights she'd seen once before. Pink and yellow and blue and lavender, those colorful lights twinkled against the snow in a slightly waving line that canted to the left. She could see that line all the way to the crest of the next hill. Fairies? Maybe, maybe not. Whatever they were, they had led her to the stones once before. She followed their lead.

The lights danced around her feet, broke apart and moved ahead as she ran. "Please take me to them," she whispered, not knowing if whatever created the lights could hear her and understand. If she didn't find Ryder and Cassidy, if she found them too late…how would she survive? They were hers. Hers to protect. Hers to save on this cold night.

She crested a gentle hill and finally, *finally*, saw the stones ahead. Tall and majestic and shimmering with power, they called to her in a way they had not before. She ran harder, all her focus on the stones. A few seconds later she saw the three standing there. Ryder and Doyle. Cassidy, standing close but not too close.

Doyle held his knife against Ryder's side. Distracted by the unexpected and unnatural snow, he tipped his head and looked up. A few flakes landed on his face and he smiled. She read his lips as he looked at Ryder and asked, "You?"

"Yes," Ryder answered. She was close enough to hear his voice when he added, "Get this over with. Do it now."

Doyle chanted a few words she did not understand—so few words, not enough, not long enough,
not enough time—and then the knife plunged deeply
into Ryder's body. Ryder fell; he dropped to the ground.
Echo screamed. Cassidy screamed. The earth shook.

Just as in her vision, Echo felt the blade as if it had
punctured her skin as well as Ryder's, but she didn't
stop running. She didn't even slow down. The sparkling
lights that had led her here disappeared. They didn't
fade away; they were just suddenly *gone*.

Alerted by her scream, Doyle turned around and
looked at her. And smiled. Murderer. Traitor.

What had once been snow gathering on the ground
and falling from the sky turned to ice. It fell, hard
and sharp. The frozen pellets that quickly covered the
ground began to grow. Ice crept up around Doyle's feet.
Ryder, prone on the ground, was not touched by the ice,
not at first. Doyle was the target. In a matter of seconds
a thick sheet of ice covered his shoes, then climbed up
his ankles like frozen kudzu, a cold vine that trapped
him in place. The ground around him began to turn
white as the ice edged toward Ryder's body.

Doyle looked at the blood on his hands, he looked at
a fallen Ryder and then—puzzled—he glanced down
at his frozen feet. The knife in his hand waved about
in an almost-wild manner.

Echo ran into the circle and dropped beside Ryder.
There was so much blood. It soaked his shirt and ran
onto the ground, bright red against the white snow and
ice. He was already so pale; his eyes were weak. So
soon, so quick, he was almost gone.

"He's all that I am now," Ryder whispered, and then

his eyes drifted closed. "He is all that I was when I walked into this circle for the last time."

Echo rose and faced Doyle, who was flailing about as if he were on fire. The ice had reached his knees, and just beyond. The knife he'd used to stab Ryder fell from his hand, clinked against the hard ice at his feet. Trapped as he was in ice, he could not bend over to retrieve it.

"I don't feel any different, and I can't do anything," he said. The ice continued to grow. "What the hell? How do I make it stop?" There was panic in his voice, in his movements. "It's damn cold, and I don't like it."

"You did not take all that Ryder is," Echo said angrily, "no matter what you thought your blasted spell would do. He's a good man with love in his heart. He cares about people, cares about this town and the people in it. You can't take that. You can't become what you're not."

Ice climbed high on Doyle's thighs. He was solidly frozen in place. "I just wanted his magic!" he shouted. "I don't want to be tied down by caring about people or places, and love...love just makes you weak."

Her heart was breaking, and still, Echo smiled. She flicked a finger against the hard ice on the side of Doyle's leg. "Weak? Who's weak now?"

Frustrated, he shouted, "I just wanted his abilities. I wanted to be a wizard."

"Unfortunately for you, Ryder doesn't have any abilities, not anymore."

Doyle frowned. Again, he waved one hand like a bad magician trying to make a rabbit appear out of thin air. He knitted his brow, moved his hands while he still could. How long before he was completely encased in ice? "I don't even have my own powers anymore!" He turned toward Cassidy, who stood—pale and shaking with the cold and the shock—several feet away. "Come here, girl. Hand me my knife! I command you!" Cassidy didn't move, and once again Doyle tried to use his old abilities, the ones he'd been born with. He looked down at his knife and squinted as he attempted to make it rise. Nothing happened.

Half a dozen townspeople swarmed into the circle. Echo had not heard them coming. Her attention had been entirely on the three she'd come here to find. Suddenly, the others were there. Behind her, beside her. One kicked the knife away. It skittered over ice and into the soft grass, where it stopped. Another, and then another, attempted to knock Doyle to the ground. After a couple of tries the ice cracked and shattered, and given the way Doyle screamed a few of his bones did the same. The ice had been quite sturdy, Echo would admit. Ice born out of pain and heartbreak.

Nevan placed a heavy booted foot on Doyle's chest and said, "I never liked you, and your vegetable soup is no better than dirty dishwater." With just a few glances, those with abilities gathered the power of the circle and erased knowledge of the spell from Doyle. He'd never be able to try to steal another's power.

With Doyle surrounded and no longer a threat, Cassidy ran to her father. Since others were seeing to a wounded and powerless Doyle, Echo joined the young girl. Together they bracketed the unconscious man they loved.

"I don't suppose healing is one of your abilities," Echo said. Ryder was alive and breathing, but barely. If he was going to die, wouldn't she know? Wouldn't she see or feel it? Maybe. Maybe not. Brigid was tending to the wounded in town, and by her own admission she was a minor healer. Ryder needed more than minor healing. He'd never survive the trip to town.

Cassidy looked at Echo with big, sad eyes. She was scared, and rightly so. So much responsibility rested in her young hands. "I don't know," she whispered. "I never tried to heal anyone before."

Echo took one of the girl's cold hands and squeezed, and she whispered as the snow stopped falling, "Now is the time to try."

By the time Gideon and Hope arrived at the stone circle, led there by a couple of tired and bruised townspeople, the worst was over. Doyle had been taken into custody by the town constable, the one who had green lightning in his fingertips. Nevan, Gideon heard the man called. Echo and a young girl—older than Emma but not by much—were hunched over Ryder Duncan's body.

Hope kept stride with him, and had since they'd left Cloughban behind. "I knew when I married you that our life would never be dull."

"A battle every five to ten years should keep things lively."

She sighed. "Lively is overrated. Dammit, I don't want the girls to fight battles, not ever."

Neither did he, but the occasional battle came with the territory. He, his wife, their girls…they would forever hide a large part of themselves from the rest of the world. They would, on occasion, have to fight for what was right.

This particular battle hadn't been much of a challenge—though he did have a nasty bump on the head. And a headache.

For now, part of his job as a father was to make sure his daughters didn't know too much about the dark side of magic. He didn't even want them to know there were battles in the world. They'd find out soon enough.

He glanced around. "Why the hell is there snow?"

Rye opened his eyes. Echo and Cassidy leaned over him, their faces beautiful and near, and...worried. Behind and well above them, the moon peeked out from behind a cloud. He wished it were the sun instead of the moon. He was so damn cold.

He'd realized Echo was close when the snow had started to fall, but he had imagined she'd arrive too late to help him. It had been a relief to know that she'd be here for Cassidy. Someone had to be here for Cassidy.

The low murmur of many voices drifted to him, but he paid no attention to them. He was entirely focused on the faces of the two women he loved.

"Am I dead?" he asked.

Echo smiled and shook her head. In spite of the smile, there were tears in her eyes. "Your daughter healed you."

"I did," Cassidy said. Her grin was wider, fuller. Older somehow. "It was hard, but I did it!" There were no tears for his gifted daughter. She'd likely never doubted for a moment that he could save her from Doyle. She smiled at Echo. "I'm so glad you got here in time. Did the fairies lead you here again?"

"Yes," Echo said suspiciously. "How did you know?"

Cassidy giggled. "Silly, there are no fairies anymore. That was me. They were pretty lights meant to

lead you where you needed to go." She glanced over
her shoulder before Echo could respond. "Granny and
Mr. McManus are here!" She jumped up and ran, and
he heard her shout, "Granny! Guess what I did!"

Echo placed her head on his chest, as if checking
for a heartbeat. He put a hand in her hair and held on.
Maybe Cassidy had healed him, but he wasn't quite
ready to move.

"I'm so cold," he whispered in her ear.

"Sorry," she responded just as softly. "That was me."

Snow and ice beneath his fingers, beneath his entire
body. Yes, that was her.

"I convinced Doyle to take my powers instead of
Cassidy's, and he did."

"You don't have any powers," Echo said without
lifting her head.

"Now neither does he, I assume." His hand settled
in her hair, held her to him.

"He's not very happy about that turn of events," she
said. She was so warm, so soft and so very much…his.

"I suppose not. Doyle was after supreme power. He
was willing to sacrifice anyone and anything to have
it all, and he came away with nothing." Rye realized
that he had always relied on his abilities, even when
they'd been dampened. Now what? He didn't know
who he was, *what* he was. Unless he, like Doyle, was
now nothing.

"Not nothing," Echo whispered.

Great. She could still see into his head, he just
couldn't see into hers.

A town like Cloughban needed a mayor who was
one of them. An independent, a gifted person. Cassidy needed someone who truly understood what she

was facing to guide her. And Echo...Echo Raintree deserved better than an ordinary man.

"I've always wanted an ordinary man," she whispered.

He didn't believe her.

Gideon and his wife arrived to put an end to the conversation, and Rye found the strength to sit up, dislodging Echo in the process.

All his life, he'd experienced a surge of energy when he was amid the stones. He'd felt the power here as if it were a physical thing. Today, he felt nothing.

Gideon Raintree was another matter. Lightning danced on his skin, and he could not stand still. His wife laughed at him lovingly as he moved back, out of the circle.

Rye looked at Echo and said, "Believe it or not, I'm glad your cousin is here."

"Me, too."

Their reasons were likely not the same. Rye gathered all his courage to say, in a calm and detached voice, "He can take you home."

Chapter 26

"Of course I have a room free!" Maeve Quinlan said as she climbed the stairs to the second floor. Showered and changed, hair fixed and makeup applied, she looked very little like the woman who had wielded an iron skillet as an effective weapon just a few hours earlier. "Not Maisy's room," she added in a tight voice. "I am shocked, shocked, I tell you, to think that she would…well, we won't discuss that unpleasantness."

Echo trailed behind, allowing Maeve, Gideon and Hope to go ahead of her.

"I will not give you her room," the landlady said forcefully. "There's no telling what kind of negative energies might be present there. Until the room is thoroughly cleaned in every way, no one can stay there." She tsked. "I imagine I'll have to sage the entire house to clear it of dark energies. That Doyle stayed here for a few nights before he rented his house out by the Conor place. Yet another reason to give the house a good, thorough cleaning."

The residents of Cloughban had never flaunted their gifts. Not in her presence, at least. Echo didn't know what most of them were capable of. What were Maeve's gifts? Beyond making killer scones.

The landlady turned, glanced past Gideon and Hope and said in a sweet voice, "I'm a witch, dear. Just your ordinary, everyday witch."

Echo sighed. A witch as well as a mind reader apparently. This was not an easy town to keep secrets in. How had Doyle and Maisy done it?

Maeve answered that thought. "Oh, they were much better at hiding their feelings and thoughts than you have ever been. If you stay awhile, I'd be happy to help you with that."

Would she be here for a while?

"I don't know, dear. I'm a mind reader, not a psychic."

Hope snapped, "Whatever you two are doing, stop it."

Gideon cast a censuring glance Echo's way. "We're all tired. Let's get some sleep and we'll head out in the morning."

Would she head out in the morning? Was this her last night in Cloughban?

Maeve escorted Gideon and Hope to a room at the end of the hall. Hope turned and hugged Echo tightly. There was love in that hug. They both needed it at the moment.

"Does it ever stop?" Hope whispered.

"No," Echo said, the word not much more than a

breath. There would always be bad people who wanted to use those who had paranormal abilities for their own profit or entertainment. And for someone like Cassidy...how could Ryder keep her safe from a world filled with people who would either hate her or crave her for the abilities with which she'd been born?

Gideon lifted a hand and gave her a tired wave instead of a hug. She returned the gesture. He'd always treated her like a little sister, had always protected her. He kept her safe, counseled her, scared away inappropriate boyfriends. But she was a grown woman now, and he couldn't protect her from everything and everyone. Though she imagined he would try if given the chance.

He had a family to take care of now. Hope and Emma and Maddy. If she ever needed him he'd come running, but it was time for her to make her own way. She needed to learn to save herself.

The door to their room closed. She imagined they'd both be asleep in five minutes, or less. Echo glanced at the door to her own room. With the exception of finding the threat to her parents there—Maisy's doing, she now knew—it had been a good home, for a while, with a comfortable bed. She was exhausted. She could use ten or twelve hours of sleep.

An unpleasant thought slipped into her head. Had that been Doyle's room when he'd stayed here? Was she sleeping in the same bed he had, under the same roof? Did she look out of the same window at night? The idea made her shiver. Still, she needed sleep...

She also needed Ryder, the man who had made it very clear that he didn't want or need her.

"Men rarely know what they want or need until we tell them, dear," Maeve said as she headed downstairs.

Echo watched her go. Witch. Mind reader. If she stayed here, if she became a part of this town, she'd be in for a life of surprises. If she stayed she'd be asking for everything she'd come here to rid herself of.

Maeve reached the end of the staircase and turned about to head toward the kitchen. Two steps, and she was no longer in view. If she was still able to read Echo's thoughts, there was no longer any indication.

For what seemed like a long time Echo stood at the top of the stairs. This was an important decision, perhaps the most important of her life. Run and hide or fight? Take the easy way out or take what she really wanted?

She'd gotten what she came here for. While she had not rid herself of the visions they were now more manageable. She could sense when one was coming on, and she was much more in control while in the visions. Control was possible. She still had more to learn, but maybe she'd make a decent prophet, after all.

The weather issue was, she suspected, connected to the stones. Once she was away from this place—*if* she was away from this place—that ability would probably fade. Probably. She hoped so! Her worry on that front came and went quickly. If she went home with a new power, she'd learn to control it as she had learned to control the visions.

The enhanced empathic ability would likely remain. She wasn't sure she liked that one much, but like the rest there wasn't much to be done for it. She'd manage. She'd study and train and one way or another she'd make it work.

The question was, would that happen here or in North Carolina? Would she continue to learn and study with Ryder or without him?

Rye had tried to convince Echo to leave Cloughban immediately—now, tonight—but she was nothing if not stubborn. If he could see into her mind the way he once had, give her a little push, convince her in a subtle, magical way that she didn't like him all that much…

But he couldn't.

Not a full hour ago, Echo had grudgingly returned to the boardinghouse that had been her home for the past few weeks. She'd made it clear she wanted to stay with him. He'd made it clear that he didn't want her here. Everyone who had participated in the day's events was exhausted, mentally and physically. She needed sleep and so did her Raintree cousins.

He needed sleep, too, but the way he felt right now… it might be weeks before he slept again.

Rye felt oddly empty without his abilities. Even dampened as they'd been for years, they'd been substantial. To be without them was like losing a sense, suddenly being blind or losing the ability to smell or taste.

Given the chance, he would change nothing. Better that he be blind than for the world to have to deal with what he might have become.

Screw the world. He would give up everything so Echo and Cassidy wouldn't have to deal with what he would have become.

Doyle, who called himself the last Ansara, was now powerless. Cassidy was safe, at least for now. For the next several years Rye would devote himself to being a father. He would teach only her if he could. Could a man with no power instruct someone like her? He would try. He would try with everything he had.

He'd continue to run the pub. He'd continue to be mayor if the people of Cloughban wanted him to do so. If they wanted someone like them, someone who was special, he would willingly step aside.

And he would do it all alone. He would not tie Echo down in this remote place. He would not tie her to the ordinary man he had become.

She had so much to offer the world; she deserved the chance to make her mark. To be a powerhouse in the magical world. Raintree princess. No, Raintree *queen*.

Yes, he should sleep. Not just for hours, but for days. The pub was closed. He was exhausted. His daughter had healed him; he would carry no long-lasting scar from Doyle's attack, but the wound had drained him in a way that could not be healed with a gifted touch. He needed rest, and yet his mind would not be still.

Cassidy had gone home with her grandmother. Rye had a choice. He could try to sleep above stairs or he could go to bed in his own room in that cottage.

Instead of doing either, he wiped down the bar in an almost-automatic manner as his mind spun with what-ifs and what-nows. Yes, he needed rest, but sleep would not come for a while.

When the door opened, he jumped. It would take some getting used to, not sensing when that door would open. Not knowing what was on her mind.

"Echo," he said. "Did you forget something?"

"Yes."

"What?"

She walked toward the bar, and him, much as she

had that first day. He'd seen trouble in her then. He saw trouble now.

"You," she said.

He should've locked the door after she'd left here with her cousins. He should've locked the place up and gone to the cottage with Bryna and Cassidy.

No, that would be the coward's way. Best to handle this cleanly.

"Go away, Raintree. Your time here is done."

She was not scared. Was she ever? Small and seemingly frail, she was one of the bravest women he had ever known. She didn't back down. "Don't tell me we don't have something special."

If he lied to her would she know? Was their connection completely severed? Earlier she'd been able to see into his head, but he'd been blind to hers. That mental link…was it entirely gone?

In case she could see more than she should, he stuck with the truth. "Perhaps we did have something special at one time, but we are both different now." She was stronger; he was weaker.

"We're not different, not deep down where it counts." She walked behind the bar. Walked into him, wrapping her arms around his waist and laying her head on his chest. She was warm and soft; she was everything he had thought never to know.

There were a million reasons for them not to be together, but he didn't want to argue with her. Not now. He didn't want to talk at all.

He grabbed the hem of her T-shirt and inched it up slowly. She shifted away from him, just a bit, to allow him to pull her clothing over her head. With a few more moves she stood before him completely and wondrously naked. Fine from the top of her head to her toes. Perfection inside and out.

"No fair," she whispered as she began to work the zipper on his jeans. "I am naked and you are not."

He needed her. One last time.

She slipped her hand inside his unzipped pants; he wrapped his arms around her and picked her up, dislodging that hand, making her laugh. He loved her laugh; it was too rare, too precious.

He carried her around the bar, to a table in the middle of the room. She'd had this fantasy once—*they'd* shared this fantasy—before they'd become lovers. Before they'd even kissed. He laid her on the table, spread her thighs, freed his erection and followed her down and down.

And into her.

This connection they had not lost. It was heaven on earth, real and unreal. It was truth and magic. He lost himself in her, body and soul. He claimed her, used her, gave to her. For a few precious minutes the world went away, and it took all their troubles with it. Nothing mattered but this. Nothing mattered but her.

She wasn't like any other woman he'd ever known. Echo Raintree was a gift. A gift he couldn't keep, but one he would always remember and hold close to his heart. Ah, he'd realized she was trouble the moment she'd walked in the door...

His trouble. His woman. His heart.

She shattered beneath him, crying out softly as her inner muscles clenched and unclenched around him. Her response sent him over the edge. He was no longer capable of thought, no longer capable of anything but *this*.

Warm and satisfied and exhausted to the bone, he held her. He'd never expected to feel this way about any woman, had never expected to love this way. She could be home, his home, in a way he had never known. Peace, in a way he had never expected. Here in Cloughban, on her blessed Sanctuary land, in the desert or the mountains or in any city in the world...

Reality returned too quickly. He could not afford to lose himself in her, could not afford to make her everything.

Echo reached up, touched his hair and whispered, "I love you, Ryder." She closed her eyes and sighed. Judging by the expression on her face, she thought all was well. She thought...

Hell, he had no idea what she was thinking.

He withdrew, stood, straightened his pants. She was the vulnerable one at this moment. Naked, sated, still lying on the table flushed with pleasure and what she thought was love.

There was only one thing he could say in response to her heartfelt *I love you*.

"You're fired."

Cassidy woke in her own bed, in her own home, with a smile on her face. She should go to school today. She really wanted to see all her friends again! There was no more reason to hide out. Not from Echo! A quick glance at the clock told her it was too late to get to school anywhere near on time. After yesterday, it was likely no one would be there, anyway.

Tomorrow would be soon enough.

She smelled Granny's porridge, and bacon and eggs, and suddenly she was starving.

Cassidy jumped from the bed and ran into the kitchen on bare feet. Granny was awake and had been for a while, by the look of it. She was dressed and her hair was gathered in a neat bun.

"Is Mr. McManus joining us for breakfast?" Cassidy asked. There was a lot of food on the table.

"No, dear. Perhaps we'll see him later today. I suspect he's sleeping late, as you did."

"Lots of people are sleeping late today!" In her nightgown, her own hair curling wildly in all directions, Cassidy ate twice as much as she usually ate for breakfast. She ate it twice as fast, too. Either the healing or the scare had worked up quite an appetite!

A small, sudden knowing robbed some of her happiness. Her da wasn't sleeping. He hadn't slept much at all last night…

"I need to see Da." Suddenly she knew he needed her. Not just as a ghostlike vision popping in to say hello, but in the flesh. He needed a hug.

Granny shook a finger. "I've warned you about those visits…"

Cassidy stood and ran toward her room. "I need to *really* see him. I can find my way to town," she added in a louder voice as she began to gather her clothes. "You don't need to come along if you don't want to."

By the time Cassidy was dressed, Granny was ready to go. She wore a rather stern expression, along with her favorite walking shoes.

"Child, what are we going to do about that father of yours?" Granny asked as they walked out the front door. That door still smelled of smoke and it hung a little crooked. It could be fixed, though. Everything that had been damaged yesterday could be fixed. Everything.

Cassidy skipped ahead. "I haven't decided yet," she called. She only knew her da *still* needed help.

Echo had never been able to see her own future, and had never really cared to. If what was coming was good, it was much more fun to be surprised. If it was bad and could not be changed, why would she want to know?

But as Gideon—garbed in a protective talisman that allowed him to drive without killing the car's electronics—drove her rental car toward the airfield where a private jet waited, she closed her eyes and attempted to see what might lie ahead for her. Something, anything. A clue, please.

How could she find and lose love so quickly? How could Ryder send her away? She knew he loved her, and she loved him. With or without magic. Wizard or ordinary man, he was hers.

He'd all but kicked her out of Cloughban. He'd even officially fired her and made her return her Drunken Stone T-shirts. She'd been naked at the time. Naked and in love and so sure they would be together forever.

Since Ryder didn't want to see her again, he'd asked her to leave those T-shirts on the sidewalk outside the pub on her way out of town.

She'd kept one. It was packed in her duffel bag. A part of her hoped he'd change his mind and come after her, maybe with that missing T-shirt as an excuse, but she didn't hold out much hope.

Would she live the rest of her life waiting for Ryder

to show up and admit that he'd made the worst mistake of his life when he'd let her go?

Somewhere up ahead, Hope drove the rental car she and Gideon had left on the side of the road on their way into Cloughban. After a couple of days away from Gideon, it had started easily enough. Hope had volunteered to drive, saying she could use a little quiet time. Maybe she'd realized that Echo and Gideon needed to talk. Alone.

They had been on the road almost half an hour before he spoke. Right back to business, dammit. "So, are you going back to the Sanctuary?"

"I suppose."

"Don't be so enthusiastic," he said dryly. "You did a good job there. You're needed and wanted. Just…don't make it snow in July. We don't need the attention."

If her heart was broken now and forever, would it snow when she thought of Ryder? Maybe. Maybe not. Away from the stones her abilities would be different. Maybe less, maybe more, but definitely different.

"It's just…being keeper of Sanctuary was always temporary in my mind," she confessed. "I was a place holder for Emma. I know, she has years before it'll be time for her to take that job, but still…it was never me. That job was never *mine*." Was that what she'd always been looking for? Something that was meant to be hers?

"What is yours?" Gideon asked, and somehow he sounded both kindly concerned and incredibly frustrated.

She had to be honest. "I don't know."

He sighed. Gideon was such a guy, not really good at the touchy-feely stuff. But he did care. She knew that. Even if he was sometimes maddening, like a big brother or overly protective father would be.

"I use my abilities to help people," he said. "Dead people, yeah, but the dead are people, too. Kind of."

"Is this supposed to be helping?" Echo asked sourly. He was trying, and she grudgingly gave him credit for that, but she was pretty frustrated herself at the moment.

"Dammit, let me finish," he said. "I tried to quit, after Hope and I got married, but this is what I do. I find murderers and take them off the streets. Hope misses it. When the kids are in school she'll probably come back. They won't allow us to partner up again. It'll be a struggle, but we'll make it work because it's who we are."

"It'll be a while before that happens," Echo said absently.

"What?" Gideon sounded confused and put out. "Madison is four and a half. She'll be in kindergarten next year…"

"But what about the boy?" Echo asked.

Gideon looked at her and she looked at him. Green eyes met in silence. They were both surprised by her words.

"Boy?" he asked after a few moments.

There had been no vision, no crippling experience that took her elsewhere, but she knew. A boy. "In eight and a half months or so," she said. "Yes."

"Hope hasn't said a word…"

"She doesn't know! Jeez, Gideon, the *eight and a half months* should've been a clue." Another Raintree baby. Maybe one with Gideon's powers, his amazing abilities. He had never said he wanted a son. He loved his daughters, doted on them, even. But he'd be thrilled…

"How many?" he asked in a voice filled with something much like terror. "We just planned on the two, but apparently we… I swear, we're careful… Never mind, we don't need to go into that." He blushed just a little. "Okay, tell me. Lay it on the line, cuz. How many kids are Hope and I going to have?"

Echo managed to laugh. "I don't know. This is life, Gideon. Be surprised now and then. Have eight kids if it suits you."

"*Eight?* Bite your tongue. Hope would kill me. Shit! She's going to insist I get clipped, I just know it."

Echo laughed. No, Gideon would not be happy when Hope insisted that he have a vasectomy but in the end he'd do it. And he'd grumble about it. A lot.

They were silent for a long moment. Gideon was probably thinking about the changes a new baby would bring to their lives. Maybe he was thinking about having a son. About baseball and football and fixing old cars.

Did Ryder want a son one day? He loved Cassidy, she knew that, but…was it enough? Did he long for more?

"Back to the matter at hand," Gideon said, all business once again. "Who are you, dammit? Where do you belong? No one can tell you, you have to *feel* it."

Feel it. She'd been feeling all her life. Good and bad, traumatic and ecstatic. On occasion she tried to block it all out, but she did know how to feel.

"I want to sing," she said softly. "I want to make music."

Gideon nodded. "Good. That's a start. What kind of music? Where?"

The answer was crystal clear, but it wasn't going to be easy. Was anything worthwhile ever easy? Wasn't what she wanted and who she was deep inside worth fighting for?

She turned to look at her cousin, studying his profile for a few seconds before she said, in the most commanding voice she could muster, "Turn the car around."

Rye looked toward the table where he'd laid Echo down last night. He wasn't sure he could ever allow anyone to sit at that table again. It was his. Hers. Theirs. He glanced at the stage where Echo had played and sang on so many nights. The space had never looked so empty to him before.

He'd lied to her about never having music in the pub. There were a couple of decent local bands that performed almost every weekend. One played traditional Irish music, while the other dabbled in soft rock. He'd paid them to back off while she'd been here because he wanted to listen to her sing. He wanted to watch her light up as she sat on that stage with a guitar in her hands.

Last night he'd been so sure he was making the right decision in sending her away, but now...he didn't know what came next. He didn't belong here, not when the powers he'd possessed had been stripped away. What if he made them uncomfortable, and they stopped coming to the pub altogether?

It wasn't as if he had many choices. He couldn't take Cassidy out into the world, not with puberty and the chaos that would bring to someone so incredibly gifted on the horizon. Her place was here. Somehow, he'd have to make it work. For her.

The pub remained closed. No one felt like celebrating at the moment. Even the grumpy trio of old men who were here six days a week was steering clear of the place. Nevan had called in reinforcements and rid himself of Doyle and his seven hired guns. They were all in a jail cell somewhere. Rye didn't know where, and he didn't care. The soldiers would receive treatment for their minor wounds and then they'd have their minds cleared of recent memories before they were dropped off in a big city somewhere in the world. Each of them in a different city, a different country.

Doyle was another matter. His memories had been removed, as well, but he would never go free. Nevan's word that the man who'd tried to kill Cassidy would never leave his lonely prison was good enough for Rye.

Some of Cloughban's own had been injured, others were shaken up by the invasion. This was supposed to be a place of safety, of isolation. Soon enough some would need to commiserate, and what better place than the village pub.

The Drunken Stone would come to life again, but it would never be the same.

He needed to find a new cook.

Maybe a waitress.

He'd get a band back for the weekend, but…no, it wouldn't be the same.

Cassidy, who was not allowed in the pub under normal circumstances, sat with her grandmother in the corner booth. He'd been surprised to see them, but he was also glad of the company. He didn't need to sit here and feel sorry for himself.

Bryna looked tired, worn out to the bone. Cassidy had bounced back more quickly than any of the adults. Kids were like that. Rye hoped she could forget what had happened to her in the past few days, but he suspected she would not.

"Da, I'm very disappointed in you," Cassidy said in a put-on grown-up voice.

There were so many reasons for her to be disappointed, but he suspected he knew what hers were. The most magically gifted being in the world, and her father was...

"Not that," she said with childish disdain.

"It's rude to read people without their permission."

"I can't help it," she said. "You're all but shouting. I don't mind that you don't have powers. Inside now you're all blues and greens and lovely yellows. Before there were black spots, but those are gone. You don't want the black spots, Da. Besides, there are still some little powers in you, some little powers that have been with you since you were born. When you recover from the curse, they'll come back to you."

Little powers. Great. His mother had not been satisfied with little powers. Would anyone else be? Would he?

He ignored that part and said, "True, I don't want black spots. So tell me, why are you disappointed?"

She slipped out of the booth and headed his way. "You let Echo go."

He hoped with all his heart that Cassidy's ability to see and understand didn't apply to *every* aspect of his life. If she peeked into things that she did not understand, she gave no indication. She was normally not shy about asking questions, so he continued to hope.

"What was I supposed to do?" he asked. "I know you like her, but she doesn't belong here."

"She *does*. Echo *does* belong here."

He had thought so, at one time. "If she belonged here she'd be here. That's the way the universe works."

Bryna scoffed, stood and headed for the rear door. "Poppycock," she said in a clear, loud voice. "Do you think the universe is going to do everything for you? The Raintree girl came to you. Of all the places in the world she might've gone in her wanderings, she ended up here. It's up to you to keep her." She snorted. "I need a nice long walk and a nap. Fix it." The door slammed behind her.

Alone with his daughter, Rye tried to remember why he'd sent Echo away. His life was in shambles; he was not who he'd always believed himself to be.

He still didn't want her family to overrun the town, but considering Gideon's reaction to the stones, he doubted that would be a problem.

Cassidy smiled. "I made Echo believe in fairies. She wasn't sure, at first, but I made her believe. I conjured some pretty lights to guide her to the stones, and she wanted to believe they were fairies. She knows better now, but I should really apologize. I told her it was me but I didn't say I was sorry. I can't apologize if she's not here."

"Do you see her future?" he asked. "Do you see Echo?" He wanted to know that she was safe and happy. Even if she wasn't safe and happy with him.

Cassidy shook her head. "Not anymore. She's too close to me now. She's a part of my circle."

It was frustrating. He wanted to know! "How can that be? You barely know her."

Cassidy shrugged, accepting in a way that only a child can be. "When I first met her, I thought she'd stay. I even had a weird thought that she was…the Oracle of Cloughban. Have we ever had our own oracle? What is an oracle exactly? I should've asked Granny. She'd know."

Oracle of Cloughban? No. Echo wouldn't come back.

"Your head is too full," Cassidy argued.

"I'm a grown-up. That happens sometimes."

Cassidy sighed and gave him a look of pure female indignation. Oh, hell, she was growing up too fast. "It's simple, Da. It's so, so simple. Clear your head and focus on what's important. Do you love her?"

"What are you grouching about?" Echo asked. "You're taking a private plane home. It's not like you're going to miss your flight. I know Hope will have to wait a bit at the airfield, but it won't be too long."

"It's not that," he grumbled.

"Then what?"

Gideon's lips tightened and his eyes narrowed, and then he said, "I have a feeling I won't see you again for a long time."

Echo glanced at her cousin's profile. She'd miss him, too, but this was her place. This was her life. "We'll visit, and you can bring the family here for a vacation."

Assuming Ryder allowed her to stay.

Who was she kidding? He didn't get to allow her anything. She'd stay. She was a grown woman who could live wherever she wanted to. The immediate plan was to settle in and hound him until he admitted that he loved her and could not live without her. That might not be easy, but it wasn't impossible, either. She would fight for him if she had to.

She wasn't a fighter. Never had been. But maybe she just hadn't run across anything worth fighting for. Until now.

"Make sure to stock up on dampening talismans before you come again," she advised.

"Don't worry, I will." He sounded no happier than he had before.

Besides, Cassidy wanted to go to Disney World...

The road was barely wide enough for the rental car. Gideon cursed when he spotted the dust on the winding road, up ahead, around the bend. One of them would have to pull off for the other to pass. Even then, it would be a tight fit.

But before they turned the bend, Echo knew that wouldn't be a problem. That was Ryder up ahead, and he was coming for her.

She wouldn't have to fight, after all.

In her head she saw a flash of an unusual rusty-red color. It was the color of the old car she'd seen parked behind the pub.

Echo whispered to Gideon, "Stop."

He did, and then he turned to her, alert in a way only a cop can be. "What's wrong? Are you having an episode? About to? What...?"

"I'll get out here. This is a wide enough spot for you to turn around if you're very careful."

She leaned over the console and kissed him on the cheek. "You really do have to come back. I can't wait to see Emma and Cassidy together."

He paled, as if that thought had never occurred to him. "Good Lord..."

"We need to start planning a big family reunion. Your kids, Mercy's, Dante's, the whole crew." Look out, world...

Echo collected her bag from the backseat, stepped aside and watched Gideon make his turn, and then she stood in the middle of the road waiting for the rest of her life to begin.

Maybe his magic was gone, but they remained connected in a primal way. To the soul, to the bone. In body and spirit. No one could ever take that from them.

He was coming for her, and apparently he wasn't alone. Along the road, close to the ground, sparkling lights in many pastel colors appeared. They weren't leading her to the stones, not this time. They were leading her home.

I love you, Ryder.

Suddenly her head was filled with his voice. *Love you, too.*

He'd heard her, understood and responded. He was not entirely without magic, after all.

Feet planted far apart and steady, duffel bag in hand, she whispered to the road—and the lights—ahead, "Come and get me."

* * * * *

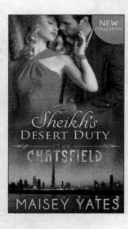

MILLS & BOON®

Seven Sexy Sins!

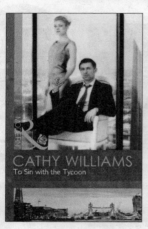

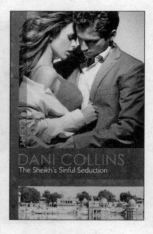

The true taste of temptation!

From greed to gluttony, lust to envy, these fabulous stories explore what seven sexy sins mean in the twenty-first century!

Whether pride goes before a fall, or wrath leads to a passion that consumes entirely, one thing is certain: the road to true love has never been more enticing.

Collect all seven at
www.millsandboon.co.uk/SexySins

MILLS & BOON®

nocturne™

AN EXHILARATING UNDERWORLD OF DARK DESIRES

A sneak peek at next month's titles…

In stores from 20th March 2015:

- **Moonlight and Diamonds** – Michele Hauf
- **Possessing the Witch** – Elle James

Available at WHSmith, Tesco, Asda, Eason, Amazon and Apple

Just can't wait?
Buy our books online a month before they hit the shops!
visit www.millsandboon.co.uk

These books are also available in eBook format!